THE ROMANOV LEGACY

ALSO BY JENNI WILTZ

The Carmelite Prophecy: A Natalie Brandon Thriller

The Sinner's Bible: A Natalie Brandon Thriller

The Red Road

A Vampire in Versailles

I Never Arkansas It Coming

THE ROMANOV LEGACY

A Natalie Brandon Thriller

Jenni Wiltz

Decanter Press
PILOT HILL, CALIFORNIA

Published in the United States by Decanter Press.
For information, contact:
publisher@jenniwiltz.com

Publisher's Cataloging-in-Publication Data
Wiltz, Jenni.
The romanov legacy / Jenni Wiltz.
443 p. ; 22 cm.
ISBN 978-1-942348-04-7 (pbk)
ISBN 978-1-942348-03-0 (eBook)
1. Nicholas II, Emperor of Russia, 1868-1918 — Family —
Assassination — Fiction. 2. Romanov, House of — Fiction.
3. Suspense fiction. 4. Russia — Fiction. 5. Spy stories. I. Title.
PS3623.I48R66 2012
813'.6 — dc23

For Sara

CHAPTER ONE

The guards shot at anything that moved. Birds, stray dogs, even street vendors who came too close to the whitewashed palisade shielding the house from view — no one was safe and there were no warning shots. Target practice, they called it.

The men "practiced" every day after lunch, calling out the name of a different Romanov and shooting wildly at a tree trunk or a tin of food set on a fence post. They called this place "The House of Special Purpose," and only the blind harbored illusions about what that purpose might be.

Marie was not blind.

She watched one of the guards through a crack in the bedroom door, which they were not allowed to close all the way. The rest of the family had gone into the dining room for supper. She stayed behind to wake her sister, Olga, who lay suffering with a headache. "Two minutes," the guard had said. "Then I will drag you into the dining room by your hair."

It was not enough time. Still, they had to try.

She glanced at Olga, feigning sleep while stiff as a tree trunk. "Olga, darling," Marie called. "It's time for supper. You must get up."

Squinting through the crack, Marie followed the guard's gaze to the pendulum clock in the hall. He was timing them. She took a deep breath and snapped her fingers.

At Marie's signal, Olga sprang to life. She reached beneath the mattress and removed a pen and sheet of paper, torn from the front of Alexei's diary. Scratching fiercely, she punctured the paper in several places and spattered her white dress with ink.

"Slow down," Marie hissed.

Olga ignored the warning. Her pen flew across the paper, giving shape to the words she'd chosen while lying in bed last night. No one must know what she and her sister were doing: not the guards, not the Cheka, not the Bolshevik censors, and certainly not their father. This letter had to slip past all of them, dismissed as the lovelorn ramblings of a doomed princess. The lovelorn part was not difficult; she would die with Pavel's name on her lips and the memory of that Crimean autumn in her breast. *Yes,* she thought. *I know how to keep a secret.*

MY DEAR PAVEL,

I MISS YOU MORE THAN YOU CAN KNOW. WE ARE SURVIVING, SO YOU MUSTN'T WORRY TOO MUCH.

BABY'S KNEE IS SWOLLEN AGAIN, BUT HE LIVES UP TO HIS NICKNAME AND WE THANK GOD FOR EVERY MOMENT HE IS HEALTHY. THERE IS NOTHING TO DO HERE BUT READ, AND I HAVE BEEN THROUGH EVERY SCRAP OF TYPE SIX TIMES ALREADY. I WISH YOU COULD SEND ME SOMETHING NEW. JUST ONE WORD WOULD BE ENOUGH. WHAT WAS THE BOOK WE READ TOGETHER IN THE CRIMEA? A SILLY STORY ABOUT A DANCING GIRL WHO BECAME AN EMPRESS. IF SHE WERE A MAN, IT WOULD NOT HAVE BEEN SO SCANDALOUS, DON'T YOU THINK? THEY WOULD HAVE GIVEN HIM THE WORLD. WHAT POWER THERE IS IN A NAME! DO YOU SUPPOSE ANYONE WILL REMEMBER MINE WHEN IT IS ALL OVER? LIKE ME, IT IS SO VERY PLAIN. VERY FITTING FOR A HUMBLE SAILOR'S WIFE, WHICH IS ALL I EVER WISHED TO BE.
OLGA NIKOLAEVNA

She stared at her signature and wondered why the letters looked so childish. Then she raised her hand from the paper and realized it was shaking. "Your turn," she whispered.

Marie flung herself onto the bed and pulled a second sheet of paper from beneath the mattress. But instead of writing, she grabbed Olga's dress sash and untied it. "What are you doing?" Olga hissed, swatting at her sister's hands.

"Leave it," Marie said. "Just keep watch."

Olga clutched the bedclothes and listened for the soldier's footsteps in the hallway. He made one more circuit from end to end and stopped in front of their door.

"Finish," Olga whispered. "Now."

The guard rapped on the door, pressing hard enough to swing it open. "What's taking so long?"

Olga swallowed the peppery lump of fear in her throat. "One more moment, please?"

The guard's suspicious eyes flickered over Olga and then Marie, hunched behind her sister. "What's going on here?" he asked.

"Nothing," Olga lied.

"What are those?" He pointed at the ink spots on Olga's dress.

Olga's lips struggled to form words. She could think of no lie he would not see through. *It is over,* she thought. *We are dead.*

"It's no use," Marie said, reaching for the ends of Olga's sash and tying them in a large bow. Olga felt her sister's nimble fingers slip the folded sheets of paper between the sash and the dress, hiding them from view. "You'd better tell him."

The guard narrowed his eyes. "Tell me what?"

"She's too embarrassed to speak," Marie said. "She fell asleep and dropped her pen. Can you believe how clumsy she is?"

Olga felt her sister's warm hands push her up from the bed. "You see?" Marie said, holding up the pen for the guard to see. "Her headache was so bad she didn't know she'd dropped it."

The guard held out his hand. "Come here," he said.

Olga looked at his open palm, its threaded crevices stained with something dark. Her throat swelled with fear. *I do not want to die,* she thought.

"Come here," he said again.

Olga shook her head. It would only anger him further, but no force in the world could make her step forward.

The guard ripped his revolver from his belt and aimed it at her forehead. "You are nothing! You are less than dirt!" Then he gathered a mouthful of spit and flung it on her. "Don't you know there is no more tsar?"

Olga felt the spittle pelt her cheeks. She bit her lip to keep from screaming, *Yes, there is a tsar! He is my father and he sits in this very house. You will be sorry when the ghost of Great Peter rises up within him to defend all of Russia from the likes of you!* But even as she thought it, she knew it was not true. Her father was weak; no shade of Great Peter lived within him. Her eyes filled with tears and blood trickled over her tongue.

Sensing her submission, the guard grasped a handful of her skirt and twisted it to pull her near. Up close, she could see the mosaic of pores and stubble on his cheeks — they reminded her of the patterned tiles on the floor of the Hermitage. *We will never see Petersburg again,* she thought.

"Is it true?" he asked. "You dropped your pen and fell asleep?"

She swallowed thickly, a mouthful of blood and bile burning her throat. "Y–yes."

The guard frisked his hand up her thigh and across her side, dangerously close to the bow of her sash. "Most women notice what is in their bed before they fall asleep. Are you not so picky, princess?"

Olga twisted her body to keep the letters out of his reach. "I had a headache. You needn't suggest more than that."

His thick palm connected with her face. "You will never again tell anyone what to do! Do you understand?"

Olga's cheek blossomed with the sting of a thousand Crimean bees. *We will never leave this house,* she thought. *Their hatred will strip the flesh from our bones.*

"Hush," Marie said, moving forward and squeezing herself between them. She smiled brightly at the guard, blue eyes wide and lashes fluttering in a pattern Olga recognized. Marie had learned at an early age how to soften a father's punishment or warm a wounded soldier's heart.

No, Olga thought. *He is not worth your care.* She put a hand on her sister's arm but Marie shrugged it off. "Olga, go into the kitchen," she said softly. "You know Kharitonov hates to be kept waiting."

Olga's knees wobbled as she stumbled past the guard. When she turned around, she saw her sister's seraphic gaze locked on the guard's pockmarked face. "You may search our room if you like," Marie said. "I promise we have done nothing wrong."

The blood and bile in Olga's throat nearly choked her as she crept into the parlor and spotted the basket used by the Novo-Tikhvinsky nuns to deliver bread and eggs. Behind her, Marie's soft voice echoed in the hallway. "Shall I show you our diaries? Our prayer books? Is there anything else you might like to see?"

Olga imagined Marie's fingers touching the man's hand, trailing up his arm, promising a favor that would banish all thought of their possible transgressions: a kiss or perhaps an embrace. Her stomach clenched and she fought a pang of revulsion for the sister who was capable of such deception.

Olga pulled their two letters from her sash and held them to her lips. *This is the only way,* she thought. *The only way I can tell him I still love him.* She had given up all hope that either recipient would be able to mount a rescue. Neither she nor Marie knew if their first letters had made it through. If they hadn't, the secret would die in this house and these second letters would be a benediction from the dead. Still, it would be enough to know that Pavel might touch the same piece of paper she had kissed with her still-breathing lips.

"Go with God," she whispered, placing the letters between the layers of cloth folded in the nuns' basket. "May He have mercy on our souls."

CHAPTER TWO

The old man rolled his head to the side and looked longingly at the carafe of water on his nightstand. He had spoken for nearly an hour and it still hadn't been enough to make his grandson understand. He should have known his breath would fail him when he needed it most.

"Yuri," he said, lifting a withered arm to reach for the carafe. His grandson came around the side of the bed and filled the glass to the rim, something the nurses never did. They knew, as Yuri did not, that a full glass of water was too heavy for many patients to lift.

"Who else knows about this?" Yuri asked.

Grigori held the heavy glass to his lips. The quick flash in Yuri's eyes told him he had just made a terrible mistake. "No one," he said.

"Are you sure it's still there?"

A hard lump formed at the back of Grigori's throat. He did not understand why their family had been chosen to carry this burden. His father, Filipp, said the tsar's own daughter had touched his hand. The tsar was God's anointed representative on earth. Surely anything his daughter touched would become holy, too. When he saw his father in heaven, he knew Filipp's right hand would glow with the same golden halo painted around the heads of Orthodox saints. "I have told you all I know," he lied.

Yuri moved from the bed to the window. He pushed open the blinds and looked at the terraced hills, stacked with low-slung houses in faded yellow and green. "All this time, it's been there waiting for me."

"It is not yours," Grigori said.

Yuri's lower lip jutted out like it had when he was a boy, refused a foil-wrapped sweet before dinner. "It will be."

"My father was wrong. He should never have kept it."

"But he did," Yuri said, "and now they're all dead. Why shouldn't I have what they left behind?"

It is as I feared, Grigori thought. *He will sell the soul of an entire country and destroy what ninety years of revolution and war could not.* "Yuri, can you not see? The gulags, the alliance with England during the war, the incursion into Korea...what do you think the Soviets were looking for? Your great-grandfather and I only survived because we did not reveal the tsar's secret. Death has always followed that family. If you break our silence, it will come for you, too."

His grandson turned from the blinds with a half-moon smile. "You always believed that horseshit, didn't you?"

Grigori let his head sag onto the pillow. He could not bear to watch greed devour his grandson before his very eyes. "I am afraid for you, Yuri."

"Don't be," Yuri said. "I'll take care of everything."

Dim fog light filtered through the plastic blinds, washing the room in lifeless gray. Grigori closed his eyes. *Forgive me,* he prayed, *for what I have just unleashed upon the world.*

CHAPTER THREE

JULY 2013
SAN FRANCISCO, CALIFORNIA

Natalie Brandon pulled the flask out of her jacket pocket and looked for a place to pour the contents. Her sister's office was devoid of any useful drinkware, so she emptied the pencil cup over the trash and filled it with a generous helping of bourbon. She looked down into the cup, where wooden shavings and broken pencil tips floated like bits of shipwreck in an amber sea. "Ahoy, matey," she said.

The sour mash swirled over her tongue. She held it there, letting the alcohol soak into the skin of her mouth. When she swallowed, she looked up at the clock. Beth was late.

She slapped a bundle of index cards onto the desk, next to a framed photo of two little girls in sundresses. The taller girl, a blonde, smiled brightly to reveal an enormous gap where her front teeth used to be. The smaller girl, a brunette, held her hand up to the camera with a face vacant of all expression. On her palm sat a fat, furry spider with one leg raised in greeting. "Medusa," Natalie said.

She stared at the pale smear meant to represent her face. Her eyes never photographed well. They were too light, without enough contrast against her skin. Combined with her long, dark hair, they made her look like a ghost.

In the photo, she wore a pink Strawberry Shortcake dress. The photographer had cut her off at the waist, but she knew exactly what else she'd worn that day: red tights and Buster Brown shoes. She could still remember the Kix she'd eaten that morning, the cream cheese sandwiches her mother had served for lunch, and every word of dialogue from that night's episode of *The Muppet Show*.

It had all seemed so harmless at first — a little girl who could recite Shakespearean sonnets from memory and calculate the grocery bill to a penny before the cart ever reached the register. But everything had changed in fourth grade. One minute, she'd been standing at the chalkboard in Mrs. Norton's class, diagramming a sentence. The next, a searing pain tore through her brain. She felt something moving beneath her skull, something with a human form and enormous, feather-covered wings.

The creature struggled to unfold itself, pressing its wings against her occipital lobe until she thought it would split open. When the creature realized her skull was the obstacle, it raised its head and looked at her from behind her own face. "I have things I want to show you, but I have to open my wings to do it," he said. "Will you let me?"

When she nodded, her body had fallen in a faint at the chalkboard. The next thing she knew, she and the creature were floating side by side above it. "My name is Belial," he said. "I live inside you now."

"Are you an angel?" she asked.

"Look around you and tell me what you think I am." He waved his arm and suddenly they were in a place where strange gray snow fell from the sky. A chimney spewed black smoke and men trudged past her wearing sooty pajamas. They were tired and they asked to stop, but a man in black whipped them until they moved again. One of them fell down and the man in black whipped him until the pajamas fell away and something red came out of his mouth. Then the man in black turned around and looked straight at her. She screamed and woke up in a hospital bed, choking on the taste of flesh and ashes.

The doctors couldn't explain it. They told her parents that her heart rate had fallen to twenty-nine beats per minute, resulting in a coma. They didn't say anything about Belial. True to his word, the angel had taken up residence in her head. He perched in the space between her brain tissue and her skull. It hurt when he moved and every time he shifted his wings, the tips of his feathers pricked her brain like needles. When she tried to explain this to the doctor, he shook his head and said it was impossible. She told him to look for Belial on an X-ray, but he found the wrong thing — all he wanted to talk about was something called the limbic system.

Her parents had shuffled her between psychiatrists, psychologists, and neurologists but none of them could find Belial either, so she gave up and stopped talking altogether.

She simply sat, uncommunicative, until they let her go. Some had diagnosed her as autistic; others said she was an early-onset paranoid delusional schizophrenic. They pumped her full of olanzapine and sent her home, leaving her embarrassed parents full of apologies for their daughter's refusal to "get well."

When she was fourteen, her parents had died in a car accident. Natalie missed the funeral because she'd set the alarm clock for p.m. instead of a.m. Black-clad Beth had barged in afterward and demanded that Natalie recite the list of Plantagenet kings in sequential order. When Natalie mixed up Henry III and Edward III, Beth flushed every pill in the house down the toilet and moved back home.

The three of them—she, Beth, and Belial—had eventually developed a comfortable working relationship. Belial dispensed angelic wisdom and acute physical pain in equal measure. Beth dosed her with cognitive therapy, and she herself had learned that alcohol was by far the most effective means of making it all just go away. There had been several occasions when alcohol failed her, but only one that had convinced Beth to take out a life insurance policy for each of them. The puffy white lines on her forearms still itched sometimes, as if the skin beneath fit too tightly.

Natalie looked at the clock again. It was after two, which meant Beth's lunch date had gone well. She refilled the pencil cup and sipped as slowly as she could until the familiar clomp of Beth's shoes echoed in the hallway.

Tall, thin, and blonde, Beth Brandon swept into the room in a cloud of Dolce & Gabbana perfume. "That's it," she said, tossing her tote bag into a chair. "No more blind dates with guys in the computer science department."

"What happened?"

"He ate sushi with his hands." She stopped, staring at the *Yale Class of '01* mug in Natalie's hands. "Nat, what are you doing?"

"Drinking whiskey."

"Out of my pencil cup? That's disgusting. Why didn't you drink it from the flask?"

"Whiskey needs to breathe, Beth."

"So does your liver."

Natalie shrugged. "Sometimes I eat sushi with my hands."

"You're different."

She'd heard those words all her life, even from Beth, who should have had the guts to tell her to just use the goddamn chopsticks. She raised the cup and drained it in a single gulp.

Beth sighed. "I'm sorry, babe, I didn't mean it. Just put down the booze. How are my talking points coming?"

Natalie tapped the bundle of index cards on the desk. As Beth's research assistant, it was her job to track down the information Beth needed for her books, speeches, and lecture notes. Rosemont University paid Natalie just enough to stay afloat, and having Beth as a boss kept her from having to explain Belial to a real employer. "Your speech is boring," Natalie said.

"Boring will pay for Seth's next year of private school. The chancellor said he'd put me on the top pay grade if this book performs."

"The chancellor's an asshole. He's going to pass you up for department chair."

Beth shrugged. "He thinks I'm too young."

"Change his mind."

"Nat, please. This is my career. Let me handle it my way."

"Your way sucks," Natalie said. "If you want the chancellor's attention, you know how to get it."

"What are you talking about?"

"You know exactly what I'm talking about."

"Come on, Nat, we discussed this before I wrote the book."

"I told you it exists. Why won't you believe me?"

Beth blinked twice. "I do believe you."

"You only blink when you're bullshitting people."

"Seriously, Nat, are we back to this again? No one has ever found any evidence that there's money out there with the tsar's name on it. If there were, someone would have talked by now. They would have found a paper trail. Entire books have been written about this."

"Book," Natalie said. "And Clarke followed the wrong trail."

"My book is about Nicholas II, not his money. I'm not a treasure hunter, Nat. I'm a professor."

"But Clarke, Lovell, Fallows, Holtzmann… they were all looking for an account with the tsar's name on it, something with deposits made before the abdication. Belial said that's not how it happened."

"How did it happen, then? Did he tell you that?"

"No," Natalie grumbled, looking down at her untied shoes. "I don't think he knows."

Don't I? Belial snickered. He flicked his wings and the movement sent bolts of lightning shooting through her skull. She sucked in her breath and gritted her teeth.

"Listen, kiddo," Beth said, "I'd love for you to be right, but I can't stake my reputation on something you don't know. The book is already written…this is the press conference announcing its release, for God's sake!" Beth sank into a folding chair next to the desk. Natalie stared at her without speaking. "Don't look at me like that," Beth said. "You know as well as I do that Stalin tore that country apart looking for extra money. If there were any tsarist accounts left, he would have found them."

"Are you saying Stalin is smarter than us?"

"I'm saying you need to admit how improbable this is."

Natalie held out her wrists. "As improbable as this?"

Beth shivered. "There's only so much I can take on faith, Nat."

"Belial said there's a password. Do you remember that confession I found? The one that said Marie planned to give the password to the guard she'd fallen in love with?"

Beth slipped off her jacket and hung it over the back of the chair. "I thought we went over this. There isn't one shred of evidence to prove Marie went through with it. It's not mentioned in any of the Romanov diaries, in statements from the guards, or the Sokolov report."

"That guard might not have talked, but his granddaughter did. On her deathbed, she swore to a priest that Grand Duchess Marie told her grandfather how to retrieve Nicholas's money. There was a password, she said, that Marie had sent him in a letter."

"A letter that never arrived. Nat, they're all lying. Why can't you see that?"

"The letter exists! It must still be out there, in someone's attic or sewn into the lining of a coat that's hanging in the Moscow Goodwill."

"How many people swore Anna Anderson was Anastasia?" Beth circled the room, a black-clad vulture in Blahniks. "I humored you the first time you brought this up and I bit my tongue the second. But I have to tell you, Nat, you're going kind of Rain Man on me with this one. There is no missing money. The guard's granddaughter lied and you fell for it. Just accept it, all right?"

She's wrong, Belial said. *Why can't you make her see?*

I'm trying, Natalie thought. Tears stung her eyes and she fought the urge to crawl under Beth's desk. "The Bank of England said—"

"Forget the Bank of England!" Beth looked up at the clock. "I have a make-or-break press conference in an hour, Nat! I have a kid to raise, an ex draining me for alimony, a chancellor breathing down my neck, and I just went on a date with someone who thinks the Weimar Republic is part of the Hoth System. I don't have the luxury of living in an alternate universe right now. If you're going to help me, fine. If not, go find someone else to listen to your nutball conspiracy theories."

"Oh, I helped you," Natalie said, glancing at the pile of cards on the desk. "I was going to ease you into it before you decided to be a bitch about it."

Beth turned the color of calamine lotion. "Nat, you didn't! Tell me you didn't!" She snatched up the cards, shuffling through them.

"You'll have everyone's attention around the two-minute mark. Be ready." She grabbed her flask and stumbled out of the room before her sister could see her cry.

CHAPTER
FOUR

Ambassador Mikhail Kadyrov reached for the steaming cup of coffee sitting on his desk. Coffee was one thing this country got right. He'd never liked the tar-black sludge his mother served at home in the Caucasus. "Olenka, you're an angel," he called to his assistant.

Thin as a rail and addicted to more than one Columbian export, Olenka knew every coffee counter in the city. "It's shade grown," she said. "Not from those stupid overgrown hybrid plants."

Kadyrov took a sip and picked up an envelope on his desk — an 11″ × 13″ manila with no return address containing one sheet of paper, its letters typed all in crisp capitals. He read it quickly. When he finished, all thoughts of coffee had vanished.

He snatched the envelope and marched it out to her. "Olenka, when did this arrive?"

She shrugged. "I don't know. What is it?"

"It was on my desk. You must have put it there."

"I didn't, I swear."

"Tell me the truth, Olenka." He looked into her eyes, layered with multiple hues of shiny gray powder. "It's important."

"I put your coffee on your desk and came right back here."

"Was the envelope already there?"

"I think so."

"Have any delivery men come into the office?"

"What's going on? Am I in trouble?"

Kadyrov felt the contents of his stomach churn. It had to be a joke. It simply wasn't possible that someone here had located what the Soviets had been unable to find since 1918. Every Cheka agent since the era of Dzerzhinsky, including his father, had been told about it—all to no end. Most of them believed it didn't exist.

But it did exist. His father had believed it. And now someone else did, too.

Beads of sweat pearled on his forehead. Who could he tell? What if this was a joke, a former KGB agent having a laugh at his expense? He'd lose his cushy California posting and be sent to a third-world hellhole. He had to choose his confidante wisely. Men had been buried for less.

The envelope was covered with his prints, but surely Valery could do what they did on American television shows: find trace elements of a rare mineral that pinpointed the author's exact location or build a profile based on word choice and handwriting analysis.

The author claimed to have an accomplice, an American professor with a reputation for scholarly accuracy. It was meant to be a threat—a veiled warning that killing the author of the note wouldn't solve anything. There was someone else who had the information, someone whose disappearance wouldn't go unnoticed.

They had to be silenced. If what the author claimed was true, a single person stood to become one of the richest, most powerful people on the face of the earth. It could never be allowed.

He reached for the phone.

CHAPTER
FIVE

The phone rang with a shrill double beep, its red light blinking furiously. Vadim Primakov kept working. He did not have time for an interruption. The Kremlin wanted to cut his agency's funding by another ten percent, putting them back at a level he hadn't seen since 1994. *That bastard Starinov is reducing us to a footnote in history,* he thought.

Founded by Yeltsin to circumvent FSK infighting, the Public Security Intelligence Bureau was meant to be an independent intelligence service staffed with people Yeltsin could trust — people who had never worked for the KGB, NKVD, or FSK. Their mandate ran from counter-terrorism to surveillance and action services. But when Yeltsin handed the reins of power to Vladimir Putin, a former FSB director, the bureau had become an unwanted stepchild. Putin had reduced the bureau's agents to fact-checkers for FSB journalists and escorts for foreign dignitaries. Now, Prime Minister Maxim Starinov was determined to finish what Putin began — dismantling any bureaucratic entity not staffed with his own minions.

Vadim knew the only way to save his funding was to attack someone else's, but wading through his stolen copy of the FSB budget would take hours. Nikulin had dropped it off at 6:00 p.m. and it had to be returned by morning. The paper was spectrally controlled, making it impossible to photocopy or scan. Eighty pages of densely populated spreadsheets remained and it was already past 9:30 p.m.

But the damn phone wouldn't stop ringing. Vadim counted eight rings, then ten, then twelve. He glanced at the LCD readout. The caller's ID and number were blocked, but the bureau's decryption software displayed the digits as it identified them. When he saw the country code for the United States pop up, he swore.

Problems in America never simply went away.

Vadim picked up the handset. "Go away. I'm busy."

"*Dobryi vyecher*, Vadim Petrovich. I am Mikhail Vasilievich Kadyrov, Consul General in San Francisco."

"What the hell do you want?"

"I need your help."

"Call your ministry. I don't work for them."

"Valery said you were the one I should call."

Vadim swore. The powerful Chairman of the Investigative Committee had erased an embezzlement charge against his daughter, making it possible for her to find work and take care of his granddaughter again. It was a small favor compared to what many others asked for; still, he should have known Valery would keep score. "What does he want?"

"I received an anonymous letter here in San Francisco," Mikhail began. "From someone who claims he has access to the lost tsarist funds in the Bank of England."

Vadim cut him short. "I'm not interested in ancient history. Tell Valery I have better things to do."

"Are you familiar with the Rumkowski file?"

Vadim shivered. No one had said those words out loud since the Yeltsin administration. He reached for the back of his phone and toggled off the automatic recording switch. "What about it?"

"Do you remember what it said?"

"Of course."

"Whoever wrote this letter claims to have the password."

Vadim frowned. "No civilian knows there is a password. That file was never declassified. The only people who've seen it are in the Kremlin or in the ground. How the hell do *you* know about it?"

"Rumkowski used my father to infiltrate the bank."

"Jesus." Vadim scribbled a note to have Kadyrov's file brought up from the archives. "What else does your letter say?"

"The writer claims two of the four grand duchesses wrote letters to people on the outside during their captivity, each with the password inside. Just before the family was murdered in 1918, those letters were smuggled out of the Ipatiev house — by this person's great-grandfather."

"Rumkowski didn't say anything about the password leaving that house."

"No," the ambassador said pointedly. "He didn't."

Alarm bells rang in Vadim's head. Something Yeltsin had said to him once, when he asked why Yeltsin had razed the mansion in which the Romanovs were massacred. "For all we knew," Yeltsin said, "the password was still in there. We had to take it apart piece by piece. It was the only way to know for sure." That had been in 1977, when Yeltsin was first secretary of the Sverdlovsk District Central Committee and Vadim a junior secretary in the Moscow City Party Committee. No one had ever said anything about looking for the password outside the Ipatiev house — until now.

Still, this lunatic letter writer was probably a fortune hunter, someone who read too many thrillers. "What does he want?"

"Asylum, citizenship, and immunity."

Vadim snorted. "Is that all?"

"He says if we don't give him what he wants, he'll sell the password to the highest bidder."

"Does he think someone will pay more than the tsar left behind?"

"Maybe there's more than money in the account."

It was a possibility Vadim hadn't even considered. "Why does this fool believe we'll do as he asks?"

"Because he's already shared his information with someone else, a professor here named Elizabeth Brandon. It seems she's well known in university circles. Her new book is about Tsar Nicholas II. It's a revisionist history, of all things."

"Now I remember why I hate Americans."

"The letter writer says he'll contact me within twenty-four hours. If he doesn't like my answer, he'll offer the password to the Chechens and then the Georgians."

"He's bluffing."

"How can we be sure? If he gets enough money from the fanatics in Grozny, he might be better off letting the rest of us fight over the tsar's inheritance while he retires on a beach in the South Pacific." Kadyrov sighed. "Vadim, I know this is a bad situation. We don't know what's in the account or if it even exists. But Rumkowski believed it. My father did, too."

"And you?" Vadim asked. "What do you believe?"

"My father wouldn't have wasted his life looking for something that doesn't exist."

Vadim tried to remember the last time he'd read Rumkowski's file. The damn thing had six levels of classification on it and he'd only ever reached the fourth. What was in the other two levels? Could there be definitive proof that the tsar's secret account actually existed? It wasn't the kind of thing he could simply ask about. People associated with that file had a strange habit of disappearing. "This ends here, Mikhail. Tell your lunatic he will have to deal with us in person."

"You're going to negotiate with him?"

"I can't let him wave those letters at the Chechens or the Georgians. Saakashvili would snatch them in an instant if he thought it would bring the Kremlin crawling back to him. When your lunatic contacts you, arrange a meeting at his home. No public places, not under any circumstances. I'll send one of my men to handle it."

"I don't want any trouble, Vadim Petrovich."

"Russia does not negotiate with terrorists, separatists, mobsters, pirates, or American lunatics who think they know this country's history better than their own."

"And Professor Brandon? Even if you kill this man, she still knows everything."

"The Public Security Intelligence Bureau will handle this. Do you understand?"

"Yes, sir. Shall I call Valery back?"

"The matter is closed, Mikhail Vasilievich."

Vadim hung up the phone. He missed the small click on the line that indicated he wasn't the only one to hear the ambassador's story.

CHAPTER SIX

JULY 2013
CUSCO, PERU

The alpaca fur lay soft as a cloud beneath his palm. Constantine Dashkov turned the blanket over to inspect the construction. The vendor wanted 300 *nuevo soles*. He would have paid twice that, but haggling was the custom and he would only insult the shopkeeper by handing over the money. "*Doscientos,*" he said.

The shopkeeper shook his head. "*Trescientos, por favor.*"

Constantine touched the leather on the blanket's underside, pretending to find flaws in the tanning. "She prefers vicuña," he lied.

"You will find no vicuña for this price."

"I did at Señor Fernandez's shop." He didn't tell the man that Señor Fernandez sold coca leaves at an exorbitant price and threw in a vicuña coat or blanket as a complimentary gift with purchase.

"Fernandez dyes goat hair and tells tourists it is vicuña."

"Is that so?" Behind the shopkeeper's hut, the Andes rose like sleeping giants, waiting to be woken. "*Doscientos cincuenta y no mas.*"

"*Bueno.*" The shopkeeper snatched the blanket from him and began to wrap it, leather side out, in thinly woven burlap.

"*Gracias.*" Constantine stepped out of the shop and took a deep breath that did not fill his lungs. The filament-thin air stretched over the jagged peaks like a piece of plastic wrap forced to cover an entire banquet table. Russian air was the opposite: thick, solid, with weight that could fill you or crush you, depending on the season. *I am done with this place,* he thought. *No more flat tires, no more insects the size of small children. I am going home.*

The vibration of his cell phone interrupted him. He pulled it from his pocket, glancing at the number. "Vadim," he said.

"Greetings, my boy." The bureau chief's tired baritone crackled over the air. "How is Peru?"

"Suffocating. But I'm on my way home now."

"I'm sorry, my boy. There has been a change of plan."

He clenched his fingers around the phone. "Don't do this to me, Vadim."

"I wouldn't ask this of you unless it were for Valery." Constantine's gut churned as he listened to the ludicrous story: a blackmailer, his professor accomplice, and the favor Vadim could do nothing but repay. "I owe him too much to refuse," the older man said.

Constantine withheld the urge to hurl his phone into the mountains. He hadn't seen his family in one year, ten months, and thirteen days. *Hurry*, his father's email had said. *We're losing her.* "Get someone else," he said. "I can't do it."

"This is not a request. It must be handled quickly and quietly, before it comes to the prime minister's attention."

"She's waiting for me, Vadim."

"You leave in an hour. The file is on the plane."

He opened his mouth to protest, but the line was already dead. Behind him, the shopkeeper held out the wrapped package. Constantine shook his head. *"Lo siento, señor.* I'm not going home after all."

※

The Global Express XRS was fueled and ready when he arrived at Velazco Astete. The bureau fielded a fleet of private jets, keeping its agents off traceable passenger manifests. Each jet had radar scramblers, missile defense, a private stateroom, and a freezer full of Russian Standard. The flight crews consisted of retired Soviet Air Defense Force pilots. Sometimes they opened the door to the flight deck and told stories about shooting down Korean planes by accident.

Constantine saluted his pilot and co-pilot as he stepped into the cabin and grabbed a bottle from the freezer. He'd emailed his father from the cab, informing him of the delay. *Tell Lana to hang on*, he wrote. *One more stop and I'll be home.*

His eyes drifted to the file on the seat next to him. It bore the bureau's seal—a double eagle clutching a scroll in one talon and a saber in the other. It contained a summary of the

Romanov murder, snippets of an old case file with a Soviet locator number, and dossiers on Elizabeth Brandon and the blackmailer, Yuri Voloshin.

The information on Voloshin came from the Russian consul in San Francisco, a man named Kadyrov. The man's background check read like a petty crime novel. His father had died when he was eight, after which he lived with his immigrant grandfather. Since the age of nineteen, he'd been in and out of prison for theft and drug charges, with no steady jobs, education, wife, or kids. Aside from his connections within the *vory v zakone*, nothing marked his presence on earth.

Professor Elizabeth Brandon proved slightly more compelling. A tenured professor at a liberal arts university, she had an impressive public record — six books, two Pulitzer nominations, and occasional editorials in the *New York Times*. She was divorced with one child, and the legal guardian of a younger sister who was a hair's breadth away from being institutionalized.

He grunted, feeling an unwilling kinship with his victim. Svetlana's doctors had done nothing but shake their heads and give her more pills. They admitted they didn't understand what was going on in her mind, yet they felt sure it could be fixed by a pill. Without the pills, they said, Lana would need to live in a "facility" where she could get the "care" she needed.

He flipped to the summary of the Romanov murder. All seven members of the deposed imperial family had been imprisoned in Ekaterinburg from April to July of 1918: Nicholas, his wife Alexandra, his son Alexei, and four daughters named Olga, Tatiana, Marie, and Anastasia. As the politicians in Moscow tried to decide what to do with them, a counter-revolutionary force—the White Army—had advanced on Ekaterinburg.

The Ural Soviet had realized it couldn't risk the former tsar falling into enemy hands. They telegraphed Moscow, informing Lenin of their decision to kill the captives. No response came back. The men of the Ural Soviet interpreted silence as acquiescence and killed the entire family, with their servants, on the night of July 16/17. They dismembered, disfigured, burned, and buried the corpses.

For months after the murder, Lenin had fed conflicting stories to the press, some stating the whole family had been killed, some that only Nicholas had been killed. He used the family's survival as a bargaining chip to keep communication open with Germany and England. Because no one found the bodies, Lenin's ruse worked. Escape rumors abounded and for the first two years after the murder, few people had any idea what really happened.

Constantine turned to the old Soviet file, begun in 1931 by an agent named Rumkowski. Stalin had tasked Rumkowski with finding tsarist funds in foreign banks and securing them for Soviet coffers. When Rumkowski asked how Stalin knew the money was there to be found, the dictator refused to answer.

Rumkowski's preliminary inquiries to major banks—Barclays, Crédit Lyonnais, Mendelsohn's—had come back negative, so he decided to play dirty. He sent agents into Europe who posed as bankers, notaries, and even a Polish nobleman to get close to various relatives of the tsar and the pretender, Anna Anderson. What they reported confirmed the suspicion that the money was there, likely in an open and unclaimed account in the Bank of England.

Later, Rumkowski had questioned the men who murdered the tsar, hoping they might have heard something in the family's last days. But by that time, just before World War II, many of the men were dead and buried themselves.

However, one guard named Ivan Skorokhodov left a granddaughter who later confessed to a priest that her grandfather had been in love with Marie Romanov. They had planned to escape and claim the tsar's fortune, held in the Bank of England. Her grandfather, who had died in 1921 of influenza, said Marie had spoken of a password. She promised to relay the password to him in writing, so that if anything happened to her, at least her beloved could live a financially secure life. That password never came, and the guard later learned that Marie and her family had been murdered.

The guard had told his daughter this story while he lay dying. That daughter told her daughter, who later confessed the sin of greed to her priest. That priest had published his memoirs in the late 1940s. Only fifty volumes were printed, and thirty-four of them had been destroyed by the KGB to keep this story from spreading.

Rumkowski had believed the priest's tale to be true. He searched the Ipatiev house timber by timber, looking for the password Marie might have left for Skorokhodov. He found nothing. In the early 1970s, when he was ready to retire, he had passed his information to Boris Yeltsin, who got the necessary permits to raze the Ipatiev house in 1977. Still, no password was found.

Over the years, other sources had pointed to England as a potential source of hidden tsarist money, from Anna Anderson to the tsarina's friend, Lili Dehn. The Bank of England had issued countless statements denying the existence of a secret account. Rumkowski believed they were lying, under a blanket order originating with King George V, who hoped to confiscate the money.

Rumkowski's leads had thinned out as people who remembered the tsar died or succumbed to dementia. No one confirmed Ivan Skorokhodov's story, and the file remained open but dormant, a nuisance that nagged at Soviet premiers desperate for money to fund the space race, Olympic programs, and the war in Afghanistan.

Constantine set the file down. Somewhere deep behind his eyes, a headache was forming. The rhythmic throb reminded him of a derrick pulling black gold out of the Baku oil fields. If Stalin himself couldn't find the tsar's money, how was anyone else supposed to?

The plane's intercom buzzed to life. "Excuse the interruption, Mr. Dashkov. We've reached our cruising altitude of 43,000 feet. Our expected landing time in San Francisco is 9:30 p.m. local time. The flight should be smooth, if you want to get some sleep."

Constantine waved his acceptance. The cabin camera displayed in the cockpit would let the pilot know he understood. He opened the small bottle of vodka and drank all of it, settling down into a restless sleep.

CHAPTER SEVEN

Olga sat alone in the upstairs drawing room, pretending to read her Bible. It lay open on her lap but she hadn't turned a page in more than an hour. The words of Jesus failed to comfort her because she could only think of the horrible end that awaited him. No matter how kind he was, the people he sought to help always betrayed him. How had it felt, she wondered, at the moment of death? Was it a relief to put down the burden of suffering? Was it a struggle not to curse the soldier who had thrown the spear? What did it all matter, since two thousand years later, the same terrible crimes were still being perpetrated?

Her eyes drifted to the empty basket on the side table. Any moment now, the delivery boy would come to fetch it and bring it back to the nunnery. The guard who had struck her, bribed with one of Marie's bracelets, would escort the boy upstairs while Marie kept the rest of the family away.

Olga moved her jaw from side to side, still feeling soreness throb in her gums. It wasn't the first time she'd been hit — it had happened to all the girls at one time or another in the past few months. Only Alexei and her mother escaped, Alexei because of his hemophilia and her mother because the men were all afraid of her. Her mother's posture and bearing were still that of an empress, even if her beauty had faded.

She knew she wouldn't be able to see the boy approach because the soldiers had painted over all the windows. Instead, she closed her eyes and listened until she heard the sound of the outer gate and a guard's voice giving the go-ahead. Raucous laughter followed the poor boy as he trudged up the steps and knocked on the front door. The downstairs guard opened it and Olga held her breath until she heard a single pair of footsteps trudge up the stairs.

The boy emerged from the stairwell and looked at the floor instead of at her. "*Dobryi dyehn,*" he said softly.

"*Dobryi dyehn,*" Olga replied, smiling in spite of herself. On this hot July day, the boy wore a scarf wound twice around his neck. "You are dressed for snow, Filipp Feodorovich."

His eyes remained on the floor. "Y–yes, your —"

"Olga," she interrupted. People who referred to them by their titles usually earned a beating from the guards. She glanced toward the far end of the drawing room where Anastasia and Marie sat on the floor, playing a card game. Marie looked up when she felt her sister's gaze and nodded.

"Here is the basket, Filipp," Olga said, putting her Bible down. "Please thank the nuns for their kindness. Their love reminds us that hope is not lost, as does your kindness in bringing us their gifts."

"T – thank you," Filipp mumbled. He reached out to grab the handle, and when his hand brushed Olga's, she gasped.

"Filipp! You're freezing."

"Y – yes, your — I mean, yes. I do not feel well. Yesterday I was sweating all day, and today I shiver no matter what I put on."

A knife twisted in her heart as she realized this boy's illness was heaven-sent. "Filipp," she said softly. "I need your help. Are you able to do something for me?"

"Of course, your —"

"Good." Olga smiled, brushing the boy's floppy hair from his eyes. "My sister and I trust you, Filipp. You mustn't let the soldiers search the basket today. If they try and take it from you, you must cough or sneeze and tell them you visited someone in the influenza ward of the nunnery."

"Yes, your —"

"Tell them the person died. Tell them that now you are ill, too."

The boy wiped his nose with his hand and nodded.

"I have to tell you a secret, Filipp." She leaned close to him, breathing in the smell of sun and straw and horse that clung to his hair. "Hidden in this basket are two letters my sister and I wrote to our friends outside. We've told them a secret in these letters, but we've left out one important part. I need you to write that part down before you send these letters."

Filipp's dark eyes shone with excitement and fever. "Of course. What should I write on them?"

Olga whispered in his ear the words that the tsar, her father, had made them swear never to reveal. They meant nothing to Filipp.

His eyes looked back at her, unaware and unblinking. "Is that all, your — ?"

"No, my dear, that is not all. Once you have done this for us, you must forget what I have told you, every word of it." She bit her lip; it was very likely the fever would do this for him. If he spoke a word of this, his ravings could be blamed on his illness.

"You can trust me, your m — "

"I know I can," she whispered, feeling a sob catch in her throat. It seemed this boy was the only one she could trust in all of Russia. These sweet, simple souls were the ones who would be hurt most by the Bolsheviks and there was nothing her family could do to stop it. They would never leave this house again, she knew it. She had imagined hundreds of times how it might feel to be shot, stabbed, poisoned, bludgeoned, suffocated, or drowned. When it finally happened, it would be a relief.

Filipp sniffed, wiping his nose with the back of his hand. She bent in close and brushed her lips against his cheek. "This is for you," she whispered, slipping a ring from her finger and dropping it into his jacket pocket. "Go with God, Filipp Feodorovich."

CHAPTER EIGHT

The night was quiet, without the usual cacophony of honks and sirens that came with living near a hospital. Natalie pulled the covers over her head and listened for the wail of the St. Luke's ambulance. The Mission was filled with people who were broken in some way. She envied the ones the doctors were able to fix.

Beth hadn't called her since the press conference, more than two days ago. She still didn't know if Beth had read her cue cards as Natalie wrote them or winged it to avoid mentioning the tsar's missing fortune. To top it off, Belial was restless, shuffling his feet and twitching his wings. *Something's going to happen tonight,* he said. *I don't think you should sleep.*

"I want to sleep," she said, shoving her head beneath the pillow. "Leave me alone."

She imagined her sister, breathless and red-faced, trying to read ahead on the cue cards and skip over the part about Marie's letter and the password. The chancellor would have been there, along with Beth's department chair. Natalie imagined them shaking their heads at Beth's disappointing performance. It made her stomach ache to think of it now. "Beth, I'm sorry," she whispered. "I don't know why I did it."

Finally, she heard the St. Luke's ambulance roar down Valencia. Red and white light spilled through her blinds and she thought about all the reasons people called for help in the middle of the night: gunshot wound, heart attack, trouble breathing. "Save them," she said. "Please." It was the closest she could come to a prayer.

Belial fluttered his wings one last time to try and keep her awake. The rippling feathers brushed her brain, stinging like jellyfish tentacles. *It's coming*, he said.

Let it, she thought, pushing the pain down into the blackest part of her soul.

❧

She woke with a hand clamped over her mouth. Her eyes flew open and she struggled, but something held her down. "I won't hurt you," a male voice said. "But I need you to be quiet. Nod your head if you understand."

As her eyes adjusted, she saw a pale face, blue eyes, and short, gelled blond hair. He wore a black turtleneck and seemed to blend into the air. She realized she couldn't see past him or around him.

Belial's smug voice filtered through the fog in her brain. I *told you it was coming.*

She ignored him and focused on the sstrange man in her room. She nodded, forcing her dry throat to swallow, and the man pulled his hand from her face. "Who are you?" she asked. "What do you want?"

"I need you to come with me."

"No."

"I'm not here to harm you, Miss Brandon. I promise."

"I have a gun," she lied.

"So do I." He smiled and pulled a Walther P99 from his holster.

A wave of panic threatened to sweep her away and she took a deep breath. "How do you know my name?"

"Come with me and I'll tell you."

"I can't go anywhere with you. I don't even know who you are."

"My name is Constantine."

Natalie tilted her head. "Like the Roman emperor?"

"Like my grandfather." He pointed the gun at her. "Now get up."

"No."

"I don't want to shoot you, Miss Brandon. Please."

She looked into his eyes, two right triangles each with an eyelid for a hypotenuse. Their narrow shape made it look like he was squinting, as if he'd grown up shielding his eyes from the sun. "You wouldn't."

"I wouldn't like it," he agreed, a faint smile curling his lips. "But I'd do it."

"I don't believe you."

"That's not my problem." He pulled back on the pistol's slide to chamber a round. "Get out of the bed before I—" He stopped in mid-sentence and swung his gun to the front door.

Belial shifted his feet. *You have visitors, little one.*

Constantine's eyes scanned her apartment and he pointed to the window. "Go," he said. "Use the fire escape."

"Maybe it's the police," she said softly.

"The police would have knocked. If you come with me, I promise I won't let anything happen to you. Do you believe me?"

He held the gun lightly, like someone who'd used it many times before. A keloid scar traced its way across his right thumb, as if someone had tried to cut it off. Natalie realized that whoever he was, he knew how to survive. "Yes," she said, as her front door splintered under a burst of machine gun fire.

Constantine squeezed off four quick rounds as Natalie leapt out of bed. She opened the window and clambered onto the fire escape. The metal was cold beneath her bare feet and she hesitated. Constantine picked her up and set her on the rickety steel ladder. "Go!" he yelled.

A bullet shattered the window behind him, raining glass shards over both of them. Natalie scuttled down the ladder. When she reached the last step, she looked down—the ground lay a full six feet beneath her. Broken glass and cigarette butts dotted the asphalt below. She looked up at Constantine. "I can't do it!"

Constantine stopped several rungs above her. "Put your hands on the last rung."

"I can't!"

He swore in Russian, blue eyes blazing. "There are men with guns behind us. Are you going to jump or do I have to throw you?"

Go on, jump, Belial urged. *I'll catch you.*

"The hell you will," Natalie said. She worked her hands down to the bottom rung, squatting on it like a frog. In her mind, she visualized a gymnast's graceful descent from the uneven bars. Then a bullet flew past her ear and she panicked. Her fingers lost their grip and she landed in a heap on the ground, like a baby giraffe falling out of the womb.

Constantine jumped and landed gracefully beside her. He reached down to pull her up. Natalie groaned and pressed a hand to her spine. "Who are they? What do they want?"

"You," he answered. Then his eyes flew open wide and he knocked her to the ground. His weight pressed her into the asphalt and she heard a bullet strike the ground near her feet. Constantine lifted his arm and fired. This time, she heard a grunt and the sound of slack flesh striking pavement.

Constantine's frame stiffened as he took aim once more. He pulled the trigger but nothing happened. "*Bliad,*" he swore, tossing the gun away. He jumped to his feet to face their second attacker, advancing on them with a pistol.

Natalie looked up in time to see him bare his teeth and hurl himself at the man with the gun. "No!" she screamed.

Belial twitched his wings. *It wasn't supposed to happen like this.*

Constantine and the attacker formed a tumbleweed of limbs as they struggled for control of the gun. They butted up against the body of the first man Constantine had killed, rolling through a puddle of blood.

Constantine scooped up a handful of blood and flung it in the other man's eyes. The attacker cried out and Constantine freed his arm just long enough to punch the man in the ribs. The blow wasn't strong enough — the attacker grabbed Constantine's free arm and used the awkward balance point to push Constantine onto his back.

Natalie sat up and looked around for help. Her heartbeat echoed inside her skull, quick and light, like the flap of a hummingbird's wings. *I could run,* she thought. *Just let them kill each other.* "Belial, what do I do?"

Deus summus salvator, the angel answered.

It was Emperor Constantine's fourth-century battle cry.

Natalie gulped and watched Constantine roll the attacker over. He extended the other man's arm forcefully, slamming the man's wrist against the pavement to break his grip. Natalie saw her opportunity and crawled closer, reaching for the gun.

The attacker twisted his wrist so that the muzzle pointed straight at her head.

"*Nyet!*" Constantine cried, raising his left elbow and smashing it into the man's nose. The man howled in pain, blood streaming from his broken appendage. Before she could stop him, Constantine wrenched the gun from his loosened grip and shot the man in the head.

Natalie screamed as plum-colored foam and blood spewed from the man's temple. Lumpy and steaming, it smelled like freshly ground pepper. The scent stung her eyes and made them water. "Jesus," she whispered.

He isn't here, little one, Belial said. *That's the whole problem.*

She looked up at Constantine, spattered with blood and standing over the body. "I'm in big trouble, aren't I?" she said.

CHAPTER NINE

Constantine took the dead man's gun and moved to retrieve his own, replacing it in his holster. "Get up," he said. "These men don't travel in pairs."

"But they're dead," Natalie said. "Shouldn't we do something?"

He squatted next to one of the bodies and peered at its uniform insignia, a sword covered by a blue diamond. "*Yebat,*" he said. "This man is Vympel." Then he moved his gaze to her scraped legs. "Can you walk?"

She rubbed her arms. "I want to go back and get some clothes."

"It's not safe. We need to keep moving." He pulled her out of the alley toward the street. She followed as quickly as she could, every step jarring her bones. First the fall, then the body slam into the pavement. Belial didn't appreciate any of it. He let his wings flutter, zinging her brain with white-hot brush strokes of pain.

Constantine led her across the street to a blue BMW 325i parked in front of a funeral home. He opened the passenger door for her and she winced when the cold leather seats touched her bare thighs.

Without a word, he started the car and headed north. The Elbo Room and Blondie's had already closed, but people lingered on the sidewalk, smoking and eating foil-wrapped burritos. Natalie looked at them longingly. She rarely went to places like that — the small spaces and the noise and the pushy people frightened her. Belial didn't like them. *They don't understand us,* he said. *We're better off without them.*

The thought of Belial made her head hurt worse. "I need a drink," she said. Constantine gave her a stern look and she blushed. "It's medicinal. I'm not a drunk."

He pointed over his shoulder. "Check my bag."

She crawled headfirst into the backseat, digging through a black messenger bag until she found three airplane-sized bottles with unfamiliar Cyrillic labels. One by one, she unscrewed the caps and poured the contents down her throat, swallowing heavily as the liquor torched her tonsils.

"Leave some for the rest of us," Constantine said.

"You don't understand." She gasped and wiped her mouth with the back of her hand. "It's the only thing that keeps Belial quiet."

"What are you talking about?"

It was too much to explain when her head was already pounding. "Nothing. Never mind. Who were those men?"

The BMW neared Duboce, on the eastern edge of the Castro. Here, too, the street teemed with partygoers. Two drunk men wove their way down the sidewalk, arms entwined, singing "Wonderwall" at the top of their lungs. Constantine turned right, onto Market headed toward Civic Center. "They were Vympel. Special forces for anti-terrorism and sabotage."

"I'm not a terrorist."

"I can see that."

"Why couldn't they?"

"I don't know."

"What did they want from me?"

"I don't know."

"What do you want from me?"

Constantine accelerated, speeding past Van Ness. "I need your help."

"Bullshit."

"It's the truth." He reached up to adjust the rearview mirror as they shot past the Warfield. A bright flash of light hit the glass and reflected into her eyes. "Get down," he said. "They found us."

Natalie scrunched in her seat as Constantine lowered his window and reached for his gun. "What are you doing?" she cried.

"Hold on to something." He pulled the emergency brake and jerked the wheel, sliding across Market Street toward Montgomery. As the car tracked perpendicular to the four-lane street, Constantine shot at the car behind them. Natalie heard glass shatter and tires squeal, and put her hands over her ears.

Constantine zoomed up Montgomery opposite the one-way flow of traffic. He swerved to dodge a honking cab and Natalie's head bounced against the glove box. She groaned and popped up in time to see the car plow toward a NO PARKING sign. "Where the hell are you going?"

Before he could answer, a bullet shattered the back window. Natalie screamed and ducked while Constantine shot back. She felt the car lurch to the left and tried to place their movement on a mental map. *Columbus*, she thought, as the smell of garlic began to fill the air and the car bounced over deeper-than-usual potholes.

Every jolt made Belial angry. Inky tentacles of pain crept out from under the shadow of the vodka. Between the ache in her head and Constantine's frantic turns, she lost track of their location. By the time the car dropped to a legal speed, she felt the contents of her last meal rising through her esophagus. "You can sit up now," Constantine said. "I lost them."

"Good timing. I'm about to lose my dinner, too." She leaned her head onto the cool glass and breathed deeply the way Beth had taught her, in through her nose and out through her mouth.

Constantine turned right onto Vallejo and snaked through a labyrinth of one-way streets. The last ended in a dirty cul-de-sac surrounded with peeling gray row houses. He parked in the garage belonging to the smallest house.

Sagging power lines criss-crossed the sky like loosely woven cambric. Broken glass and piles of burned garbage littered the street. The house's windows and doors were covered by rusted metal bars. Half of the porch floorboards and even more of the roof appeared to be missing. "This is the safe house," Constantine said. "We stay here tonight."

Natalie gulped and followed him to a tiny door on the left, an old tradesman's entrance. The flimsy lock yielded and he hurried her inside. A dim bulb crackled to life, unfettered by a housing or shade, illuminating a single room with a galley kitchen and a door that presumably led to a bathroom.

Twin beds covered in rotting green chenille jutted out from the far wall. Matching curtains hid the lower panes of two dim windows. A rounded refrigerator and Depression-era stove kept company with a rusted dining set upholstered in vinyl. The walls were a grimy shade of beige, somewhere between old lace and used teabag. Everywhere Natalie looked, she saw upturned cockroaches.

Constantine checked the door and window locks. "I wish I had someplace better for you. Our prime minister revoked the agency's permission for action services, so whatever we keep abroad has to be unnoticed and undesirable."

"Mission accomplished," she said. She sank onto one of the beds and a mushroom cloud of dust enveloped her. Belial fluttered his wings as if he could sweep it all away. The pain tore through her temples and she gasped.

"What's wrong?" Constantine asked.

"Nothing," she lied, forcing a smile as she sat up. "I just want to know what's going on."

"You don't look well."

Natalie gritted her teeth. "I've been chased out of my apartment, shot at, and nearly killed. The least you could do is tell me why... and who the hell you are."

"My name is Constantine Dashkov. I work for the Public Security Intelligence Bureau of the Russian Federation."

"What does that have to do with me?"

"You have information we need."

"I don't have anything. I told you that already."

"Professor Brandon, this will be easier for both of us if you cooperate."

Natalie looked up, clasping the bedspread until her knuckles shone. Behind her eyes, Belial's shoulders began to shake and it took her a moment to realize he was laughing. "Not good," she said.

"What is it?"

She tried to twist her lips into a smile, but moving any muscles in her face hurt too much. "I'm not who you think I am."

"I called you by name in your apartment. We both know who you are, professor."

Natalie opened her mouth to explain, but nothing came out. She wished she were telepathic instead of…whatever the hell she was. *What am I, Belial?* she asked. *Do you even know?*

I do, he answered.

Then help me, she begged. If she told Constantine the truth, would he let her go or just start chasing Beth? She couldn't think. Forcing ideas into her swollen brain felt like pushing a bedspread through a keyhole. "I'm not who you think I am," she repeated.

Constantine put a hand under her chin. He tilted it up to look her in the eye. "Pretending you're someone else won't make me go away. You know that, don't you?"

"I'm telling you the truth."

"If you're not Professor Brandon, who are you?"

"Beth is my sister."

He tightened his grip on her chin. "Our records indicate that apartment is leased by Elizabeth Brandon."

"She rented it for me. It's her signature on the lease."

"Then why do her employment records also list that location as her residence?"

"She makes students cry on a regular basis," Natalie said. "Would you want hundreds of pissed-off undergrads knowing where you live?"

Anger flooded her veins and the urge to throw up returned, drenching her in a wave of sweat. Belial soothed her, caressing her with his wing. *You're getting upset, little one. I think you should let me handle the rest of this.*

She ignored him, grabbing the edge of the mattress and clutching it until she felt the springs dig into her fingertips. If Belial took control, she'd never find out what they wanted from her sister. She used the pain to stay focused, staring into the Russian man's blue eyes. "Why do you want Beth?"

I don't think you heard me, Belial said, flicking her with a wing. Natalie blinked back tears and kept her gaze focused on Constantine.

"I'm not going to hurt her," he said. "I just need information."

"What information?" Spots danced in front of her eyes, floating past her like waltzing mushroom caps. It was Belial, pressing on her optic nerve.

"A man claims to have a password that allows him to access Tsar Nicholas II's funds in the Bank of England. He said he shared his information with your sister, who verified its authenticity. I need to find out what he showed her."

"He lied," she whispered. A drop of sweat rolled into her eye, burning it with salt. She blinked it away but when she opened her eyes, everything had already gone black. Her fingers and toes tingled and when she commanded them to move, nothing happened. *Not now, Belial,* she begged. *Please not now.*

But it was too late.

I'll handle everything, Belial said. *You just rest.*

He thrust his wings up against her skull, pressing them outward until she was sure her head would crack open. "I'm sorry," she whispered, as the world around her vanished.

CHAPTER TEN

Constantine watched the girl's eyes roll back in her head. She collapsed onto the bed and he pulled her upright. Sweat glistened in the creases of her forehead and he gasped at the heat radiating from her skin. He swore and laid her back down.

Images from the horrible days following Lana's return flashed through his mind. Sullen and withdrawn, she'd locked herself in her room for three days. When he finally broke down her door, she lay sweating and unconscious, in the grip of a terrible fever. She shook and spasmed like the girl in front of him, her skin concealing all the fires of hell.

He ran to the bathroom and pulled the cold water handle of the claw-footed tub, releasing a stream of dirty water. In the freezer, he found two plastic trays filled with frost-burned ice cubes and emptied them into the water. "Hold on," he said, brushing sweat-damp hair from her cheeks. With one arm under her shoulders and the other beneath her knees, he carried the unconscious girl to the bathroom.

Her body twitched when he lowered her into the cold water. He scooped it over her arms and chest, exactly as he had for Lana. The dirty water beaded like gray pearls on her skin.

Constantine straightened her legs to make sure they were covered and dug beneath the sink until he found a washcloth. When he plunged it into the water, a dead spider fell out, floating like a jellyfish in the sea. He fished it out before it could touch her and placed the cool cloth on her forehead.

This was all his fault. He'd seen the professor's headshot in the file. He should have realized the woman in the apartment looked nothing like the woman in the photo. He'd been too focused on finishing the job so he could go home.

He tried to remember what his file had said about the professor's sister — something about sanitariums. Looking down at the girl in the tub, he realized the file was probably right. Every one of her nails lay ragged, bitten off in pieces above the quick. Her masses of dark, tangled hair hadn't seen a comb or scissors in quite some time. When open, her eyes were ghostly blue-white, not so different from the color of her skin. They reminded him of a frozen Siberian lake, primeval and dangerous.

He touched the back of his hand to her cheek. It was still too hot. What if he left to fetch a doctor and the next Vympel death squad found her?

He picked up her hand to take her pulse, but something else caught his attention: vertical white lines, running nearly the length of each forearm. Constantine recognized them immediately. Lana's lines ran horizontally.

He'd killed dozens of people in his years working for Stealth and then the bureau, but he still wondered what made people turn their weapons on themselves. And if they failed, as Lana and this girl had, did that make them feel better or worse? Did they realize life had more value than they thought, or did they just keep trying? For Lana, it appeared to be the latter.

He traced the girl's scars with the tip of his index finger.

A low moan rumbled from her throat in response. Her legs twitched in the water, splashing him. He lifted her out of the tub, laid her on the bed, and dried her with a towel. When he came to her face, he patted her cheeks gently, but they were wet with tears a moment later.

"What's wrong?" he asked.

"It hurts," she moaned.

He tossed aside the towel and sat on the edge of the bed. The girl moved slowly, crawling into his lap and clutching fistfuls of his shirt in small, white-knuckled hands. She pressed her head deep beneath his arm, as if she could burrow into his side. He tried to pull her up but she resisted, clinging to him until he let her be.

Her eyes leaked tears in wordless sobs as the pain worked its way through her. It came in waves, like a pregnant woman's contractions, except that each one left her with more time to breathe before the next one seized her.

Over the course of an hour, they left her exhausted and weak, fingers cramped into curls where they clutched at him. He had never felt more helpless in his life.

When at last she lay quiet in his arms, he bent his head to her ear and whispered, "Is it over?"

The girl nodded, unable to open her cracked lips.

"What do you need? Do you want some water?"

She nodded again and he extricated himself from the tangle of her arms and found a glass in the kitchen cabinet. He rinsed it and filled it with tap water. "Here," he said, holding it as she swallowed greedily.

When she finished, she looked up at him with fire-bright eyes, skin shining with oil and sweat. "Thank you," she said.

"For what?"

"You could have left me."

Constantine thought of Lana, discovered by a night watchman after Lazovsky and his men had left her unconscious and bleeding on the pavement outside a warehouse. There was no honor in a man who left a woman to die on the street. "I couldn't."

Her lips stretched in a small, ghostly smile. "You've made that choice before."

"Yes."

"For a woman?"

"Yes."

She clutched the empty glass in her fingers. "Who is she?"

"I think she's a lot like you."

"Do the doctors tell her she's crazy?"

"Yes."

"Do you believe them?"

"Something bad happened to her and she can't find her way back to us. Is that what happened to you?"

She shrugged. "One day, he just appeared."

"Who appeared?"

"An angel called Belial. He lives in my head. Sometimes he tries to get out — that's what just happened." She closed her eyes and sighed. "I guess it could be worse. Could be Lucifer, right?"

Constantine gulped. "I think you need more water." He took her glass and refilled it until water ran over the top and down the sides. Lana never talked about abstract things like angels and demons. But Lana wasn't there — and he wouldn't see her until he finished this job.

When he brought the glass back to the girl, he held it an inch beyond her fingertips. "What's your name?"

"Natalie."

"Natalie, what does your sister know about the tsar's money?"

She leaned forward and took the glass. "Beth doesn't know anything. She doesn't believe it exists."

"How can you be sure?"

"Because I tried to convince her two days ago and we haven't spoken since."

"The blackmailer mentioned your sister by name. Why?"

"She just published a biography of Nicholas II. Someone probably saw her name attached to the subject and bluffed."

"People who break into embassies and blackmail ambassadors don't usually bluff about things like that."

"I wouldn't know." She paused. "Do you have any more vodka?"

"Are you crazy?" As soon as he said it, he wished he hadn't.

"Alcohol helps. It slows Belial down so I can out-think him."

Constantine blinked. "You said you tried to convince your sister the tsar's money is there. How do you know?"

"Belial told me." She drew her legs to her chest and wrapped her arms around them. "You mentioned a password. I've only seen one source in the whole world that talks about a password. Either your blackmailer found that source and is using it to bluff, or he's telling the truth."

He watched the color flood back into her cheeks and it frightened him. "Calm down. I don't want you to faint again."

"What if we can solve a mystery that's almost a hundred years old?"

"Not 'we.' You wouldn't be involved if it weren't for me."

Natalie swung her feet off the bed and planted them on the floor. He jumped, ready to catch her if she fell. "I'm fine now," she said. "See?"

He put an arm around her waist to steady her, resting it above the soft curve of her hip. Drops of water from her tangled hair fell onto his sleeves. Although she'd lost the sudden fever, her body remained hot to the touch. "I don't believe you."

"The men in my apartment. Do they also think I'm Beth?"

He nodded. "They must have followed me straight to you."

"So she's safe as long as you don't tell anyone you made a mistake?"

"Yes."

"I want you to keep it that way."

"You would take her place against a Vympel death squad?"

"I would take her place in hell."

Constantine looked down at her pale skin. He realized the blue tone beneath its surface came from iron or steel. "Now I believe you," he said.

"Promise me nothing will happen to her."

"I can't."

She grabbed his wrists. "Belial told me the money is there. I'll help you find it if you promise me those men won't hurt my sister."

"I told you I can't." If a small-time gangster like Lazovsky would destroy Constantine's sister just to get to him, what would Vympel do if they believed Natalie and her sister had information they needed? He stared at her face, trying to find a way to explain how dangerous this was. But as he looked at her, his brain replayed the image of her in the bathtub, sodden clothes clinging to every curve.

He released her abruptly and escaped into the bathroom. "I'll find you some dry clothes," he said, slamming the door behind him.

He stared at his reflection in the mirror. *She's just an ordinary informant. Stop pretending she's Lana.* Then he closed his eyes and pressed his hands to his head, but all he could see was Natalie Brandon's eerie blue gaze. What was it she believed lived behind her eyes? An angel? Maybe that wasn't so strange. The women who knelt before the icons in the Arkhangelsky Sobor believed a divine essence inhabited a painted piece of wood. Why shouldn't it inhabit a person, too?

He bent down and rummaged in the under-sink cabinet. Tucked in a small wicker basket, he found a pair of men's jeans and a white T-shirt. He carried them back out to her.

"This is all we have," he said, shaking them out. "They're a little dirty."

"I like things that are dirty," she said. "You saw my apartment."

He turned his back while she dressed, listening to the sound of the scratchy denim sliding up over her hips. "Okay," she said. "You can turn around now."

The T-shirt hung loosely over her breasts, dark nipples visible through the thin cotton. He gulped. Natalie glared at him and pressed her scarred forearms to her chest. "Are you staring at my arms?"

"There's nothing wrong with your arms," he said, guiding her back to the bed. "I know someone who has scars, too, remember?"

"Why did she do it?"

"I don't know."

"Why don't you know?"

"She won't talk to me. I want her to, but she won't."

"Did you tell her that?"

"Yes." He paused. "How did you get yours?"

"Why do you care?"

He touched one of her scars and felt the soft, puffy skin. "It might help me understand why she did it."

"Are you going to shoot me if I don't tell you?"

"No. I wasn't going to shoot you earlier, either."

"I didn't think so," she said. "None of it was my fault, you know. It was Dante's."

"Dante?"

"Belial brought him to me. Dante said he needed me to transcribe a message for him. He said it had to be in blood."

"Dante," Constantine said again. "Why didn't you say no?"

She looked straight at him. "When Italy's greatest poet tells you to do something, you do it."

"Of course," he replied, as if her answer were the only logical one. "So what did you do?"

"I went to the kitchen, picked up a knife, and held it across my wrist like a violin bow. But Dante said I was doing it wrong and corrected me, like this." She held an imaginary blade parallel with her ulna. "I used the blood for ink, writing every word he said on my kitchen wall."

Constantine pointed at her right arm. "What happened to that one?"

"Canto XXXIII. That fucker is long."

Constantine bit his tongue.

"I wrote down everything he said, which turned out to be from the *Inferno*." She shook her head. "The bastard could have just told me to look it up. I almost ran out of ink."

"Ink," he repeated, shaking his head. "But someone must have saved you."

"Beth had been calling me for an hour straight. When I didn't answer, she called 911 and took a cab to St. Luke's. As soon as I woke up, I asked her to copy down Dante's message. She compared what I'd written to the real thing and found something that didn't belong. It was the German word for coward."

"I don't understand."

"Neither did we. But Beth found out that a previously undiscovered manuscript of the *Inferno* had just come up for auction. It was supposedly written by Dante himself. They authenticated it with lasers and Raman spectroscopy, and the starting bid was set at $15 million."

"What did that have to do with it?"

"The man selling the manuscript was named Feigling."

"I don't follow."

"Feigling means coward in German."

He felt the blood drain from his cheeks. "You're kidding."

"I never kid about medieval poetry. Beth raised hell with the president of the auction house, telling them they had a forgery on their hands. They ran another round of tests and the results were different. Turns out the manuscript was forged. They told Beth it was a German man, someone who made his living forging everything from manuscripts to passports."

"I remember hearing about that case." He shook his head, staring at her with begrudging respect. "He got caught because of you? How did you know the manuscript was a fake?"

"I didn't."

"You must have known something about it. Something that triggered your dream."

"I didn't know the damn thing existed." She narrowed her eyes. "Did your file say anything about me?"

"Just that Elizabeth Brandon has a sister who'd been in and out of a sanitarium as a child. How did all of this start?"

"Belial showed up and put me in a coma when I was nine. When I came out of it, I asked the doctors if I could see him on the X-ray. That's when they shipped me off to the funny farm for kids. Someone decided I was schizophrenic and it stuck."

"Did they give you any medication?"

"They gave me all of it. I barely knew my own name for five years."

"What happened?"

"Beth." Her features relaxed into the purest smile he'd ever seen. "She saved me."

"Does she think you're schizophrenic?"

"She thinks I'm like Joan of Arc, visions and all. Maybe it's the same thing."

"What do you think?"

She shrugged and twisted away from him. "It's bigger than me. I'm just the puppet."

"Then who's the puppeteer?"

"You know what happened to Joan of Arc, don't you?"

He recognized the bitterness in her tone and knew where it came from. Lana believed what happened to her was her fault, too — that she deserved to be beaten and raped and left for dead, even though he was the one Lazovsky wanted. "It's not your fault this thing happened to you. You know that, right?"

Her smile was like a jack-o-lantern, scooped out and hollow. "I know lots of things."

"Whatever made you this way, it's not your fault. It's a disease."

"Is it?" She shrugged and shifted position on the bed. "I don't even know what's inside me. Sometimes I think I can find out."

"How?"

"Sometimes I'll flick a lighter and hold my finger inside the flame. Or I'll hold it to my arm or my leg."

"To be like Joan?"

"To see if God or Belial can feel it." She dropped his gaze and picked at the decaying chenille bedspread. "Beth thinks I'm smarter than she is, but she's a million times what I'll ever be. Maybe I had to be this way so she could be who she is. But if that's true…" She clenched her fingers. "I still want to know that's the reason."

"Natalie, look at me." He put two fingers under her chin and tilted it toward him. "None of this happened as a cosmic trade for your sister's success. Sometimes things happen for no reason." She tried to pull away but he held her face in his grasp, brushing her cheekbones with his thumbs. "It's not your fault."

"You don't believe that." She leaned her forehead against his and suddenly, her lips were just inches away.

"I do. Somewhere inside, you do, too." He watched her eyes thaw like the ice they resembled, slipping from something hard and cold into something liquid, something he couldn't grasp if he tried. He closed his eyes and gently brushed her lips with his own, intending to pull away when she was comforted.

But something happened. Instead of pulling away, she opened her mouth to him. Hungry and angry, her tongue swept his in a honeyed frenzy. She slipped shaking hands around his neck and pulled him closer. The heat from her body swept through him, setting his blood on fire in an instant. He kissed her back and imagined pressing her down into the creaking bed. "Natalie," he said, pulling back. "We can't do this."

Her heavy breath moved her hair where it had fallen over her face. "You asked me to believe you. Do you believe me?"

Her eyes, melted pools of Siberian ice, held more fear and pain than he could fathom. Maybe the best way to help her wasn't to try and change her. Maybe the best way was simply to do what she asked — believe in her.

He let her pull him down onto the bed and covered her body with his.

CHAPTER ELEVEN

Beth Brandon lay in bed with a book in her lap. On the cover, a half-naked redhead writhed in the arms of a pirate who looked like Fabio. She wished she were the type of professor who read Foucault or Goethe for fun, but on most days, she could barely manage Jared Diamond. Life was already full enough of guns, germs, and steel.

In the past week alone, she'd picked Seth up from the principal's office for fighting, disciplined a grad student for writing sexual comments on a freshman student's paper, badgered Scott into sending May's child support, and biffed a speech to the university regents after Natalie hijacked her cue cards.

To top it off, someone had prank-called the house twice that night. Occasionally, an enterprising student found her phone number and begged for an extension on a paper, but these calls weren't like that. The other person never said a word — all she could hear was calm, soft breathing. She hated to think someone might be watching the house. Seth was never home alone, and even if he were, Roosevelt would bark at any intruder. Still, she couldn't bear to think of her son being in danger. She added another item to her mental to-do list: test the security system.

She turned back to the pirate book and read one paragraph before a noise in the hallway caught her attention: slippers shuffling on polished hardwood, making their way to her door. Seth's small fist knocked twice before he turned the knob. "Mom?" he said, poking his pale head into her room.

"What's wrong?" Her heart hurt when she thought of how often he'd come to her with questions about his father, why he never called, and when he would get to go down to L.A. and visit. She arranged her face into a smile while her brain formed quick answers to a barrage of dangerous questions.

He shuffled inside and scrambled up onto the bed. "I can't sleep. I tried listening to my iPod, but it didn't work."

"Wanna sleep in here tonight?"

"Maybe. If Roo can come, too." His soft blond hair fell diagonally across his forehead and he brushed it up out of his eyes. "Are you busy?"

She held up the romance novel so he could see the cover. "Babe, I'm reading a book about pirates that doesn't mention anything about vitamin deficiency, disease, rats, or the lack of basic hygiene on a pirate ship. I think it's safe to say I'm not busy."

Her son nodded, well versed in the falsehoods of popular representations of pirates. "Shark Week started tonight, Mom."

"Did they talk about great whites?"

"It was hammerheads. Aunt Natalie said she'd watch it with me, but she never came."

Beth felt a quiver of arrows pierce her heart. Every doctor who'd reviewed Natalie's file had insisted she be kept away from Seth, but Beth could never bring herself to obey them. "Oh, sweetie," she said. "I think it was my fault. I'm sorry."

Seth's brown eyes blinked at her solemnly. "Did you tell her not to come?"

"We had a fight. She probably thinks I'm still angry at her."

"You're not, are you? I mean, you said you're sorry, right?"

"No, I didn't."

"Why not? You make me say I'm sorry all the time."

"I guess I thought I wasn't sorry," she said. "But I am."

"Then you need to tell her. I don't want you guys to fight."

"I don't want to fight with her, either."

"So can you call her? And find out if she's coming over tomorrow? It's important. They're gonna talk about mega-mouth sharks."

Beth sighed. "It's not that easy, babe."

"Yes, it is. You just pick up the phone and call her. Ask her if she's coming tomorrow…please."

"All right." Beth put down her book, wondering why she needed her eight-year-old son's prompting to apologize to her sister. Her cheeks burned as she realized how stupid it all was. So what if her speech had been less than stellar? If she was that dependent on cue cards, the problem was hers, not Natalie's.

She reached for the phone and hit the speed dial for Natalie's number. It rang four times before Natalie's machine picked up. "Nat, it's Beth. Look, I'm sorry for getting mad at you the other day. I know you're trying to help, and I shouldn't have snapped like that. I just want to make sure you're okay. I've got someone here who really wants to know if you're coming over to watch megalomaniac sharks tomorrow—"

"Megamouth!" her son yelled. "Mom, get it right!"

"—so call me, or just come over, okay? I love you, sis." She hung up the phone and smiled for Seth. "You're my witness. I invited her over for sharks." She glanced at the clock radio on her nightstand: 2:30 a.m. It was odd that Nat wouldn't answer this late at night. She couldn't be out and about, could she? What if something had happened to her?

"Hey, kiddo, why don't you go back to bed?" she said, in a voice that sounded falsely bright, even to her. "If Nat calls back, I'll tell her you say hi." She held her breath, wondering if Seth would call her bluff.

He looked at her for a moment, the questioning expression in his eyes so much like his father's that she felt tears gather beneath her lashes. *I wish you could have seen the best of him instead of the worst*, she thought. Then he nodded and slipped off the bed. "See you in the morning, Mom," he said, smiling as he closed her door.

"I love you," she said.

Beth lay back and listened for the click of Seth's door. It came just as the phone rang again. She snatched it up, eager to tell her sister how brave Seth was in the face of her absence. "Nat?" she said.

But no one answered. All she heard was slow, gentle breathing. "Who is this?" she asked. "If you don't stop harassing me, I'll call the police."

In the background, she heard something familiar — a foghorn, blaring out into the night. One, two, three blows. She held the phone away from her ear and realized she heard the same noise outside her window. The caller was watching the house.

She slammed the phone down and ran to her bedroom window. She threw aside the curtains and looked down at the street. It was empty. No cars, no pedestrians. "I know what I heard," she said. "I know you're out there."

The next number she dialed was 911.

CHAPTER TWELVE

JULY 2013
SAN FRANCISCO, CALIFORNIA

Constantine watched Natalie sleep, curled in a fetal position on one of the grimy beds. Her lips were rosy and softly swollen. After one frantic embrace, she'd drifted off in his arms as his fingertips traced the Cyrillic alphabet on her skin. Part of him felt relieved. The girl couldn't separate fact from fiction. He had no business sleeping with her, even if she thought it was what she wanted.

His eyes drifted to the puffy silver scars on her arms. Her story about Dante and the German forger couldn't be true. But why invent such a lavish story to explain a suicide attempt? Lana never explained anything — she just kept trying.

He remembered the day his sister had come home from the hospital after Lazovsky's attack. She'd smiled, gone into her room, and closed the door behind her. Without a sound, she'd calmly sliced the flesh from her cheeks and fed it to her tiny dog. It was morning before they found out what she'd done.

Constantine understood certain kinds of death, like the star-bright explosion of pain delivered so well by bullets, bombs, and knives. He didn't understand it when it came from the inside out. How did these women silence the scream of their own flesh, the cry for life when confronted with death? Obeying that cry was all that had kept him alive in Chechnya.

He shook his head to clear the images of blood and death. It was time to do his job. He grabbed his phone and dialed Vadim. "Pour a drink," he said as his boss picked up. "We have problems."

"Greetings to you, too, Constantine Alexandrovich."

"Find the analyst who did the intelligence work for that file."

"Why?"

"So you can fire him. He sent me to Natalie Brandon, not Elizabeth Brandon."

"Did you kidnap the wrong woman? Constantine, we're not even supposed to be in that goddamn country!"

"There's more. Someone followed me here."

"Impossible. No one knows about this but the two of us and the ambassador."

"Then whoever prepared that file is on Starinov's payroll."

"Starinov! Why do you suppose he's the one following you?"

"Because the men I killed were Vympel."

"Are you sure?"

"I saw their insignia, Vadim."

Originally a KGB special ops squad, Vympel had disbanded amid the confusion of communism's fall and Yeltsin's messy assumption of power. In the late 1990s, the unit had been resurrected by Maxim Starinov, a protégé of Putin.

Starinov had returned the squad to its roots — a brutal *spetsnaz* unit specializing in foreign espionage. The squad functioned as Starinov's personal army, with no government mandate or oversight. During the second Chechen war, Starinov sent Vympel men dressed as Chechen rebels to kidnap and murder Red Cross workers. When he ordered Vympel to end the hostage situation at School Number One in Beslan, they fired thermobaric rockets into a school full of frightened children without hesitation.

Nine months ago, the bureau's hackers had intercepted an email from Starinov to the heads of the GRU and the SVR, informing them that the reconstituted Vympel unit would fall under his personal jurisdiction. His personal army was now being paid for by Russian taxpayers and given unprecedented access to the country's best weaponry and technology.

"So it's true," Vadim said. "How many of them were there?"

"I killed two. I don't know how many more he sent."

"They'll come after you with everything they have."

"That's not what scares me. They're watching us from the inside, Vadim. If they had their own intel, they'd have gone for the right sister." Constantine thought about the brief he'd been given—information about the Romanov execution and portions of the Rumkowski file. If he was right about the leak, Starinov knew everything the bureau knew. "That bastard is using us to find the tsar's money, isn't he?"

"And he'll kill you when you find it." Vadim took a gulp of vodka. "He must believe the tsarist cache exists or he wouldn't risk sending Vympel into the United States."

"If we get it first, maybe we can strike a bargain."

"How long can you avoid the next Vympel death squad?"

"As long as I have to," Constantine said, turning to look at Natalie. "But there's something else." He told his boss about Natalie and her connection to the German forger. "It can't possibly be true, but she believes it."

"Are you saying she can just *ask* Nicholas and Alexandra where they hid the money?" Vadim scoffed.

"She's not a psychic," he said. "It's something…different. But Natalie says her sister never met Voloshin. They've never heard of him or seen his copy of the Romanov letters."

"Do you believe her?"

Constantine watched the gentle rise and fall of her chest, and the curl of her hands next to her breast. "Yes," he answered.

He heard the sound of breaking glass as Vadim chucked his bottle across the room. "So it was all a bluff? Why in God's name would Voloshin do something so foolish?"

"Because it worked," Constantine said. "A professor's name was enough to make us all believe him. But if Voloshin's never met the real Elizabeth Brandon, he won't know Natalie isn't the professor. Let me take her to the meeting. I don't know enough about the tsar or his money to see through Voloshin's bullshit."

"We need the professor, the one Voloshin mentioned."

"Natalie is her sister's researcher. Everything her sister knows, she knows."

"You aren't going to give me a choice, are you?"

"You didn't give me one. Lana's still waiting."

"Kadyrov set the meeting for 1 p.m. at Voloshin's house."

Constantine jotted down the address and the time. "If Natalie thinks Voloshin's story is good enough, we'll give Starinov something to bargain with."

"A target is what you'll give him. He'll send the angels themselves after you."

"Let him," Constantine said. "We already have one on our side."

CHAPTER THIRTEEN

Vadim hung up and reached for the bottle of chalky antacid tablets in his drawer. The vodka had been a bad idea. Just hearing the word "Vympel" made his stomach leak like a Soviet faucet. He knew he couldn't fight Starinov head-on — the bureau didn't have the money. All they had was a brief head start and the cooperation of Constantine's lunatic girl. Starinov was going to obliterate them and there was nothing he could do about it.

He thought of his daughter, Liliya, and granddaughter, Marya. They would be cooking supper right now, simmering things in a pot and making the house smell of meat and paprika. Marya would set the table and fold yellow cloth napkins into unidentifiable shapes that she insisted were zoo creatures. Liliya would put far too much spice in the stew and their noses would run while they ate.

A sudden pang of longing dwarfed the burn of his ulcer. He wanted to embrace them and tell them how much he loved them. If the worst happened, he wanted to die knowing he had made peace with the people dearest to him.

He hefted his briefcase and left the office, a whitewashed brick building north of the Kremlin, just off Bolshaya Nikitskaya. Nondescript except for two false towers and a dormer window, the building looked more like a well-to-do merchant's home than a government agency's headquarters. He liked it that way: no glass-walled skyscraper and no view of the vulgar riverboats draped with banners advertising tourist hotels, nightclubs, and websites. He detested the young billionaires of the Ostozhenka who wasted all their rubles on Rembrandts, Bentleys, and models who looked like starving choir boys. The city he loved was the ancient one, a colorful place with brightly painted homes and silver samovars in every parlor. That Moscow was the true soul of Russia, old and powerful and boisterous, like a drunk *boyar* at the table of Ivan the Terrible.

Vadim trudged down Bolshaya Nikitskaya, past the ornate red-brick theater and the beautiful blue opera building. An afternoon shower had left puddles on the sidewalk. He avoided them as best he could. Liliya wouldn't be happy if he splattered mud up and down his slacks. In good weather, street vendors sold fruit and snacks for commuters on their way home, but the storm had driven most of them away. There were no Greek nectarines for Marya today.

When he reached the traffic signal at Nikitsky Vorota, he turned east on Tverskoy. He thought about what Constantine had said about the spy in their midst. There were twenty analysts who might have prepared Constantine's brief. Even worse, sometimes field agents prepared briefs if they had relevant knowledge. That drove the number of possible culprits to over a hundred. He would have to ask Pavel for a sweep of employee computers and phone records. The log would take days to inspect, and by then the culprit might have leaked even more information.

He turned onto Malaya Bronnaya, alert to the noises of his beloved city. Car honks, dog barks, children's laughter, and puddle splashes. He curled his lip at the last. *Some lucky bastard who doesn't have a drill sergeant for a laundress,* he thought. But the further he went, the more the sound disturbed him. The splasher kept pace with him, neither overtaking him nor falling too far behind. People minding their own business rarely kept such a studied pace — they sped up to reach a crosswalk or slowed down to take a call.

In an instant, he decided not to go home. He didn't think the splasher meant to kill him; Vympel would never be so sloppy. But whoever it was obviously needed information about him and there was no sense in providing it.

Directly across the street stood a line of residential buildings, some renovated with freshly painted exteriors and some in a lesser state of repair, with crumbling brick façades and flaking paint. These were the easiest targets, decaying wood doors with flimsy locks that he could easily force open. All he needed was to enter one and get access to a cell phone.

He trudged north, hands shoved deep into his pockets. He slowed his pace, as if the long walk were too much for him, and listened again for the sounds of pursuit. The rustle of a nylon raincoat as it brushed against a man's legs, the barely audible scuff of boots on uneven pavement: yes, someone was still following him.

Two blocks north, he spotted an old brick building with an open door and an idling Lada at the curb. He pushed back the sleeve of his coat and looked at his watch, as if he were surprised to see the car. Reaching into his pocket, he pulled out his cell phone and called his voicemail. "Hi Kolya, it's me," he said loudly, turning in the street. "Are you going somewhere tonight?"

He gave the imaginary Kolya time to offer a response. "Well, I'm almost to your house and I saw the car running so I wanted to make sure we're still on."

He counted to ten while Kolya told him that while he wished he could accompany Vadim to their favorite Japanese restaurant, he'd forgotten about his niece's dance recital.

"That's too bad," Vadim said. "I guess we'll go out some other time. But since I'm right here, I'll pop in and wish your niece good luck at her recital." Then he disconnected and walked through the open door.

Once inside, he pushed the door until it was nearly shut, removing the home's hallway from public view. He saw a closet and bathroom on the left, a living area on the right, and a staircase at the end of the hallway. A green buffet table held ticket stubs from the Helikon opera house and a Nokia phone. He picked up the phone and shut himself in the closet.

The glow of the phone's tiny screen provided enough light to type out a text message to Liliya. He told her to keep Marya inside until he returned, to open the door for no one. A second text went to his head of security, Pavel Chubais, with the emergency code for a full building sweep. He was about to leave the closet when he had another idea.

The only way to save Constantine was to convince Starinov the boy was already on the money's trail. What would convince Starinov they'd found something? Who was left to trust, if every agent and every analyst were under suspicion?

He sent two more text messages, crossed himself, then exited the closet and left the phone exactly where he found it.

CHAPTER FOURTEEN

Filipp blinked, unable to see past the blinding white light in his eyes. His arms lay useless at his sides, like two dead sturgeon on the fishmonger's table. He turned his head to the side and waited for his vision to clear.

"Awake, are you?" a woman asked. Cold fingers fell to his wrist, checking his pulse. "I suppose you'll survive."

"Where?" he gasped.

"You are in the convent of the Sisters of the Blessed Sacrament." Scrubbed clean, her ruddy face was unlined and devoid of all warmth. Her hair lay flat beneath her white wimple. "I am Sister Marfa."

He forced another word from his bone-dry throat. "Water."

"You've had plenty," Sister Marfa replied. "But I will fetch you some more."

Filipp closed his eyes as the nun held a glass to his lips. The liquid trickled down his parched throat. "What happened to me?"

"You fell ill, right after you left that house. The guards brought you here and you've been in this bed ever since."

"Ever since?"

Sister Marfa raised an eyebrow. "It has been more than a month. The fever held you like a mother suckling a child."

My hand, he thought. If washed, it no longer bore the touch of the tsar's daughter.

As his memory descended from the realm of fever and flight, he remembered what else he might have lost. The basket was of no importance. He had transferred the letters and ring to his coat, afraid the guards would tear away the basket's fabric lining before sending him through the gate. Filipp looked down at the plain chemise draped over his chest. "My clothes," he said.

"They're here," the nun assured him. "Disinfected, of course."

His heart beat hard enough to break his ribs. What if the nuns had destroyed the grand duchesses' letters? The Great Father's family asked one simple thing of him and now he might have ruined it all.

A sob gathered deep in his chest and he met Sister Marfa's gaze head-on. He did not trust this red-faced nun. "Do the sisters still bring eggs to the Great Father and his family?"

Sister Marfa tilted her head, her small gray eyes narrowed. "They are no more," she said smoothly.

Filipp scrambled to sit up. "What did you say?"

"They are gone," she said, pressing him back down.

"But where have they been taken?"

"Nowhere you may follow."

A cold sweat gathered along his breastbone. "What?"

"The guards told us our services were no longer needed. We heard from no one for several days and then hell descended on us." She turned her hands into fists, clenched tightly at her sides. "Guns and cannon raining smoke and noise upon us like the end of days. The Bolsheviks had run away, and the White soldiers meant to rule the town. They spent days banging on doors, looking for people, dragging away some but not others."

Filipp made his voice as hard as the knot in his chest. "Where have the Great Father and his family been taken?"

Marfa smiled. "To the earth, maybe? No one can say. Someone saw a bloody girl hauled up some stairs, another saw soldiers digging a pit in the forest, some peasants say they saw two trains pull from the station, going in opposite directions." She shrugged. "But anyone who thinks they saw something disappears. They do not come back."

He understood the warning. "What is happening to this place?"

"God alone remembers Russia, and it is only to visit plague upon us."

"But surely you must have hope?"

"I have nothing but what He gives me." Then she rose. "Someone will bring you bread after vespers."

He closed his eyes until Sister Marfa was gone. Then he set his feet on the floor, feeling his legs shake beneath him.

He could not wait for someone to bring him bread. They might have decided to turn him in by then. There was a coldness in Sister Marfa's eyes that he remembered seeing in the eyes of the guards surrounding the tsar. She was one of them, a Bolshevik.

He stumbled across the room to the wooden wardrobe and carried his clothing back to the bed, knowing he was too weak to stand. He lay down and slipped the garments on. When he came to the jacket, he reached inside the pocket for the pieces of paper he'd taken from the basket.

His thick fingers touched a pocketknife, his watch, a money clip (money gone, of course), and…there, yes…a folded wad of paper. Unfolding it carefully, he inspected the contents: market list, pharmacy receipt, letter from his mother, and two torn pieces of paper, one covered with swirly writing, the other with a spidery, slanted hand.

He said a prayer of thanks and returned the papers to his pocket. He knew he had to take them far from the people who had imprisoned the tsar and his family.

His hand, pale and blue-veined, looked no different for having been touched by a grand duchess. Still, it was a sign from God that he had been chosen. Even though he had failed to post the letters, God spared him from the fever for a higher purpose. There was more he had to do, and he would be kept alive long enough to do it. He remembered the words the grand duchess had spoken in his ear and thanked God he had not yet committed them to paper.

His shaky fingers fastened the toggles on his coat. If it was still summer, he would look ridiculous, but he didn't have the strength to carry it. Overheated and underfed, he would simply claim to be suffering from the fever — people would stay away.

His fingers swept the seam of the coat's right-hand pocket. He found the spot where his mother's stitching had given way. There, between the lining and the wool, lay the ring that had come from the hand of Grand Duchess Olga herself. He smiled and left it where it lay.

"Goodbye, Sister Marfa," he said, arranging the pillows and blankets to look as if he lay huddled beneath them. Then, without enough strength to pull himself out of the window, he opened the casement and let himself fall headfirst into the soft grass below

CHAPTER FIFTEEN

JULY 2013
MOSCOW, RUSSIA

Liliya's sharp eyes canvassed Vadim's legs from knee to ankle. She pointed at the brown specks near the cuff of his slacks. "You stepped in a puddle, didn't you?"

Vadim hung his raincoat in the foyer. "I just told you someone tried to follow me home. Is that the first question you wish to ask?"

"Yes," she snapped. "It's harder to remove a stain than it is to pull a trigger. I'll wash the pants. You entertain your granddaughter."

Vadim obeyed, changing into a sweatshirt and jeans. He tried to clear his mind, hoping to give Marya at least a few minutes of undivided attention. The world would still be crashing down around him in half an hour. He owed her that much.

He found her in the living room, entranced by a television program featuring a pink puppet and a blue puppet devouring cookies at an alarming rate. He watched from the hallway, taking in the gentle halo of blonde hair tied up in two scrawny pigtails. Her feet dangled from the sofa, encased in glittery pink socks. He still had trouble accepting how close they had come to losing her.

For six months last year, she'd lived with a foster family while he scrambled to erase Liliya's conviction for embezzlement. The court-appointed case worker had not allowed Marya to live with him once she realized who he was — spies made poor parents and worse grandparents, she'd said. The case worker's ruling had left him no choice. He'd mortgaged his soul to Valery Zyuganov, head of the Moscow Criminal Intelligence Department, in return for Valery's help circumventing the charges. Still, because of the system's impenetrable bureaucratic cogs, his granddaughter had spent her fourth birthday with strangers.

I will leave her something better, he vowed. *I will make a safer world for her to live in.* He cleared his throat. "Hello, pumpkin."

Marya flung herself off the couch and into his arms. He felt the warmth of her tiny fingers as they squeezed his shoulders in as big a hug as she could offer. "Your mother says I'm to entertain you while she does my laundry," he said.

Marya's blue eyes widened to the size of saucers. "Can I have a horsey ride?"

He got down on his hands and knees and waited for Marya to climb onto his back. She clutched his sweatshirt with hands that smelled of crayon, shrieking in delight as he crawled through the room. He rounded the coffee table and reared like an angry stallion at the footstool. Experience had taught her to hang on tight and she locked her ankles around his ribs. When his left knee began to ache, he pulled up alongside the couch and gently tipped her into the cushions. "That's enough, my girl. You'll have me headed for the glue factory."

From the kitchen, Liliya shushed him with a piercing whistle.

"Not that horses have anything to do with glue," he said quickly. His eyes wandered to his laptop and he wondered if Constantine had checked in yet. "There's something I have to do, *lastochka*. Do you think you can finish watching *Ulitza Sezam* by yourself?"

"Didn't you just work all day? I want you to watch with me."

"We'll watch together while I check on something."

Marya settled herself at his side, leaning her head against his arm. Her eyes glazed over as she scanned the rows of numbers on his computer. "What are you doing, Grandpapa?"

"Looking for something that's difficult to find," he said, scanning the phone records.

"Can't someone help you?"

"No, sweetheart. No one can."

She patted his arm twice. "It's okay to ask for help. Mama said so."

"Did she now?" Vadim glanced into the kitchen, where Liliya dabbed at the spots on his pants with a sponge. "Your mother has learned something, I see."

He wondered if Liliya might be right. Valery Zyuganov had helped him before. Would he do it again? There wasn't much the Director of Moscow's Criminal Intelligence

Department didn't know. The three of them, Vadim and Valery and Maxim Starinov, had come a long way since their days together at Sokolniky's School Number One.

He stood up and walked to the living room window overlooking Patriarshy Prudy. From his third floor apartment, he had an elevated view of the pond and its lush surroundings. Night had dimmed the day's energy, leaving only quiet couples to linger on the wrought-iron benches, holding hands and tucking heads against each other's shoulders. God willing, Marya would be one of them someday.

He tugged on the window's velvet curtain, leaving a space just wide enough to observe the street below. Then he reached for his phone and dialed.

Valery answered on the second ring. "Vadim Petrovich, I hadn't expected to hear from you. How is that precocious daughter of yours? I hope prison wasn't too tough on her."

"You got her out before the worst of it, and I will always be grateful. But that isn't why I called. I need to ask you something, Valery."

"I can't promise I'll answer, but go ahead."

"Why did Starinov send Vympel after one of my men?"

The line went quiet.

"You know what I'm asking about," Vadim continued. "We're all chasing something that doesn't exist."

"It doesn't matter what I know."

"Why did Starinov send Vympel after my agent?"

"The man bombs his own subway system to create sympathy for war in Chechnya. If he thinks killing your agent will get him what he wants, he'll do it." Valery sighed.

"Your boy is in trouble, Vadim. Their orders are to kill him on sight."

"Can you stop it?"

"It's out of my hands."

"Talk to Starinov."

"And tell him what? That we think he's wrong? Men have died for less."

Vadim scanned the row of cars parked on the street. He caught a flash of light inside one, as if someone sitting in the driver's seat had swiveled a phone to his other ear. "Tell him that God condemns all acts of murder," he said.

"You and I know that God means nothing to him."

"That's not what he told a certain president of the United States."

"He said what a silly man wanted to hear. You didn't imagine he believed it, did you?"

So many lies, Vadim thought. *How will Marya ever know whom to believe?* "I sent a second agent into the field, Valery. I won't stand by and see them killed by their own countrymen."

"I suggest you take comfort in the fact that your daughter and granddaughter have been returned to you. It is the best that can be done. Kiss them goodnight for me."

Valery hung up. At the same moment, the bright rectangle of light in the car below went out.

CHAPTER SIXTEEN

JULY 2013
SAN FRANCISCO, CALIFORNIA

The first thing Natalie noticed was a tingling in her arm. Hung off the edge of the bed, it wouldn't move when she tried to brush her hair from her face. "Rise and shine," a man's voice called.

Looking down, she saw the thin silver band linking her wrist to the metal bed frame. "You handcuffed me?"

Constantine knelt beside her, dressed in a dark gray suit and white shirt. His blond hair was carefully spiked, a perfect imitation of the work-hard-play-hard bankers who populated the Financial District during market hours. He held a mug of steaming coffee. "I'm sorry about the handcuffs. I couldn't take the chance you would run away while I was out."

"Why did you leave?"

"We needed supplies. It was safer to go alone."

She shook her wrist, rattling the cuffs. "I have to go to the bathroom."

He nodded, pulling a key from his pocket. She caught a whiff of soap and alcoholic aftershave. "We can't stay here much longer. There are fresh clothes for you in the bathroom."

She looked down at her T-shirt. Bits of memory shook loose from her fogged brain as the full impact of the previous night settled over her. "You killed two people," she said. "And I distinctly remember wearing pants at some point."

He looked at the floor and tightened his grip on the key until his knuckles shone white. "That was wrong. I'm sorry."

She'd meant it as a joke, but he seemed genuinely uncomfortable. He crouched before her like a Taliban prisoner about to be beheaded. Then it hit her: he was ashamed of himself for having almost slept with her.

Natalie flung back the covers and stalked into the bathroom, slamming the door behind her. In the mirror, she watched her cheeks and throat explode in bright red splotches that looked like poison oak. Against her will, her eyes clouded with tears. *Even kidnappers are ashamed of me,* she thought.

She took a deep breath and repeated the mantra Beth had given her as a child: "God grant me the serenity to accept the things I cannot change, courage to change the things I can, and wisdom to know the difference." It had been years before she'd realized Beth had cribbed it from AA.

She thought of all the elementary and middle school teachers who must have wondered what the hell went on in the Brandon household after school. Still, Beth's intuition had been right. Sometimes, if she caught it early, a moment of concentrated thought centered on this phrase could force Belial to lie down and be quiet.

She repeated the mantra until the bathtub faucet ran hot, then slipped the stopper into the drain and waited. Behind the wall, pipes clanged like an out-of-tune organ. Just thinking of her sister made her feel homesick. She'd missed the start of Shark Week with Seth because she'd been too proud to apologize to Beth. Now two men were dead and Nicholas's money was behind it all — even her argument with Beth. *This is a dream*, she thought. *It has to be.*

She tossed away her T-shirt and underwear and slipped into the steaming water. Affixed to the wall, a rusted metal rectangle held a bar of soap. The letters on the soap's surface were still crisp, with no erosion. She frowned and looked into the garbage can. She saw a barely used bar of soap and two paper wrappers.

She turned the soap over in her hands. Constantine hadn't been ashamed of *her*. He'd been ashamed of himself, enough to give her a fresh bar of soap so that nothing that had touched his bare skin need touch hers.

A fluttery feeling tickled the pit of her stomach. No one but Beth had ever anticipated her reaction to something so small. A wave of longing crushed her when she realized she couldn't tell her sister, the only person who would understand what it meant.

She wondered if the police had found the dead men in the alley yet. Once they realized her apartment was all shot up, they'd connect the dead men with her disappearance and start looking for her. How long could she and Constantine evade the police? Surely in a city so full of people, two of them could remain unseen.

That's what you think, Belial said, stretching his wings.

"Good morning to you, too," she said, rinsing the soap from her skin. Behind her eyes, the angel smiled. *Get dressed, little one. We have work to do.*

Constantine had left her a striped oxford blouse, black skirt suit, and leather pumps. The skirt fit snugly and the shoes pinched her toes, but once she put them on, she looked like an average office worker. A smaller bag held an assortment of drugstore makeup. She reached for a black crayon to trace her eyes and smeared her lips with something dark and sticky.

When she emerged, she saw the table set with a single place: one plate of scrambled eggs and toast, one cup of coffee, and a paper napkin folded in half, tucked beneath the plate. Constantine stood at the sink washing an iron skillet, his suit jacket discarded and sleeves rolled to the elbows.

"Is this for me?" she asked, pointing at the plate.

"Hurry, before it gets cold."

"Where's yours?"

"I already ate. You look very pretty."

"I feel like I have a placenta on my lips. Why are we dressed like this?"

"You're supposed to be a professor, remember?" He set the skillet on a dish towel and came to sit beside her. "We're meeting a man named Voloshin to see what kind of proof he has that the tsar's fortune exists. He's the one trying to blackmail the ambassador."

She paused, fork halfway to her mouth. "So I didn't make it all up. This is really happening."

"Why would you think it wasn't real?"

"Sometimes I get confused between what really happens and what Belial shows me." She set her fork down and picked up the toast. "Once when we were little, I watched a dark-haired man kidnap Beth. I screamed for someone to chase him and when no one did, I took off after him."

"What happened?"

"Beth tackled me halfway down the street. She'd been standing next to me the whole time. The neighbors stared and pointed and my mother never let me play in the front yard again."

"Didn't your parents try and help you?"

Images of needles and rosaries and leather restraints flashed through her mind. "Not hard enough."

"Where are they now?"

"Dead."

Good riddance, Belial muttered. He shifted his feet and set off a tremor of rolling earthquakes in the back of her skull. She ignored them as best she could, scooping up the last bit of scrambled egg and washing it down with coffee. "Beth took care of me. It was better that way. Belial hated my parents."

"Why?"

"They did everything they could to get rid of him. He and Beth have a much better working relationship. Can I ask a question now?"

"Yes." He took her plate and brought it back to the sink, plunging it into the soapy water.

"Where did you learn to speak English so well?"

"Satellite TV."

"Shut up."

He smiled, crinkling the skin at the corners of his eyes. "The security company I worked for brought in private tutors for us. That's how it all started."

"Why did they do that?"

"If we spoke English, we could masquerade as Red Cross workers to get closer to our targets. Then in Chechnya, we stole TVs and satellite antennas for our safe houses. We watched *NYPD Blue* and *The Practice* to learn how to interrogate in English."

"How long were you in Chechnya?"

"Two years."

"What did you do there?"

"I killed people."

He bent his head Taliban-style and she softened. "I saw the soap in the garbage. You didn't have to do that."

"I did."

"If I didn't push you away last night, it was because I didn't want to."

"I'm responsible for you now. I know better, even if you don't."

Anger flared in her belly. "Don't you pity me. Don't you *ever* pity me."

He sighed. "We need to go. Are you ready?"

"*You* kidnapped *me*, remember?" She got up and paced, hating the way her toes squished together in the pointy dress shoes. "Tell me one thing. Where does this guy say he got the password?"

"A pair of letters, written by two of Nicholas II's daughters."

"A pair," she repeated. "That's new." The guard's granddaughter's tale mentioned one letter, from Marie to Ivan. "How'd he get them?"

"His great-grandfather smuggled them out of the Ipatiev house."

"Who wrote the second letter?"

He turned his head sharply. "What do you mean?"

"I'm positive Grand Duchess Marie wrote one of them, but I've never seen anything that mentions a second letter."

"What are you saying?"

"He's either telling the truth or the world's worst liar."

"Let's find out," he said, grabbing her arm and propelling her out the door.

CHAPTER
SEVENTEEN

Yuri Voloshin lived one block southwest of Russian Hill Park in a court filled with pretty Victorians. Natalie stared at the houses, most with children's bikes lying in the front yards. "Tell me again what's supposed to happen," she said.

Constantine flicked his head from side to side, looking at house numbers as the BMW crawled down the street. "We get the Romanov letters from him and try to verify their authenticity as best we can. Then we get the hell out of here."

"What happens to Yuri?"

"I don't know yet."

"Are you going to kill him?"

"I said I don't know."

"I think you should."

"Why is that?"

"He put everyone on this street in danger. He put Beth in danger. She has a son, for God's sake. What would have happened if Vympel found Beth instead of me? Just for that, he deserves to die."

Belial, quiet until now, raised his head. *I can help you,* he said.

Constantine pointed at the least attractive house in the cul-de-sac, a tired brown Victorian that wore its drooping gutters like a scarf. A short driveway angled down into a one-car garage with a yellowed NO PARKING sign nailed to its door. "That's it," he said.

He parked across the driveway, blocking the garage. Natalie followed him to the porch and looked at the spiny green welcome mat, missing its plastic daisy.

Constantine rapped on the door and Natalie closed her eyes. Would Belial be able to tell if this man was lying just by looking at him? *Please, Belial,* she thought. *Help me.*

But no one answered Constantine's knock.

Natalie looked out at the street. "Maybe Vympel got him already."

Constantine knocked again, louder, and something moved behind the door. The handle turned, opening wide enough to reveal a sliver of pasty skin and a single dark eye. "Yuri Iosipovich Voloshin?"

"Who wants to know?"

Constantine kicked the door open and shoved his way inside. Natalie followed, closing the door behind them.

"Who the hell are you?" Yuri growled. Short and stocky with bulging eyes and thick lips, he didn't look like the type to break into a foreign embassy. He looked more like a child molester.

"I represent the government you're attempting to blackmail," Constantine said.

"Did Kadyrov send you?"

"Russia sent me. You will never speak to Kadyrov again. Now show me the letters."

Yuri reached for a lighter and a pack of Marlboros on the sideboard. His nails were each a perfect quarter-moon of white. Rounded and buffed, they shone like a newly waxed car. "You don't see shit until I get what I asked for."

Constantine palmed the Walther. "Is this what you asked for?"

Yuri blew a puff of smoke into Constantine's face and shifted his gaze to Natalie. "Is he like this with you, too?"

"Worse," she said. "I woke up handcuffed."

"I bet you did. What's your name, sweetheart?"

The kitchen is full of knives, Belial said. *Sharp ones.*

Natalie forced her lips to smile. "I'm surprised you don't recognize me. After all, you told the ambassador we worked together."

Yuri blinked. "You're Professor Brandon? I saw your picture online. It doesn't look anything like you."

"I got a makeover."

"You looked better as a blonde."

"So did your mom." Then she turned to Constantine. "Hurry up and kill this guy. I need a drink, if you know what I mean."

Yuri shook his head. "You can't kill me, sweetheart. Not if you want those letters."

Oh, I want them, Belial said. *And I already know how to find them. Go ahead, little one.*

Natalie stepped closer to Voloshin. She placed her palms on either side of his face and stared into his eyes, watching for the signs Belial had taught her. Voloshin clamped his lips shut and breathed heavily, flaring his nostrils. His pupils dilated and contracted in rapid succession. "You're scared," she said. "And you should be."

"Of you?" Voloshin said. "You look like a PTA mom."

"Belial taught me to read people like you. He says you kept those letters here, someplace you can get to them easily." She snorted. "You probably put them in a sock drawer or a wall safe behind a shitty painting."

Yuri's pores released the smell of fear, sharp as unwashed flesh. Belial nodded his approval. *Very good, little one. We can kill him now.*

No, she thought. Angry at her refusal, Belial tapped her with his wing, setting off a firestorm behind her eyes. She gasped and dug her fingers into the side of Yuri's face.

Constantine pulled her back. "Are you all right?"

"It's Belial," she said. "He wants to kill him."

"Go check the house. If you find money or weapons, take them."

Natalie hurried into the kitchen and pulled open the freezer door. She reached for the plastic vodka jug and gulped until the burn numbed her to Belial's wings and words.

As the pain subsided, she glanced at the yellow appliances and faded floral wallpaper. A Russian-language calendar hung on the wall, displaying the wrong month — there weren't enough days. On the counter, a cracked bar of Lava soap lay in a plastic dish.

She tilted her head, remembering Yuri's pristine fingernails. He wasn't the one getting down and dirty. And why hadn't he flipped the calendar to the right month? If the Romanov letters had been with this family for ninety years, why were they surfacing now? Someone else obviously lived here, or had at one time. Someone who got his hands dirty and still used a Russian calendar. Why wasn't that person here, participating in the negotiations? She didn't think he was dead. Yuri didn't seem like the sentimental type who would keep a dead man's soap.

She flipped through the calendar until she figured out which month it had been left on: June. The other person had been in the house until just last month. She put down the vodka and headed for the staircase, where years of footsteps had worn a gray path up the center of the mustard shag carpet.

Upstairs, she found three bedrooms. The first was a makeshift workout room with dusty free weights and an over-the-door resistance system she recognized from late-night infomercials. The second room, she guessed, belonged to Yuri — it was filled with Patrick Nagel posters and dirty laundry. But the third bedroom lay virtually empty. A row of black garbage bags lined the sliding closet door. She could still see indentations in the carpet where pieces of furniture had rested for quite some time.

She tore open the first plastic bag and lifted out a flannel shirt with tortoiseshell buttons. The cuffs hung three inches past her fingertips. It smelled warm, like almonds and musk. The rest of the bag held more clothing, including a pair of pants with a photo in the back pocket. Its white border had been trimmed with pinking shears and although the points were dull and bent, the subject of the photo looked brand new: a 1964 Ford Falcon, parked in front of the house. Yuri, she calculated, hadn't been out of diapers in 1964.

As she inspected the bags, she realized there were several things missing: pajamas, socks, underwear, T-shirts, and sweats. The bags contained only work clothes, a few jackets, and blue jeans. As soon as her mind created the list, she knew. The missing items were the types of things her mother had sent with her to her first sanitarium.

A feeling of helplessness washed over her as she thought about what Yuri had done. He'd packed off his father or grandfather so he could steal his family's legacy without anyone interfering.

She ran back to Yuri's room and yanked open the drawers of his dresser, searching for anything to confirm her hunch. It wasn't hard to find, tucked against the right hand side of the top drawer.

The letter, written on Seashore Oaks stationery, was filled with the kind of handwriting that wasn't taught anymore, with slashes across the vertical length of the number seven and long curlicues on the first stroke of the number one. It made her want to cry.

PLEASE COME. IT IS LONELY AND I HAVE BEEN ILL. THE NURSES DO NOT ALLOW ME TO VISIT WITH THE OTHERS WHILE I AM SICK. I REMEMBERED THAT I DID NOT CLEAN

OUT THE GARAGE. IF YOU SPEAK TO THE DOCTORS ONCE
I AM WELL, YOU COULD ARRANGE FOR THEM TO LET
ME COME HOME, JUST FOR A WEEKEND. PLEASE, YURI, I
MUST SEE YOU.

"The hell with this," she said, shoving the letter and photo into her jacket pocket.

She hurried downstairs, eyes locked on Yuri like a heat-seeking missile. She went up to him, fist clenched, and socked him on the jaw. "You didn't tell him, did you?"

Yuri threw up his hands to defend himself against a second punch and looked to Constantine. "What the hell is she talking about?"

"Professor," Constantine said. "What's going on?"

Natalie ignored him. All she could think about was a lonely and helpless old man who would die alone because he'd been sold out by his own family. "You were going to keep the money for yourself and leave him to die in that shithole!"

"You're crazy, lady."

"Belial was right about you. He wants me to slice you open with a knife, and believe me, I know how. See?" She held up her forearm, pushed back her sleeve, and ran her finger the length of her scar.

Yuri pulled his arm back, as if to hit her.

"Go ahead," Natalie said. "You'll only make it worse."

"I'll do it!" Yuri cried, his arm quivering.

"All right, that's enough." Constantine tossed his gun away, picked Yuri up around the waist, and body slammed him to the floor. "If you touch her, I will kill you. Do you understand?"

Yuri's eyes filled with angry tears. "I trusted your government. I was trying to do you a favor."

"Blackmail is not a favor. Give me the letters now."

"You can't just steal them from me."

"The way you stole them from your family?" Natalie asked.

"I didn't know about the money until he was already in a home!"

"I don't believe you," Natalie said. She picked up Constantine's gun and handed it to him.

"This is your last chance," Constantine said, pressing the Walther to Yuri's temple. "Where are the letters?"

Yuri's cheeks were red and puffy and Natalie saw sweat stains beneath his arms. "In the safe," he growled. "Behind the painting."

"I knew it," Natalie said.

Constantine rocked back on his heels. "That wasn't so hard, was it? Now go get them."

Yuri rolled to his feet and made the sign against the evil eye as he passed her. She flipped him off and watched him scuttle toward the eastern wall of the living room. He lifted an ugly seascape from its nail and leaned it against a console table.

Natalie saw the safe and her heart began to pound. She was in the same room as letters written by two of the Romanovs. *Beth is never going to believe this,* she thought.

She stepped up to Yuri's backside and peered over his shoulder. A black combination safe had been built into the wall. After three quick twirls of the dial, Yuri lifted the latch. He pulled the door forward and Natalie held her breath as he reached into the square black hole. But he didn't pull out a piece of paper — he pulled out a revolver and pressed it to Natalie's head. "I want my reward," he said. "I want what Kadyrov promised me."

Constantine aimed the Walther. "You won't get it by killing her."

"Are you sure about that?" He jabbed Natalie's forehead with the muzzle. "You — reach into the safe and grab the box."

Natalie gulped and looked at Constantine. When he nodded, she followed Yuri's directions and pulled a document-sized metal box from the safe. "Is there more?"

"No," Yuri said. "Now go to the front door."

Natalie clutched the box to her chest. "Where are we going?"

"Shut up and walk!"

Again, her eyes sought Constantine's.

"Do it," he said.

She shuffled forward as slowly as she could. Constantine's blue eyes locked on Yuri's trigger finger. The barrel of the gun was cold where it touched her skin. Drops of liquid plunged from her shoulders to the band of her bra.

The door was only inches in front of her.

She reached out for the brass knob and gasped when it began to move.

The door flew open, knocking her backward into Yuri.

"Candy gram," a deep voice boomed.

CHAPTER EIGHTEEN

The pounding on the door sounded like a medieval battering ram. Beth woke with the pirate book on her lap and one hand curled around Seth's baseball bat. Flashbulb memories of the night before popped into her head: the prank calls, the 911 operator, the calm but patronizing deputy dispatched to assure her she wasn't in any danger.

A second set of violent knocks echoed in the downstairs hallway. "I'm coming," she grumbled, reaching for a fleece bathrobe.

Seth cracked his door as she passed, one hand grasping Roosevelt's collar. The dog barked and Seth hushed him with a nip to the shoulder. "Mom, what's going on?"

"Nothing," she said. "Stay with Roo, okay?" She knelt down to pet Roosevelt, thinking the ordinary gesture might comfort her son. But the dog, always energetic in the morning, jumped up to meet her and scratched her across the cheek. "Ow," she said, as Seth pushed Roosevelt back. "I'm serious, kiddo. I'll be back in a sec. Why don't you guys practice 'sit'?"

She waited until Seth closed his door and then stumbled downstairs, groping for the doorknob. The morning sunlight blinded her and she raised a hand to shield her eyes. A uniformed man stood on her porch, clutching his belt. "Good morning, ma'am. Inspector Lopez, SFPD," he said, holding up his badge. "I need to ask you a few questions about an incident that happened at an apartment leased in your name. We think it might be connected to your 911 call last night."

"What are you talking about?" she said, rubbing her eyes. "What incident?"

"Do you currently rent unit number six at 1490 Valencia?"

"My sister lives there. Is she all right?"

"Ms. Brandon, when was the last time you saw or heard from your sister?"

A heat wave rocked her from head to toe. She'd had hundreds of nightmares that began this way, with a police officer asking her to come and identify Natalie's body. Beth swallowed hard and forced her voice to remain steady. "Three days ago. I called her last night around midnight, but she didn't answer. Tell me she's okay."

"Your sister is missing, Ms. Brandon. I need you to tell me where she might be."

Beth sank against the doorframe and clutched it until her knuckles shone. "I knew this would happen someday."

"Ma'am, what do you mean, you knew this would happen?"

"It's my sister," she said, trying to stay calm. How much could she tell this man? Would he understand if she tried to tell him about Nat's condition? "She's…not like other people."

Lopez shifted his stance. "Is she disabled?"

Beth looked up at the policeman but his hard eyes revealed no sympathy. To him, this was just another call. "She sleepwalks," Beth lied. "She doesn't know what she's doing."

"I know what a sleepwalker is, lady. But let me tell you, a sleepwalker didn't shoot up your sister's apartment."

"Shooting? What the hell happened?"

"We got the call early this morning. Shots fired, breaking glass, heavy footsteps, that sort of thing." Lopez shrugged. "The neighbors thought it might be a robbery."

"My sister doesn't have anything worth taking."

"No one outside the apartment knows that. I'd like you to take a look and see if anything's missing. Based on your 911 call last night, we think someone was watching your place while their buddies robbed your sister."

"Give me five minutes," Beth said, slamming the door before he could reply. She ran to the phone and dialed her neighbor, wincing at the early hour. When June's husky voice answered, the words tumbled out in a rush. "June, I'm sorry to call so early, but Seth and I need a big favor."

CHAPTER NINETEEN

Ivan Tarasenko watched the blonde sister slide into the cop car parked in her driveway. "She's moving," he said.

There was a moment of silence before his headset transmitted a response. "You are sure?"

"*Da.* She is with a policeman. Do you want me to follow her?"

"*Nyet.* Maintain your current position."

Ivan sank into his seat. The van stank of paint and cleaning chemicals and it was beginning to give him a headache. Sergei hadn't said anything about a stakeout during the mission briefing in Moscow. They'd been told it would be in and out in less than two hours, but they'd arrived twelve hours ago and still had no cargo.

The first target, a dark-haired girl, had gotten away. Two squad members had died trying to prevent her escape, which made Sergei grumpy and the rest of the group nervous. When a search of the girl's apartment had revealed her sister's address and phone number, Sergei assigned stakeout duty to Ivan. They'd all hoped the dark-haired sister would come here to hide, or at the very least, call to tell her sister where she'd gone. Neither had happened so far.

In the meantime, the rest of the squad had gone to pick up the second target. Ivan hoped they were having better luck. Personally, he thought it would be a good idea to grab the sister who lived here and hold her for ransom. The house was obviously expensive. Surely the family had money tucked away somewhere for just such an occasion.

Ivan began to plan the attack in his head. He could enter the house through the side gate, hide inside, and snatch the woman after the policeman brought her back. She had just taken her child and the dog to a neighbor's house, so she would be all alone when she returned. Even if Sergei told him to let her go, he could still have a little fun with her before turning her loose. He imagined her warm body pressed against his, struggling frantically. Every move she made to try and escape would bring him closer to pleasure.

Ivan smiled. Yes, that would definitely make up for a stakeout with no results.

CHAPTER TWENTY

Natalie fell backward as the front door swung open. A tall man holding a briefcase stepped through. His dark eyes flicked from Constantine's gun to Yuri's. "Well, aren't you a cheerful lot," he said in a British accent.

"Who the hell are you?" Yuri asked.

"An interesting question," the stranger replied. "Who the hell *am* I? Who the hell are any of us, really? It's hard to put a label on a consciousness that's constantly evolving." He paused to inhale. "There, did you see that? I just evolved." He looked down at Yuri. "You did, too, although it's a bit harder to notice."

"Viktor," Constantine interrupted. "What are you doing here?"

"I'm the cavalry, darling. Vadim re-routed me and said you needed help." He winked at Natalie. "Introduce me to your pretty friend?"

"Maybe later, when there isn't a gun pressed to her head."

"To business, then," Viktor said. "You are Mr. Voloshin, I presume? I am Viktor Igorovich Zhilin, authorized by the Public Security Intelligence Bureau of the Russian Federation to issue you a single payment of ten million dollars in exchange for your Romanov artifacts." He paused, giving Yuri a conspiratorial grin. "I'm told you asked for asylum, but with ten million dollars, the world is your asylum, isn't it?"

Yuri's eyes drifted to the briefcase. "You got ten million in there?"

"Strictly speaking, no. But if you remove the gun from the pretty girl's head, I'll show you what I can do to get it." Viktor set the briefcase on a table and flipped it open to reveal a laptop. "I have a secure satellite connection and a shadow installation of our bureau's wire transfer software. You're familiar with wire transfers?"

Yuri nodded.

"Then let's get started." Viktor stepped toward Yuri and pushed the barrel of the gun from Natalie's head. "That's a good lamb." Then he pointed at Constantine. "You too. Weapons down."

"Not until you get his gun further away from her."

"It's called good faith, dove. He trusts us and we trust him."

"I don't trust him. Get it away from her."

"Oh, have it your way."

In one swift movement, Viktor wrenched the gun from Yuri's hand and clicked on the safety. "Are you happy now?"

Constantine lowered his gun. "No."

"I suppose you hate puppies and rainbows, too."

Natalie took a deep breath. She grasped the banister for support with one hand and held Yuri's box to her chest with the other.

Yuri, robbed of his weapon, glared at the newcomer. "If you're here to give me money, hurry up and do it."

"The customer is always right," Viktor said. He glanced around the room, taking in the brown corduroy couch and gondola-print wallpaper behind it. "Well, perhaps not always. I'll initiate the wire transfer to a bank of your choosing. When it's complete, I will ask you to sign a receipt."

"Do it," Yuri said.

"I'll be in the other room," Natalie said. "With the vodka." She stumbled away, still clutching the box. Her head hurt, she was drenched in sweat, and she wondered why Belial hadn't said a word while Yuri held the gun on her. Belial only disappeared when he was planning something.

The jug was where she'd left it on the kitchen counter. As she unscrewed the cap, Belial flicked her with a wing. *You're going to need me soon. You don't want to do that.*

"That asshole could have shot me. Where the hell were you?"

I have my reasons.

"Don't we all," she mumbled. She slid to the floor, holding the box with one hand and the vodka with the other.

In the living room, Viktor talked Yuri through the wire

transfer. "Now," Viktor said, "as soon as I've verified your possession of the letters, I'll type in all those lovely little zeroes."

"They're in a box," Yuri said. "That crazy bitch has it."

"Excuse me for just a moment, then." Three footsteps later, Viktor appeared in the kitchen. He smiled, revealing slightly crooked teeth. A shock of thick black hair dipped into his eyes and he brushed it away like a self-conscious schoolboy. Natalie ignored him and took another swig of vodka. "You should slow down," he said. "Only bricklayers and circus freaks drink like that."

"I know what I'm doing."

"Do you?" He knelt beside her. For the first time, he saw her eyes up close. The smile fell from his face and he crossed himself in the Eastern Orthodox fashion. "*Durnoj sglaz.*"

Natalie recognized the protection against evil eye. "I'm not a witch."

"I'm sorry, it's just…your eyes make you look like a *rusalka.*"

"*Rusalki* have green eyes. I thought Russians knew these things."

"Who are you?"

"I'm the professor."

"You're Professor Brandon?"

She nodded. "I'm a tenured professor employed by Rosemont College. My specialties are early modern European history, World War I, and dating computer science nerds who eat sushi with their hands. Sometimes I have blonde hair and wear expensive shoes."

"You're not what I expected."

"Sorry to disappoint you."

"On the contrary," he said, slipping to the floor beside her. "I've never met a professor who could win a drinking contest. May I offer a word of advice?"

"I take one thing from strangers, and it's not advice."

"When I walked through the door, love, you had a gun to your head. Does that sound like someone who doesn't need advice?"

"Do you have anything useful to say, or do you just walk around talking like Elton John all day?"

Viktor grinned. "Constantine and I are used to each other, but I forget that others aren't."

"We were doing just fine without you."

"Lamb chop, I don't know if you've noticed, but all the great tragedies start out 'fine.' You know… Oedipus has eyes, Romeo's alive, Charles is in love with Di."

"Do you have a point?"

Viktor sighed. "You looked straight at him the minute I pried that gun away from your head. I know that look. But I also know he's hiding something. A woman."

Natalie took another swig from the bottle. "That's all you've got? That's as weak as your accent."

"There's someone he calls and writes to every time we're in the field. He tries to hide it, but it's someone he cares for deeply."

She leaned her head against the cabinet. "Constantine is a grown man. He can take care of himself."

"But can he take care of you?" He leaned toward her and the heat of her breath mingled with his. Viktor's lips were dark, naturally suffused with color. *That's what vampires look like,* she thought, leaning forward for a closer look. Interpreting her move as desire, he opened his mouth and placed it over hers. As soon as she felt the soft pressure of his lips, he flew backward, jerked away by a hand twisted in his collar.

"Get away from her," Constantine growled.

Shit, Natalie thought. Did Constantine think she'd wanted to kiss Viktor? She hadn't, not at all. It was the strangeness of it all, the vodka, the relief of having Yuri's gun barrel removed from her forehead. It was stupid and she already regretted it.

Viktor shrugged and straightened his collar. "Always a bridesmaid, never a bride. I suppose I'll go keep the customer satisfied."

Constantine extended a hand to Natalie. "He didn't hurt you, did he?"

Her hand disappeared when he encircled it with his fingers and pulled her to her feet. "It wasn't what it looked like," she said.

"You don't owe me an explanation."

"But last night, I wanted…I mean, we almost…that's not who I am."

He placed his lips on her forehead. "I know."

Natalie collapsed against him, imagining he would put his arms around her. But he didn't. He let her rest against him for a moment and then he released her, holding out his hands for the box. "It's time."

She surrendered the box and followed him back to the living room, where Yuri was tethered to a banister with a plastic zip tie. "Those are my letters," he growled. "I want my money."

Constantine ignored him. "Who wants to do the honors?" he asked as he set the box on the coffee table.

"You do it," Natalie said. To her, the Romanovs were fairy tale creatures, as shrouded in myth as the denizens of Troy or Illyria. She had never believed she would come this close to them, to touch something they had touched. Her stomach tingled with nervous anticipation as Constantine slowly lifted the lid.

Inside the box lay several sheets of paper, a purple velvet bag, and a stack of yellowed photos and postcards. *Belial,* she thought, *even if these turn out to be fake, let me always remember what it was like to believe.*

"Christ's toenails!" Viktor said. "Half the Russian army could be on our tail by now." He reached past Natalie and jerked the papers out from under the velvet pouch. He sifted through them and handed her two sheets with the same date scrawled across the top: July 13, 1918. "Voilà. Are they real?"

She took the letters and held them side by side. She couldn't read Russian well — Beth had a translator from the university's Russian department for that—but she'd studied the children's schoolroom primers and correspondence in three languages and knew the quirks and the signature of each. She looked for the characteristics she knew, the swoops and swirls that differentiated one girl's handwriting from another's. "This is Marie's," she said, holding up the letter in her left hand. "And this is Olga's."

"I told you," Yuri snapped. "I told you I had them."

"We never doubted you," Viktor said. He typed in the transfer amount of $10,000,000. "I'll need the bank and account number you wish to use."

Constantine used a knife to free Yuri, who typed in his account number and bank name as requested. "How do I know this is going to go through?" Yuri asked. "I want proof."

"Of course you do, sweet pea. Once my system shows the transfer as complete, I'll receive confirmation on my phone. With a transfer this large, your bank won't be able to process the entire sum right away. Give them a few days to recover from the shock."

Viktor's computer scrolled through hundreds of lines of visible code. Upon completion, the computer beeped and flashed a dialog box filled with Cyrillic characters. A moment later, his phone beeped. He pulled it from his jacket pocket and held it out for Yuri to see. Yuri nodded. "Now what?"

"It's up to you, pet. I can hack into their system to show you they've received the order, or you can use my phone to call them."

Yuri narrowed his eyes. "I don't trust your computer."

"*Quelle surprise,*" Viktor said, handing over his phone.

While Yuri dialed, Constantine packed the letters back into the strongbox and handed it to Natalie.

Viktor cleared his throat. "Are you sure you don't want to hang onto that?"

"She won't let anyone else have it," Constantine said. "Besides, she's not the one you need to worry about. It's the voice inside her head."

"She hears voices?"

"Just the one, really."

"I'm right here," Natalie said. "I can hear you."

Suddenly, Yuri let out a whoop. "It worked! They said they see it and they'll get approval from the regional VP to start processing it as soon as possible."

"You see?" Viktor beamed. "You'll never get anywhere in life unless you learn who you can trust." He took one last piece of paper from his briefcase — a receipt — and acquired Yuri's signature. "That completes our business," he said, turning from Yuri to Constantine. "What do you say, old chap? Shall we take our treasure trove home?"

"The sooner, the better."

Yuri stepped forward to open the door for them. "Nice doing business with you." Then he scowled at Natalie. "Not you. You're still a crazy bitch."

"See you in hell," she said. "They have better knives there."

The bullet whizzed past her and struck Yuri in the head.

Natalie screamed as Viktor and Constantine pulled her to the ground, covering her with their bodies as the tinny clap of assault rifle rounds shattered the morning's silence.

CHAPTER TWENTY-ONE

The soles of his shoes had come off weeks ago, sometime after leaving Changchun. Filipp continued barefoot along the dusty trail used by White Russians fleeing Siberia into China, a trail that led all the way down to the port city of Dalian. He had no intention of following it all the way — he suspected the Okhrana had agents posted at every Chinese harbor.

Just ahead lay the city of Shenyang, situated on a dry, ugly plain. He paused and looked longingly to his left. Fog hung low over the rolling emerald mountains and he wished he could abandon the dusty trail for their protection and isolation. If he tracked eastward, he could cross the Hamgyeong Mountains and slip down into the Korean peninsula undetected. Surely the Bolsheviks couldn't patrol the *entire* continent.

His stomach rumbled and made the decision for him. If he were to have any chance of eating or acquiring shoes, he had to risk a trip through the city. His last meal, two days ago, had been a paste made of rotten rice and another traveler's discarded tea leaves. He licked his lips and rested one hand over his coat pocket, seeking the outline of what lay hidden in the lining.

He'd fled Ekaterinburg on foot like many of the cowardly Bolsheviks who feared reprisals from Admiral Kolchak, the man leading the monarchist counter-revolution in Siberia. Once, he met a group of Kolchak's soldiers and came within a single breath of asking them to take him to the admiral. But his heart had warned him against it just in time. The White soldiers were no better off than the Bolsheviks. What was to stop them from killing him, stealing the grand duchesses' letters, and selling them? So he'd kept his mouth closed, eaten a meal beside the soldiers' campfire, and continued alone.

Outside Harbin, he'd camped with deserters from the Bolshevik army. They told him that the ambitious admiral had confiscated the tsarist gold reserves then stored in Omsk. Filipp feigned outrage to please the deserters, but in his heart, he understood Kolchak's reasoning. The murdering Bolsheviks could not be allowed to fill their coffers with the Great Father's gold. Still, he did not feel Kolchak could be trusted. The man printed his own money and seemed more interested in creating his own empire than in finding out what had happened to the tsar and his family.

Throughout northern China, he'd encountered impoverished White Russian refugees. Some pressed onward without knowing why, while others built tin shacks near the border with Russia and waited for a future that would likely never come. He had stayed with one such family for a month while he recuperated from an illness, after which they confessed to owning pieces of porcelain and jewelry stolen from the tsar's palace at Tsarskoe Selo. He'd excused himself and gone for a walk, wondering how he could get the money to buy the artifacts from them. *Surely*, he thought, *I cannot leave the Great Father's things scattered all over China. I will collect them for his family and keep them safe, just like the letters.*

But when he'd returned to the family's hut later that evening, he found it in disarray. Every member of the family had been shot in the back of the head. *Okhrana*, he thought. The Bolshevik secret police were everywhere, hunting down émigrés and reclaiming what they believed to be state property. He had gathered his meager possessions and fled into the night.

Filipp swallowed heavily at the memory. *People meant danger.* Those three words had kept him alive for nearly two years. But now, without food or salve for his cracked and bloody feet, the time had come.

He trudged down the hill into Shenyang and stumbled down its side streets, searching for an open shop or restaurant. Night had fallen an hour ago and he did not know whether local custom permitted the types of evening amusements available in larger cities. Finally, a mile down the high street, he found it. Tucked beneath a layered canopy of red and green tiles, he saw a weathered sign with Russian characters carved beneath the Chinese ones.

Years ago, Russia had leased parts of this area from the Chinese, only to lose them in the disastrous Russo-Japanese War. Perhaps the man who owned this shop would remember those days and look upon him kindly. *Or,* Filipp thought, *perhaps he will sell the description of yet another fleeing Russian émigré to the Okhrana.*

His belly rumbled again and he knocked on the door. Almost immediately, a black-bearded Chinese man appeared. *"Jiuyang,"* Filipp said, bowing his shoulders. Then he continued in Russian. "Blessings be upon you, sir."

Short and stout, the merchant had a round face offset by a long moustache. "And you also, stranger," he replied. "You are in need of a place to rest. Please come inside."

Filipp thanked him and obeyed. Inside, the small store held shelves filled with boots, hats, gloves, outerwear, blankets, and saddles. It smelled of leather and incense. Behind a linen curtain, he could see the shadow of a woman and a small boy.

"Have you come here to shop?" the man asked.

"I have no money," Filipp said. "Would you be willing to trade?"

"Let me see what you have."

Filipp set his knapsack on the merchant's counter and opened it. The merchant nodded, his sharp eyes inspecting Filipp's hat. "That is beaver fur, is it not?"

Filipp forced a smile to his lips and a lie through his teeth. "I am from Perm, where the animals are trapped and skinned."

"Perm," the merchant said. "I heard rumors about that city."

"I am but a traveler. No one speaks to me of such things."

"They say your empress and her daughters may be held captive there. Perhaps your emperor, too." The merchant tapped his long yellow fingernails together. "After all, no one knows what happened to them. Have you heard this rumor?"

Filipp wiped sweaty palms against his trousers. "N–no," he said. "The only rumor I have heard is that they are all dead."

"Then where are the bodies?" the merchant asked. "Many travelers I've spoken to believe they are all still alive."

"I know nothing. I have been away from home for nearly two years now."

The merchant's eyes glimmered with greed. "But that is precisely when they disappeared. Surely you must have heard something. Or have something."

I knew it, Filipp thought. It happened everywhere along his route — Russian émigrés frantically selling their possessions as they fled from the Bolsheviks. Some of them sold stolen goods they claimed were the Great Father's. Merchants and pawnbrokers had become used to acquiring jewels and gold for a pittance. They were never pleased with travelers who had no such treasures to give.

The warmth of the bamboo floor had finally begun to penetrate his feet. He wiggled his toes and realized that for the first time in weeks, his heels didn't hurt. "It has been a terrible journey."

"You are much the worse for wear," the merchant agreed. "You need a hot meal and a new pair of slippers."

"Yes," he whispered.

"There is a fresh pot of soup with dumplings in my kitchen. My wife has made too much. She always does, even though I tell her we are expecting no one. Can you smell it?"

"Yes," he whispered.

"I also have a pair of slippers that might fit you. They have an otterskin bottom, lined on the inside with soft fur. Very good for walking. Do you do much walking, traveler?"

Filipp felt his heart knock in his chest. What if the rumors were true and the Great Father and all his family were dead? He did not want to believe anyone could murder such beautiful, helpless girls… but if they lived, why had they not been seen since that terrible summer? He had comforted himself with the fact that no bodies had been found, yet he knew there were ways of making bodies disappear. Surely, if the tsar and his daughters were in heaven, they would not begrudge him a bowl of soup, a cup of tea, and a new pair of shoes. Would they not want him to be cared for, after all he had been through on their behalf? He felt his eyes moisten as he looked up helplessly at the merchant. "F–food," he mumbled.

"Yes?" the man prodded. "Have you something to offer me?"

"I h–have one thing," Filipp said, swaying on his feet. The incense was fogging his brain and he fought the urge to lose consciousness.

"What is it? I promise I will give you a fair price."

He ordered his hand to reach for his knife and slit the lining of his coat. But his hand did not obey. Instead, it reached into his breast pocket for his great-grandfather's watch. "I have this," he whispered, placing it on the counter.

The watch had been made in St. Petersburg by the same old man who made watches for Tsar Alexander I. It had been passed down in his family beginning with his great-grand-father, who died over a hundred years ago. He'd promised his father to keep it safe forever — those were the last words his father heard and he'd died with a smile on his lips. Tears slipped down Filipp's cheeks. *I'm sorry, Father. But the Great Father's children have no one else. Please understand.*

The merchant picked up the watch and inspected it.

"It was made by the watchmaker for Tsar Alexander I," Filipp offered, knowing his desperation would reduce the watch's value.

"Yes," the merchant said. "It is very finely made. But are you sure it is all you have to give?"

God help me, Filipp prayed. "Yes."

The merchant snatched the watch off the counter. "Very well. Come with me and claim those slippers before you fall down."

Filipp did not even ask how much he would receive for the watch. He followed the merchant into his storeroom, heart heavy with loneliness, fear, and hunger.

CHAPTER TWENTY-TWO

Natalie's ears rang with the echo of gunfire. Pressed to the floor beneath Constantine's body, she fought the impulse to claw her way free from the claustrophobic tangle of limbs. She wanted to turn her head, but couldn't. Her current line of sight went straight to Yuri's forehead, dotted with a smoking red-black hole.

"Pull him in!" Constantine yelled. "He's blocking the door!"

Suddenly, Yuri's body slid out of view and the front door slammed shut. Constantine's weight lifted as he rolled toward the front window and punched through it with his elbow. Palming the Walther, he squeezed off six shots before a return volley sent him back to floor level.

Natalie gasped for air and held Yuri's box to her chest.

"Any more bright ideas?" Viktor asked, dropping Yuri's legs.

Constantine pointed toward the back door. "Run like hell."

"What if they've already got it covered?"

A second round of gunfire knocked the rest of the glass from the front window. "We don't have a choice," he said. "Get her out of here. I'll cover you."

"No!" Natalie shrieked.

"Come on, love. He'll be fine." Viktor reached for her hand.

She jerked it back and looked at Constantine. "I'm not leaving without you!"

"Go," Constantine growled, his gaze locked on the street, pistol aimed through shards of broken glass. A drop of sweat trickled from his hairline to his jaw. "Now." He squeezed the trigger and let loose a second barrage.

"That's our cue," Viktor said. He grabbed her wrist and dragged her to the back door. "Head for the fence," he said, flinging it open.

Natalie stumbled as a spray of bullets catapulted bits of grass and dirt into the air. Viktor sprinted past her. At the fence, he knelt and cupped his hands. Natalie tossed the box over the fence and stepped into the boost, using her weight to roll herself over the top.

Viktor vaulted over the fence, landing in a deep crouch. "Are you okay?"

She nodded, reaching for the box and peeking through the gaps in the fence. "Why isn't Constantine following us?"

"He will."

"Go back for him," she whispered. "Don't leave him."

"Those bullets came from less than a hundred meters away. They'll tear us to pieces if we go back." He pulled her down a side yard, pivoting to cover all directions with his gun. "Time to organize some transportation."

She followed him onto a driveway, squinting in the sunlight. Belial shifted his feet, setting off an electrical shower of sparks in her head. *You mustn't linger, little one. They're coming for you. You don't want to die, do you?*

"No," she said, gritting her teeth.

Viktor raised his head from the window of a Reagan-era Monte Carlo parked on the street. "No what? This one's perfect. It has no class whatsoever. We'll blend right in." He bashed the driver's side window and opened both doors. "Hop in."

She obeyed and latched her seatbelt, fighting a rising tide of nausea.

"I see someone's done this already," Viktor said, pointing at the naked steering column. "Darling, I need you to look beneath your seat and find me a screwdriver. I'm sure that's what they used."

Natalie set the box on the floor and felt beneath the seat, ignoring everything sticky or furry. "Something died down here," she said, closing her fingers over a long metal rod.

"As long as we don't follow suit." Viktor jammed the screwdriver into the steering column. With a few quick jerks, the car's engine sprang to life.

Natalie leaned her forehead against the window and stared toward Yuri's house. "Where is he?"

"He's coming. He has to be."

The tingling in Natalie's skull sharpened. Belial was shaking his head. *You can't let them have that box.*

"I know," she moaned, rocking in her seat.

It belongs to me.

"Shut up, shut up, shut up!"

"Who the devil are you talking to?"

"Not the devil," she said.

A burst of gunfire erupted from the house behind them. Natalie sat up straight. "Please be him," she whispered. "Belial, please let it be him."

The side gate flew open, banging against the garage wall. A suited figure flew through it, sprinting for their car. Natalie scrambled to open the rear passenger door. She flung it open just in time for Constantine to dive through headfirst.

"Go, go, go!" he shouted.

Viktor hit the gas pedal and the car rocketed down Polk Street. He ran the stoplight at the end of the block and spun left onto Bay.

"Are you all right?" Natalie asked. She pointed at a dark, wet patch on Constantine's left shoulder. His face had already gone pale and waxen.

"It's fine," he said. "It went through."

Viktor swore and swerved to the right to pass a slow-moving Toyota Prius in the fast lane. He cut the Prius off to get in the left turn lane, angling toward Van Ness. He glanced at the traffic signal as it turned green and stomped on the gas. He stomped on the brake just as quickly when a horde of pedestrians stormed the crosswalk, moving against a DO NOT WALK sign.

"You're kidding," he said, glancing down the street at the endless rows of suited businessmen and skinny-jean-wearing hipsters.

"It's San Francisco," Natalie said. "It's our civic duty to jaywalk."

"Go," Constantine ordered. "They'll move."

Viktor inched forward until one of the passing men pounded a fist on the hood of the car. "Watch it, asshole!" His amber eyes glared at Viktor and then Natalie. Belial shuddered, the tips of his wings tapping Natalie like exploding mortar shells. *I see the mark of death upon him.*

"What do you mean?" she said.

An angel played a trick on him, hiding the cancer behind a benign cyst. I believe you call it "hide and seek."

"Jesus," Natalie whispered. She felt sick to her stomach.

Viktor snorted. "This whole time, you've been talking to Jesus?"

"No," she said. "To Belial."

"There's that word again. Is anyone going to tell me what it means?"

Constantine struggled to sit up. "Where are you going?"

Viktor pointed at a passenger plane rapidly dropping in altitude. "We've got the letters and we've got the girl. We can get the hell out of here if we make it to the airport before Vympel."

"We need a place to hide."

"Are you saying you want to fly coach?"

"Wait!" Natalie said, turning to face Constantine. "I need you to translate the letters for me first."

"Darling, you're the professor of Russian history," Viktor said. "You're the one we need to decipher the letters."

"I'm not—" Before she could finish, Belial tapped her with his wing. *Look left, little one.*

She turned her head and saw a motorcycle cop watching the flow of traffic. The stoplight above flickered from yellow to red. "Viktor, stop! There's a cop!"

Viktor slammed on the brakes where Van Ness met Market, swinging his head between the litany of signs prohibiting various turns from various lanes at various times of day. "What in the name of all that's holy is a HOV? And why can't I make a left turn in the morning? Land of the free, my ass." He waited for the light to turn green and sped through. "I want out of this hellhole, Con. Tell me we're going to the airport."

"She's right. We need to read those letters first."

"I was having a great time in Colombia until Vadim called, you know. My orders were to get you out of that house. I did it and now I want to go back."

"My orders are to retrieve the letters and find the password. I can't do that until I know what they say. What if they're fakes?"

"It doesn't bloody matter, does it? Voloshin's dead. Besides, isn't that her job?"

"Leave her out of it, Viktor."

"I can't. Apparently, neither can you."

"She isn't what she seems."

"Not daft, you mean?"

Constantine pressed a hand to his wounded shoulder. "Just find us a place to stay and I'll explain everything."

"Let the record state that I have a very bad feeling about this."

"We all do," Constantine said. "But unless you have other leverage over Vympel, we don't have a choice."

CHAPTER TWENTY-THREE

JULY 2013
SAN FRANCISCO, CALIFORNIA

Beth's hand shook as she slipped her key in the lock. *Keep it together,* she thought. *The cops are still watching you.* She turned the key, waving to the sergeant as she slipped through the door. A few seconds later, she heard Lopez's patrol car back up and drive away. Only then did she give in to the fear and anger racing through her. For once, she was grateful that Seth and Roosevelt weren't there to greet her.

"Nat," she moaned. "What the hell happened to you?"

Her sister's bed had looked like an open-face feather sandwich, torn apart by dozens of bullets. There wasn't any blood, but Natalie's dresser and bookshelf had been overturned, her few possessions strewn around the living room.

Lopez seemed convinced it was a robbery and wouldn't listen when she insisted that Natalie had nothing to steal.

Neighbors clocked the shots at 2 a.m. Beth knew Nat had trouble sleeping, so it was possible her sister had heard someone coming and simply fled before the attack occurred. Still, Lopez's detectives hadn't found any evidence of Natalie or her attackers anywhere in the outer Mission. He'd quizzed her on Natalie's habits and interests to try to narrow down possible hiding places, but she'd remained purposefully vague. At the time, she'd thought she was protecting Natalie. But what if she was wrong? Was it possible Nat could hurt someone?

"No way," she said out loud.

Prove it, her conscience replied.

She dropped her purse on the escritoire and went upstairs to her home office. In the corner stood a mahogany filing cabinet, five drawers of two-dimensional paperwork that encapsulated three lives: hers, Seth's, and Natalie's. She pulled a file from the bottom drawer, labeled "Natalie," and spread its contents on the floor.

The doctors were always so careful when they handed her copies of her sister's assessments. They made sure never to touch her hands, as if Nat's strangeness might be something genetic and communicable.

Some of the older papers had begun to yellow and curl. The ink had spread and faded, but all the hypocrisy and false empathy remained.

Patient's coma remains unexplained. MRI reveals overdeveloped hypothalamus with extraordinary power of suggestion — possible cause of the somatic delusion described.
— Dr. Edward Hinman, St. Mary's Medical Center, 1991

Patient displays signs of recurrent psychosis with certain long-term deterioration in functional capacity. Administered immediate dosage of Thorazine; recommended long-term treatment plan with continued use of antipsychotics and mood stabilizers.
— Dr. Thomas Gridley, SF General Hospital, 1994

Patient exhibits anhedonia, avolition, affective flattening and dysphoric mood, characteristic of moderate to severe schizophrenia. According to family member (sister), symptoms worsened with Prolixin.
— Dr. Samantha C. Thompson, Cal Pacific Medical Center, 1995

Patient is unresponsive and uncommunicative. Persistent auditory hallucinations severely affect patient's communication and judgment. GAF score: 32 out of 100.
— Dr. Emil Berg, SF Community Health Network, 1999

Patient admitted after suicide attempt. Despite persistent auditory hallucinations, patient displays advanced metabolic function in frontal cortex. Performs exceedingly well in higher thought process tests, including abstraction and concept formation. Family member (sister) reports improvement after discontinuing Clozaril in favor of behavioral therapy.
— Dr. Jabez Harger, St. Luke's Hospital, 2002

Not one of those doctors could tell her why Natalie chose an angel as her hallucination of preference. Not one of them could tell her how Natalie knew the things Belial told her. They couldn't give her one good reason why any of it was happening at all — except to tell her that a very selfish little girl had probably woken up one day and decided to steal the spotlight from her normal, well-adjusted parents and sibling.

"Assholes," Beth said, crumpling the papers in her hand. Medical degree or not, no one knew her sister the way she did. She'd seen Natalie fall prey to inexplicable fevers, bouts of depression, seizures, and enough self-loathing to crush the most egotistic Hollywood star. No matter what Belial told her or showed her, the only person she'd ever harmed was herself.

Beth knew, in the deepest core of her soul, that Natalie would never hurt anyone else. As long as she believed that, Lopez didn't need to know what the doctors had said. But Natalie was still alone and someone was still chasing her — someone smart enough to watch Beth's house, too. She thought of Seth and Roo, safe at June's house. How long could she leave them there without raising suspicion?

If she called Scott and asked him to take Seth, Scott would want to know why. He'd been trying to get custody for two years now and as far as the state was concerned, his only drawback was his lack of steady employment and income; they knew nothing about the cocaine.

If Scott discovered the extent of Natalie's paper trail, he'd use it to prove Beth put Seth in danger. So far, her only hold over him was the exorbitant alimony she paid him every month. With Natalie as his ace in the hole, he might choose to forgo alimony for a chance at sole custody and child support. "Over my dead body," she snarled, envisioning one of Scott's dealers patting her son on the head.

As she gathered up the contents of Natalie's file, she heard a strange sound next door in Seth's room: the hiss and crackle of static, as if a walkie-talkie had been turned on. As soon as she heard it, the sound vanished.

Seth didn't have a walkie-talkie.

Suddenly, she wished she'd kept the dog with her. She wouldn't have hesitated to investigate before last night, but now that she knew someone was watching, even an ordinary noise was cause for alarm.

She had no weapons other than kitchen knives and garage tools. She wondered if she should just leave and check into a motel with Seth and Roo until the police found Natalie. *Oh, no you don't*, she thought. *This is your house and you will take charge if it's the last damn thing you do.*

She dropped the stack of papers in her hand and went to investigate.

CHAPTER TWENTY-FOUR

JULY 2013
SAN FRANCISCO, CALIFORNIA

The motel's air conditioning had been set at full blast despite an outdoor temperature of less than seventy degrees. Natalie put Yuri's box on the floor next to the bed and rubbed her arms to stave off an explosion of goosebumps. "How long can we stay here?"

"Long enough for someone to tell me what the hell's going on," Viktor snapped. "Who is she, Con?"

Constantine dropped the room key on the nightstand. "She's not the professor."

"Perish the thought."

"She's the professor's sister."

"Is that true?"

Natalie nodded. "Yuri lied to everyone. He never spoke to my sister about the Romanov letters. Beth doesn't believe Nicholas's money exists."

Viktor raised one thick black eyebrow. "But you do?"

"Belial told me it does."

"You keep using that word. If you don't tell me what it means, love, I'll be forced to assume you don't like me very much."

Natalie felt her cheeks burn. Explaining Belial to Constantine was one thing…he'd witnessed her seizure and stayed with her. But Viktor seemed more self-interested. What if he decided she was a liability? Would Constantine side with him?

Belial pressed his wings against her skull. *Are you embarrassed by me? After all I do for you?* She grunted and clamped her jaw shut.

"What's the matter with her now?" Viktor asked.

"You might want to sit down for this." Constantine pulled his gun from his waistband and collapsed onto one of the beds. He told Viktor everything about their flight through San Francisco, including her part in apprehending the German forger.

Through it all, Viktor leaned against the wall, arms crossed over his chest and one heel propped against the ochre wallpaper. "Vadim didn't tell me any of this. I may owe you an apology, Miss Brandon."

"I may accept it," she said. "Can I ask a question now?"

"Just one."

"Did you really give Yuri all that money?"

"I wouldn't give him the money to call a cab."

"But Yuri called the bank."

"Yuri used my phone, programmed to dial the North American desk, where a native English speaker told him what he wanted to hear. A real bank would have told him that any incoming wire transfer of that size would be routed through the Federal Reserve, triggering a bureaucratic apocalypse of paperwork." Viktor shrugged. "He's a blithering idiot and I used that against him."

Constantine touched his shoulder and winced. "What, exactly, did Vadim tell you?"

"That you were trying to get the Romanov letters from a civilian who used them to blackmail Kadyrov."

"Why didn't he warn you about Vympel?"

"Must have slipped his mind." Viktor marched to the bed and back, then punched the bathroom door. "Goddamn it! I should have known he'd only re-route me from Colombia to send me into something worse."

"If it's any consolation," Constantine said, "I found out about Vympel the hard way, too."

Viktor shook his head. "It's not. But someone still needs to patch you up. I'll go and fetch supplies."

Constantine reached into his pocket and tossed Viktor a roll of bills. "Vodka. Lots of it."

Viktor caught the money and slammed the door on his way out.

Natalie watched him through the window, spotting his lanky frame in the parking lot as it moved toward the Monte Carlo. "Is he going to be all right?"

"He's never gotten along with Vadim."

"Can you trust him?" she asked, closing the curtain.

"Of course. We've worked together since Stealth." Constantine patted the space next to his leg. "Come here so I can look at you while I'm still conscious," he said. "Once Viktor gets his hands on me, I'll be out cold."

Natalie blushed. She had no experience talking to men who weren't shrinks. She'd already ruined everything by throwing herself at him, but at least now she understood that the flutter he caused within her was thin and evanescent. Like a sparkling filament, it would crumble if she beat at it. *Let it go*, she thought. "You mentioned Stealth before. What is it?"

"A private security company. Because we'd been trained by retired KGB agents, dozens of us contracted out to go to Chechnya. Then Vadim found us."

"Does Viktor think I'm crazy?"

Constantine grinned. "Viktor is crazy. He pretends he's British."

"Why?"

"When I met him in Stealth's training camp, he hung a picture of Kim Philby next to his bunk. It got worse when he started watching *AbFab* on satellite TV."

Natalie nodded. She remembered reading about Philby, a decorated member of British intelligence who defected to the Soviet Union. He became a Soviet hero after his death, complete with state funeral, posthumous medals, and a postage stamp. "Children cling to their heroes," she said.

"And who's your hero?"

"Beth."

"What's she like?"

Natalie ran her fingers over the slick polyester bedspread. "Everything good went into her."

"She probably feels the same way about you."

"How do you know that?"

"That's how I feel about Lana."

"The girl who tried to kill herself? The one Viktor says you're hiding?"

The smile fell from Constantine's face. "Viktor said what?"

"He warned me about you at Yuri's."

"Before or after he tried to kiss you?"

She shrugged. "I thought he looked like a vampire. Why don't you tell him it's your sister?"

"It's none of his business."

"It's none of mine, either."

"You're the only one who might be able to talk to her." He reached out and touched one of her scars. "She's done this three times now. One day, she'll get it right. I was supposed to go home to be with her."

"What happened?"

"Vadim sent me here instead."

Natalie hung her head. "I'm sorry."

"Lana won't listen to me. I just can't get through to her."

Natalie bit her lip. Constantine had taken a bullet so she could escape Yuri's house. Anyone willing to do that for a stranger would surely love a sister, even one who was broken inside. "She listens. I know she does." Then she took a deep breath. "You could just go. I wouldn't say anything. I'll tell Viktor I fell asleep and don't know where you went."

"And leave you here, with Vympel looking for you?"

"If it were me, and I didn't have Beth…" She shook her head. "I wouldn't make it."

"If I did that, I'd be no better than the people who hurt her."

"Who were they?"

"People who wanted to get to me. She had nothing to do with it."

"Maybe you'll get to kill them someday." Natalie let out the breath she hadn't known she was holding. "But I'm glad it's not today."

Constantine smiled, creasing the skin around his eyes. "I thought you hated me for threatening to shoot you." He pulled her near, close enough for her to feel his breath on her skin and count the hundreds of tiny pores dotting his cheeks. This close, she felt like she could actually see what he was made of—the atoms, the molecules, the bond between them that allowed them to form hair and skin and sweat.

"No," she said softly. "I don't hate you."

He traced the diagonal of her cheekbone, trailing his finger to the collar of her blouse. She sighed and he pressed his lips to her neck. The shock of his touch made her shiver. She held her breath and closed her eyes as his lips traveled closer to hers.

Then she heard the plastic room key slip into the electric lock.

"The prodigal returns," Viktor said, bursting through the door with a collection of plastic bags. He glanced toward the bed and raised an eyebrow. "Did I interrupt something?"

Natalie sat up straight, painfully aware of the fact that she'd almost kissed Viktor an hour or two ago, and here she was with Constantine, sprawled out on a bed. "No." She got up without meeting Constantine's eyes and flopped onto the other bed. "Not a thing."

"Good." Viktor tossed one of the plastic bags onto the space she'd vacated. "Because this one's all mine. Let's get you out of these wet things, shall we?"

Constantine smiled. "I bet you say that to all the girls."

"Good grief," Natalie said. "You two really did learn English by watching TV."

Viktor helped Constantine peel off his blood-soaked shirt. "Did I mention that I'm not only the hair club president, I'm also a client?"

Her eyes drifted to the floor, where she'd deposited Yuri's box. *That's not a very safe place, is it?* Belial said. *You're going to want to hide that.*

"Why?"

"Why ask why?" Viktor answered. "Try Bud Dry."

"Make it stop," she said.

Do as you're told.

She stood up and stretched, using her toe to slide the box out of sight beneath the bed.

"Now for the fun part," Viktor said, tossing the bloody shirt onto the floor. He dumped the bag's contents onto the bed: disinfecting pads, tape, gauze, iodine, bottled water, and sandwich bags. He cleaned the skin around the wound with an antiseptic pad, smiling at Constantine's compressed lips. "Don't pretend it doesn't hurt. Scream if you like." He glanced over his shoulder at Natalie. "As long as it won't disturb the psychiatric ward."

Belial ruffled his wings. *I don't like him. I want him to leave.*

"Hush," she said. "Leave him alone."

"I thought you wanted me to fix him," Viktor said.

"I wasn't talking to you. Keep working."

Viktor moved to the sink and mixed a solution of iodine and bottled water in a resealable sandwich bag. Then he used his pocketknife to poke a tiny hole in the bottom of the bag.

Constantine roared as Viktor held the bag over the wound and squeezed. Natalie fought the urge to look away. *This happened to him because of you,* she thought. *Watching him suffer is your punishment.*

Viktor patted Constantine's shoulder with a towel and applied a dressing and bandage. "Finished! Now let's all have a drink."

Constantine groaned. "I thought you'd never ask."

Natalie hopped up to rummage through the bags. She found the bottle and poured into the motel's plastic cups, handing the first to Constantine. His fingers brushed hers and she turned away quickly, handing a second cup to Viktor. He stared at her empty hands. "I expected you to be joining us, based on your previously demonstrated alcoholic tendencies."

"I am," she said. "Mine's the bottle."

"Of course it is, love."

Constantine drained his cup in two gulps. "Any sign of Vympel?"

Viktor curled his lip. "Let's talk about something more cheerful, like leprosy or the holocaust."

"Viktor."

"I didn't see anything." He paused. "Do you think we can still trust Vadim?"

"It doesn't matter. He can't do anything to help us. That password is the only leverage we have."

"Speaking of which, what happened to the box?"

Natalie's heart froze. Why had Belial told her to hide it? And how was she supposed to keep it hidden when they were all in the same room?

I promise you I'm right, he whispered. *I will never lie to you.*

She looked Viktor in the eye. "It's in a safe place."

"Safe from whom? I thought you couldn't wait to get your hands on those letters."

"Belial said we should wait," she lied.

"Then by all means, let's do what your imaginary friend says." He turned to Constantine. "Are you going to allow this?"

"If she says wait, we wait."

"Do you know what happens if we wait? Vympel comes knocking on the door!" He turned to Natalie. "What does your imaginary friend say about that? Is he prepared to die?"

"Technically, he's already dead. I don't think he's worried."

He threw his empty cup against the wall and slumped into a chair. "Are you listening to this, Con?"

"We all need to rest," Constantine said. "Let's sleep for two hours and then we can be reasonable again." His head sank onto his pillow. "Viktor, you take first watch. Wake me up in an hour."

Viktor retrieved his gun from the nightstand and repositioned himself in the chair. "I don't want to hear another word out of you," he said, pointing the gun at her. "You or any of the imaginary creatures that live inside you. Are we clear?"

She flipped him off and rolled onto her side, tucking her chin to her chest and waiting for the beat of her fearful heart to subside.

CHAPTER TWENTY-FIVE

Filipp lay weak and exhausted, clutching the bedspread embroidered by his wife. Now that the end had come, he wanted to hold something that reminded him of her. "Milla," he whispered. His son, Grigori, shifted in the bedside chair.

A thunderous boom shook the glass in the window. The last time he'd heard artillery blasts on the edge of town, his entire world fell apart. He could still feel the thick Siberian air in his lungs and see the Bolshevik soldiers polishing their pistols outside the merchant Ipatiev's house. On the bedspread, his son's hand lay near his, tan and unlined. It symbolized all the strength he lacked, and Filipp clasped it firmly. "It was this hand she touched," he said.

Grigori smiled, crinkling the skin beside his gray eyes. "I know."

"You think you do," Filipp said. "But there is more."

"You mean the part where the grand duchess kissed you?"

Filipp opened his mouth to chide his son, but couldn't gather the breath. He coughed violently and Grigori pulled him upright in time to disgorge a clot of blood into a bowl. "Don't try to talk. I'll bring you some tea."

"No," he said, looking up at his son. "There is more, and we have little time."

"You're serious," Grigori said, sinking into the chair.

"The last time I saw her, Grand Duchess Olga Nikolaevna entrusted me with letters to take from that horrible house."

Grigori's face grew pale. "Papa, what are you saying?"

"She told me a secret, something she wanted me to write on the letters before I sent them. But I failed her." Filipp looked away so his son could not see the depth of his shame. "I fell ill. By the time I recovered, the Great Father and his family were gone."

"That wasn't your fault, Papa. You couldn't have saved them."

"What about the people who would have received those letters? Could they have saved them?" Filipp shook his head. "God could not be so cruel. I believe He intended for me to keep them all along. Now it falls to you to carry these words until the Great Father rises again."

"The tsar is dead, Papa. You know he is."

"Then where is his body? Where are the rest of them?" He felt tears collect in the corners of his eyes. "You did not see them, Grigori. They were such beautiful girls. Who would not wish one of them to survive?"

"Wishing does not make it true."

"God chose us to guard their secret. Why would He not choose one of them to survive?" His wet eyes flickered to the shrine in the corner of his bedroom. On a rectangular table, he'd propped up photos of Nicholas II and his family, along with a few of their belongings he'd bought from impoverished émigrés: a belt buckle, a hairpin, a brooch, a pair of earrings. "If even one of them remains alive, we must give their legacy back."

"A few rusty trinkets?"

Filipp's rheumy eyes swept the room. "I cannot speak it. The walls have ears."

Grigori leaned in closer. "Tell me what she said."

Filipp felt the telltale rattle in his chest. The North Korean army was closing in on Taesongdong, and everyone knew they would be followed by the Soviets. His son — and the letters — must be gone by then. He opened his lips and let his tongue form the words he had never before uttered.

"Good God," Grigori said. "But that's — "

"Hush." Filipp clamped a hand onto his son's shoulder. "You must never speak it aloud."

A second blast shook the ground beneath the house. Filipp imagined tanks rolling across the countryside, crushing people and animals beneath their treads, stealing the breath from their lungs. Suddenly, the entire war made sense. "I should have seen it," he gasped. "The Soviets know we are here, my boy. They have sent the North Koreans to seek us out."

"Don't be ridiculous, Papa. Just try and rest."

"I know what happened in the gulags! I know what they were looking for. Do not underestimate what they will do to claim what they believe is theirs. Do not let them find you here."

"I won't leave you. I can't."

"You must!" Filipp said. "We were chosen for this. It is why God spared me that summer."

"You survived because the nuns cared for you."

"I survived because God willed that it be so! The Great Father and his family ask this of us from their seat in heaven. I ask it of you as a father's dying wish. Will you refuse me?"

Grigori felt dizzy and nauseated. Everyone knew the tsar was dead. Why couldn't his father see that? What was he supposed to do? He had known no home but Korea and the outside world gaped like the edge of a map, leading to black pits of death and despair. "I'm afraid."

Filipp tried to smile but could barely move his lips. "God will not take away the danger, but He can take away your fear. Go put on the uniform, my son."

Grigori stepped into the next room. At the back of the closet, Filipp had hidden the uniform and dog tags of an American soldier, killed on the road to Panmunjon during the U.S. and Soviet withdrawal from the 38th Parallel five years earlier. He realized his father had always planned for this moment, and wondered how much of his father's life had been lived in the service of the dead tsar.

Grigori replaced his Korean tunic and pants with the scratchy soldier's jacket and trousers. He draped the dog tags around his neck and made his way back to his father's room, where a bright, fresh blood clot lay on the pillow beside Filipp's mouth. "Papa!" he cried.

Filipp couldn't take in enough air to cough. He gasped and wheezed, gripping Grigori's arms with the strength of a man half his age. Grigori watched his father's lips turn blue. He held Filipp to his chest, sobbing like a child until the frantic twitches ceased.

Minutes later, he unclasped his arms and closed the sky-blue eyelids. He kissed Filipp's lips and crossed his hands over his chest. Then he went to his father's bureau, removed the grand duchesses' letters from the false-bottomed drawer, and tucked them inside his jacket. He scooped up the contents of his father's shrine and placed them in a burlap sack. This was all he would take with him into the world, into the bombs and bayonets of the approaching North Korean army.

CHAPTER
TWENTY-SIX

The noise of a jet engine thundering overhead woke her. Natalie gasped and sat up straight. The bedside clock read 9:35 p.m.

They'd gone to sleep far more than an hour ago. As her eyes adjusted, she recognized the forms of the two men: Constantine in the other bed and Viktor, snoring, slumped in the chair. *First watch, my ass,* she thought. Viktor had no excuse for not waking her to take a second watch if he felt himself drifting off.

Belial snickered. *He doesn't trust you, little one. Are you surprised?*

She pulled the covers over her head, but sleep wouldn't return — not as long as the box remained hidden beneath the bed. She had never been this close to something so important. If the letters in that box were genuine, it was the find of the decade. If they were genuine and contained the password, it was the find of the century. She didn't care about the money. All the rubles in Russia couldn't evict Belial from her head. What mattered was the truth. The ghosts of the Romanov girls had been her childhood companions, better than anyone real or invented. If they had done something as shocking as betray their father's secret, she had to know.

She flung back the covers and reached under the bed for the box. She pulled it up and removed the lid, flaking rust particles onto the sheets. *Dried blood*, she thought. She blinked twice to clear the image, then inhaled the scent of old paper wafting from the open box. It worked on her like incense in an Orthodox priest's censer. She felt drunk, transported, part of something bigger than the four walls that surrounded her.

On top of the paper lay a velvet bag. She opened the drawstring and poured the contents into her hand: a belt buckle, a jeweled hair pin, earrings, a brooch. They emanated waves of shimmering light, like the halos of Byzantine saints.

It was the light that interested Belial. *What have you got there, little one?* He peeked out through her orbital sockets. What he saw made him jump, slamming his head against her skull. *Where did those come from?*

"From the box. Are they real?"

My brother's hand has been upon them. I can feel it.

"Your brother?"

Lucifer.

The angel shuddered and Natalie fought the urge to throw up. She reached for the stack of paper beneath the pouch. On top were dozens of postcards: thick, sepia-toned stock printed with photos of the imperial children. They felt raw beneath her fingertips, jagged and torn like flesh slashed by a dull bayonet. A few receipts lay between the cards, handwritten on napkins and other scraps. A name, an item or service received, an amount dispensed, a signature. She couldn't read the Cyrillic text, but the signature was the same on each.

At the bottom of the stack, she found the two letters she'd glimpsed earlier that day. She unfolded them gently and stared at the handwriting. *Olga,* she thought, running her hand over the first piece of yellowed paper. The grand duchess had signed her name in English, even though the rest of the letter was in Russian. Her eyes devoured the unclosed top loop of the "g," the wide space between the two last letters of her name, and the period after it — exactly how she signed letters to her family.

She couldn't read the body of the letter, but she could decipher the name in the salutation: Павел. There was only one "Pavel" to whom Olga would have written during the last days of her life: the man she loved, a sailor named Pavel Voronov. Separated by rank, her mother's disapproval, and Pavel's hastily arranged marriage, Olga never fell out of love with him. She'd loved him enough to bestow her last written words on him.

No one else in the whole world knows this, she thought. Her heart ached for the girl. A realist susceptible to black fits of depression, Olga understood better than the rest of the girls what would happen to them. A letter to a married man, a deeply unsuitable match for a tsar's daughter, meant only one thing: Olga knew the end was near.

Such lovely girls, Belial sobbed. *Why did he have to kill them?*

Natalie blinked away her tears and reached for the second letter, written in Marie's hand. Natalie recognized her flamboyant signature, with multiple lines criss-crossing beneath her name. She had signed in Russian, unlike her sister. Marie was the family's romantic, the one who dreamed of nothing more than a husband, children, and family to call her own. Her letter was addressed to Иван.

Ivan Skorokhodov, she thought. The guard Marie fell in love with, the one whose granddaughter swore to a priest that the grand duchess intended to send their family the password. *It's all true,* she thought. What, Natalie wondered, had brought Olga and Marie together to write and smuggle these letters from the Ipatiev house? How did they even broach the topic between them?

She stared at the indecipherable Cyrillic scrawled on the page. Which word was the password? Did they specify a bank or a city? How would the men know where to begin looking for the money? Would it be a race to see who claimed the cache first, or were there different passwords for different accounts? Maybe each of the girls had their own account, to dispose of as they pleased. If so, did anyone know the passwords to Anastasia's or Tatiana's account?

Her fingers traced the edges of Olga's letter. At the top left hand corner, they felt a glob of something that was once gelatinous — a dab of brown binder's glue that clung to the paper.

Belial raised his tear-streaked face. *What's that on your finger?*

"Glue," she whispered.

A nervous tickle ran up and down her spine.

There wasn't supposed to be any glue.

By 1918, the family had used up the paper they brought with them into captivity and tore unused pages from old diaries, stitching them together to make new books, which they cheerfully presented to each other as Christmas and birthday gifts. Both Nicholas's diary and Alexis's diary for 1917 had hand-sewn pages. It was possible the girls had ripped pages from a book they brought with them from Tsarskoe Selo, but those volumes would have been high quality, bound with leather and stitched by hand.

That rat bastard Yuri had lied about everything.

CHAPTER
TWENTY-SEVEN

The boys had built the ramp themselves. Grigori had supplied the wood and tools, watching as Yuri and his friends occupied the backyard shed until nightfall. In constant use since its completion, the ramp had given rise to the street's most popular Saturday activity: watching the boys pedal like mad and fly off the ramp, praying they would land safely.

It was never supposed to happen like this, Grigori thought. Yuri should have been in the capable care of Julia, his mother, and Iosip, his father. But Grigori's wife, son, and daughter-in-law had all been taken away in a single day. One last-minute trip to Stinson Beach, one misjudged turn on a dark road, and one intoxicated driver hurtling up the road toward them. Everything vanished in a ball of fire and a twisted wreck of metal.

Grigori peeled back the curtain of the living room window and looked for his grandson. He spotted the bright blue bike as it flew up the curve of the ramp, over… *no, it can't be.* Grigori squinted to make the image clearer. There was a small boy huddled on the ground beside the ramp, shaking with fear.

Yuri's bike sailed over the cowering child and landed in the middle of the street. He skidded to a stop in front of three neighborhood boys who clapped and whistled their approval. Yuri slapped their raised hands and whooped in triumph. Then he held out his hand.

All three boys reached into their pockets and pressed a bill into his grandson's palm. They ignored the sobbing child beside the ramp. "Want me to go again?" Yuri asked.

Grigori ran out of the house and knelt beside the crying boy. "Hush, *malchik moy*, it's all right. How old are you?" The boy reached out to Grigori, clasping the older man's leathery fingers with his baby-soft ones.

"Th–three," the boy sobbed.

Grigori recognized him, a stepbrother of Yuri's friend Bobby. Bobby's father had remarried that summer, bringing his new wife and her two small children into his home. "The boys won't bother you again," Grigori said. "Run along home now."

The child scrambled to his feet and hurried down the sidewalk. Grigori strode into the street and picked up the ramp, tossing it onto the lawn. He'd get the axe and chop it up as soon as he dealt with his fifteen-year-old grandson.

"Hey," one of the other boys called. "Isn't that your grandpa?"

Yuri turned, saw Grigori, and spat into the street. "What the hell do you want?"

Grigori gave Yuri the stare his own father Filipp had used whenever he failed to lock the chicken coop at night. "Give me that money," he said.

Yuri scowled. "What money?"

"The money you just put in your pocket. You're not to terrorize that poor child anymore, do you understand? All of you."

The other boys exchanged a wary look and began to back away. "You're busted," one of them hissed, picking up his bike and pedaling for home. The others followed.

"Don't go with them," Grigori said.

"I'll do what I want," Yuri snapped. He pivoted his bike and put a foot on the pedal. "You're not my father."

Grigori gripped Yuri's arm with all his strength, white knuckles holding the boy in place. "Have I not taught you to protect those younger and weaker than us?"

"Great job," Yuri said, nodding his head at Grigori's tight grip.

"Our family is different. You know this, Yuri."

"Enough with the sacred-mission bullshit. No one cares."

"You don't mean that," Grigori said. He set his jaw, but on the inside, his heart fell like a stone hurled into a pond. His grandson pretended to understand nothing of war, death, and the Soviet menace. How had he failed to make Yuri understand? "You know the letters exist, Yuri, but you do not know what they mean. When I tell you what really happened, you will care. You will see we have avoided death only by following the path laid out for us."

"What about my dad? Did the letters kill him, too?"

"Your father did not know the truth yet," Grigori said softly. "It was a car accident, nothing more."

Yuri's black eyes glittered. "He said you were crazy. Did you know that? Every time he came back from your house, he'd shake his head and tell us how batshit crazy his old man was."

Grigori lowered his head. "Your father and I did not see eye to eye. But he understood our purpose. He was ready to accept it. The day will come when you, too, must decide where you stand. With the evil, or against it."

"Fuck off," Yuri said.

Grigori looked into his grandson's eyes and saw only anger. The boy missed his father, but without an outlet, the grief was eating him alive. He didn't know how to let go.

Grigori released the boy's arm and watched Yuri pedal furiously down the block. For the first time, he forced himself to think about what would happen if Yuri could not be trusted.

Perhaps it is time for a test, he thought. He would wait for Yuri to grow up, and he would try to trust his reckless grandson. But not even a blood connection would blind him to the purpose of his sacred task — protecting the tsar's secret. There was only one thing he could think of that would both test Yuri's devotion and keep Nicholas's secret safe.

He left the bike ramp on the lawn and went into the house, wondering where he had put his wife's old books and calligraphy pens.

CHAPTER TWENTY-EIGHT

Natalie pulled the covers over her head and squeezed her eyes shut. She dreaded telling Constantine the truth. It was all a hoax. Just thinking about it made her want to cry.

The Romanov letters, had they been real, were worth dying for. They'd given her a purpose, which was more than any of her shrinks had been able to do. For one moment, however brief, she'd known something no one else in the world could know. Now it was gone and she had nothing. She put a hand over her breast, where the velvet pouch lay tucked inside her bra. The Romanovs' possessions were sacred to her and she had no intention of leaving them behind.

Belial was restless, too, drumming his fingers against her brain. *Something's not right*, he said. *Something's not right.*

After an hour of tossing and turning, she gave up. If she rummaged through the other bags Viktor had brought, maybe she'd find more vodka. There was no other way to get Belial to calm down.

She swung her feet off the bed and stopped. Something was wrong. There was a strange noise in the hallway — light footsteps in rapid succession that stopped just outside the door, followed by a series of metallic clicks.

Belial paused. *What's that noise?*

She heard a latch click open across the hall, followed by the abrasive whir of an air conditioner. The noise didn't go away because the door didn't close.

They were just standing there, waiting.

"Viktor," she whispered. "Viktor, wake up!"

The first blast shot out the deadbolt and a chunk of the doorframe. A second destroyed the electronic lock. Viktor woke instantly, flailing in the chair and diving for cover.

The intruders kicked in the door and stormed the room, their shadowy bodies silhouetted by the hallway's flickering fluorescent light. Viktor raised his gun and fired. Constantine, slower to react, sat up in bed and reached for the pistol on the nightstand. He fired and one of the black-clad figures groaned and fell backward. Another dropped to the floor and crawled on his belly toward her.

Fight him, Belial ordered. *I'll help you.*

From the bed, she kicked out at the dark, crouched figure. Her heel caught his face, but he recovered quickly, grabbing her ankle and pulling her to the floor. Her tailbone slammed against the thin carpet and she cried out.

Hit him with the box, Belial said. *It's useless for anything else.*

Her fingers swept beneath the bed, reaching for the box. She swung it against the attacker's head, but the corroded metal did little damage.

Perhaps you'd better let me handle this.

Belial gave her no time to respond. He rose to his feet, pressing against her skull with enough force to split it in half. When he spread his wings, her vision went black. She screamed with a rush of pain and fear.

Belial's energy animated her, moving her body as he willed it. All her senses had gone dark, leaving only a thick blackness and a pulsing electric hum. Her arms and legs carried her toward the attacker instead of away from him. She screamed at Belial to stop, but her voice echoed inside her hollow body.

Belial made a fist and slammed it into the attacker's face. *His rage blazes forth like fire and the mountains crumble to dust in his presence! The Lord is good!*

Natalie felt a dim ache, centered on her jaw. The attacker had struck back. Instinctively, she told her body to pull away, but it didn't obey. Her synapses refused to carry her commands. Belial had turned them all off.

Sensations reached her in their dimmest form, long after they actually happened. Something wet blanketed her face and hands. She imagined it was blood. There was something thick and heavy at her feet that didn't move. Then she felt herself being lifted. She squirmed, trying to crawl away from whatever had her in its grip. *No,* she screamed inside. *Belial, let me go!*

Suddenly, a voice made its way through the black fog. "Natalie! Natalie, look at me! Are you all right?"

Her body jerked uncontrollably, like falling from a cliff in a dream. The pulsing hum in her brain vanished and her eyelids flew open as she gasped for air. Everything hurt: her hands, her face, her head.

"Are you all right?" Constantine asked. His anxious face hovered next to hers.

"What happened?

"Vympel. They took Viktor and the box. Good God, what did they do to you?" He tilted her head to the side and touched her jaw. Lightning bolts of pain shot out from the place his finger touched.

"You're hurt, too," she said. The dressing taped over his wound was saturated with blood.

"Natalie, what happened?"

"Belial," she said. "It was Belial. I couldn't control it." She looked down at her red, scraped knuckles and felt tears gather in her eyes.

Constantine pulled her into his arms. "I was afraid they would take you, too, but they gave up once they had Viktor."

"Why did they take him?"

Constantine's blue eyes darkened, turning a shade of gray she hadn't seen before. "I don't know. But we have to get him back. And we have to get out of here before your police show up."

Three dead bodies lay on the floor, two near the door with bullet wounds and one at the foot of her bed. The man's face was a pile of red mush. She felt like she was going to throw up.

Constantine slipped back into his bloodstained shirt and gathered the rest of the supplies Viktor had bought. He took her hand and pulled her down the stairwell to the parking lot, populated by less than a dozen cars. The Monte Carlo was untouched.

They got in without speaking. Natalie handed Constantine the screwdriver and he started the car. He revved the engine once and took off down the street, passing an ambulance and police car headed for the motel. Natalie held her breath until they had gone several blocks, toward the freeway entrance. "Where are we going?"

Constantine's profile, illuminated in yellow streetlight glare, looked sharper than she remembered it. "I don't know."

"Are they taking him back to Russia?"

"Maybe. It depends what those letters say." He made a fist and punched the steering wheel, honking the horn. "I should have copied them. God, I was so stupid."

"The letters are fake," she said softly.

"What?"

"That paper didn't come from the Ipatiev house."

"How do you know?"

"They ran out of paper," she said, feeling a sob stick in her throat. "They had to slit blank pages from their books. The real thing would either have a super-straight edge, after being cut with scissors, or a jagged one from being torn out of a hand-sewn binding."

"So this was all for nothing?"

She felt a tear slide down her left cheek. "I didn't want this to happen. I'm sorry."

His foot pressed the gas pedal to the floor and he merged onto the freeway at a hundred miles an hour. "Why the hell didn't you tell me?"

"It was already too late. It wouldn't have changed anything."

But as soon as she said the words, she knew they were lies. What if she'd woken the men once she'd made her discovery? What if they'd left immediately? Vympel would have found an empty room.

Belial sighed. *This is all your fault, little one.*

"Haven't you done enough?" she snapped. She turned in her seat and sifted through the plastic bags. When she found the second bottle of vodka, she opened it and began drinking.

Is this how you thank me for saving your life?

"You killed someone, Belial," she said. "With my hands. I'm going to drink this whole bottle if that's what it takes to make you go away."

Constantine gripped the wheel with angry white knuckles. "He's talking to you, isn't he?"

Natalie nodded and raised the vodka bottle.

I was going to tell you the truth about those letters. But if you'd rather sulk...

Natalie jerked the bottle from her lips, spilling some down her chin. "What truth?"

I thought you wanted me to go away.

"Belial, what truth?"

The grand duchesses' signatures matched. You saw it yourself. Under what conditions are a forger's best works produced?

She thought about it, imagining herself as the forger. Then it hit her. "Belial," she whispered. "You wouldn't make me think this if it weren't true, would you?" But he didn't answer. He simply folded his wings and crouched down beneath them, silent and immobile.

"Natalie," Constantine said. "What the hell's going on?"

She felt her heart quicken inside her rib cage. "We still have a chance. Turn the car around."

CHAPTER TWENTY-NINE

The sun had not yet set, but the blue velvet curtains in prime minister Maxim Starinov's office had been drawn for hours. He preferred darkness to light. Light gave hope to people who came to ask him for things, and he wanted them to know that nothing in Russia would help them get what he would not give.

The wood-paneled walls held portraits of Ivan, Peter, Lenin, and Stalin: the great men who made Russia fearsome in the minds of her enemies. He would be another like this, the man who gave Russia back to herself after her sloppy affair with Western-style capitalism.

Starinov turned his attention to the stack of folders sitting on his desk. Each contained a dossier on an FSB agent. Periodically it became necessary to sort the wheat from the chaff, or even the wheat from the wheat. It mattered less who was sorted than that the sorting be done. Without fear, men became lazy.

He picked up a pen and glanced through the dossiers. If he read something that displeased him, he drew a slash across the photo. One by one, he made his way through the stack. When he was through, the man sitting quietly in the corner would pass the files to Vympel.

Starinov picked up the last file. "Galen Ibrahimovich Popov," he read, waiting for the man in the corner to comment. The agent in question was one of his. Surely he would not let his own perish without offering a trade.

"Not him," the man in the corner said quickly.

"But Popov's last three attempts at recruitments have failed."

"He is my brother-in-law. I brought him into the agency."

"I suppose I can offer you a bargain," Starinov said. "Popov can be spared if you give me another name."

The man pressed his lips together. Beads of sweat gathered within the fine hairs of his neatly trimmed moustache. To his credit, the man held eye contact as he processed his options.

"Time is short," Starinov pressed. He held the pen in his right hand, poised to make the final stroke. "What is your answer?"

The man's mouth opened just as the phone rang.

Starinov glared at the blinking red light on the console. "I am not through with you," he said, leaving his pen uncapped on the desk. He picked up the handset, watching the man in the corner shift uncomfortably in his chair.

The voice on the line transmitted through crackles and pops. "Your Excellency, this is Lieutenant Colonel Sergei Kyrillovich Borovoi. You asked me to report directly to you once our objective had been achieved."

Starinov felt a thrill of anticipation in his chest. His eyes flickered to the portraits on his wall. "You have the letters?"

"*Da.* I request your permission to extract Professor Brandon."

"Vadim's agent didn't pick her up?"

"There was a mistake in the file, Your Excellency. Dashkov got away with the wrong woman, the professor's sister."

"Does he know this?"

"He must, sir. But we have Professor Brandon under full surveillance and she has received no communication from Dashkov or her sister."

"Are you certain? No email or text message?"

"No, sir."

Starinov hesitated. It was unlike Vadim to let his agent disobey a direct order. If the boy had not checked in yet or admitted his mistake, Vadim would have no idea the wrong sister was in custody. But he knew the way Vadim ran his operation. Vadim's agents confided in him completely — Vadim insisted on it.

Borovoi sensed his hesitation. "What are your orders, sir?"

"Bring the letters and Professor Brandon to me. I will deal with the rest."

"Yes, sir. And … sir?"

"Yes?"

"Dashkov has killed five of my men. Please take that into consideration."

"I will," Starinov said, hanging up. He waited for the green light to flash briefly, an indication that the digital recorder had captured the call in its entirety. The recording would be transferred to his chief of staff, who would use the digital signature of Borovoi's phone to track him. If something went wrong, the cleaners could at least be given a GPS coordinate.

"Now," he said, tight smile on his lips. "Where were we?"

The man in the corner did not answer.

"I believe you owe me a name. Have you thought of one? Or shall I supply one for you?"

The man looked up, hopeful. "Yes. Anyone."

"Vadim Primakov."

"What?" The man shook his head. "But... he's a director."

"No one is above suspicion. Not even you, Valery Vakhanovich."

"Vadim is a friend." Beads of sweat fell like tears down Valery's face.

"If it helps you at all, Primakov has been lying to us. He is playing his own game, with his own rules."

"This is about the Romanov letters."

Starinov nodded.

"Vadim asked for my help. He wanted me to help his agent and I refused."

"I have very little sympathy for Primakov's man, considering he has already killed five of mine. Nor for Primakov himself, who failed to bring the existence of the letters to my attention. That does not make me happy."

Valery shivered. "Of course not."

"Enough of this," Starinov grumbled. "You may save your brother-in-law or you may save Primakov, a man who may be a traitor to Mother Russia. At the very least, he has been a traitor to me. The decision is yours."

Valery clamped his lips shut. His eyes shone with moisture.

"It's a shame," Starinov said, picking up the phone. "Your sister is ill, is she not? Your brother-in-law's salary pays for the drugs that keep her cancer from spreading." He sighed. "But then again, living with cancer isn't really living, is it? Perhaps you're making the right decision after all." He held up Popov's file and began to dial.

"Wait," Valery whispered, blinking quickly in the dim light. "What do you want to know about Vadim?"

CHAPTER THIRTY

Seashore Oaks Nursing Home sat high on a ridge, five miles inland and lifted well into the fog bank. Natalie saw nothing but gray in every direction. It was like nuclear winter — the worst possible place to send a loved one to die.

Constantine parked the Monte Carlo in front of the entry vestibule. She stared at the building with loathing. *Don't go in there,* Belial said. *You know what they do to people like you.*

"I know," she whispered. "But it's the only way."

"Is it Belial?" Constantine asked. "What's he saying?"

She forced her throat to swallow. Every muscle in her body felt tense, locked in place to keep her from exiting the car. "The doctors. They all want to lock me up."

"Natalie, they won't lock you up."

She turned to face him and felt her eyes fill with angry tears. She hated that the doctors could make her so afraid. But if there was one thing Belial insisted on, it was that she stay away from hospitals and doctors. "How do you know?"

He flicked aside his jacket, revealing the Walther in his waistband. "I won't let them."

Don't be stupid, little one. A gun is no match for thousands of vials of haloperidol, chlorpromazine, droperidol, thioxene, iloperidone…you have to find another way.

She balled her hands into fists and pressed them to her forehead. "I'm doing this, Belial. There is no other way." She looked down at her newly purchased handbag, inside which lay the miniature trove of Romanov artifacts she'd stolen from Yuri's box. The bag felt empty without the letters. "We need this."

Her eyes wandered to the automatic sliding doors of the vestibule. A white-coated doctor trotted out to a parked car and fumbled with his keys. Belial tensed, ready for trouble. *They sent him out here to spy on you. He's going to run back inside and tell them you're coming. They'll be ready.*

She grasped the door handle so tightly that ridges of white bone rose up over her knuckles. Constantine put a warm hand on her shoulder. "Are you all right?"

"What if the doctors find out I belong in there?"

His hand moved from her shoulder to her cheekbone. He let his index finger slide down the curve of her cheek. She closed her eyes and leaned into his touch, feeling his warmth radiate through her body. "You don't belong in a place like this," he said. "All you have to do is pretend we're husband and wife, visiting an old man. Can you do that?"

His blue eyes met hers head-on without fear or doubt. She waited for that moment of distancing, the one when most people shut themselves away from her to protect themselves. It didn't come.

She opened her mouth to speak, but the back of her skull erupted with the heat of a lightning strike. *Pretending is all you're going to get, little one. You know that, don't you?*

"Yes," she whispered, blinking back tears. "I know how to pretend."

Natalie followed Constantine through the sliding doors into a reception room. He smiled at the woman behind the desk. A plastic nametag identified her as "Myra." Her hair was black at the roots, with blonde permed curls that cascaded to her shoulders. "Good morning, Myra," he said, thickening his consonants to make the Russian accent unmistakable. "I'm here to visit my uncle."

"What's your uncle's name?" Myra asked.

"Grigori Voloshin." Constantine spelled it for her as she typed.

A white-coated man emerged from the hallway on her right and passed directly behind her. All his attention was focused on the chart in his hands and he scribbled as he walked. *He's writing something about you,* Belial growled.

"No," she said. "Cut it out."

"What was that?" Myra asked, looking up at her.

"You'll have to excuse my wife," Constantine said, putting an arm around her shoulders. "She just found out her grandmother is ill."

Myra curled her lip, revealing front teeth stained with coral lipstick. "You're having a run of bad luck, aren't you?"

"What do you mean?"

"Your uncle is sick, too. We can't allow you to see him."

"Why not?"

"The only approved visitor on the list is his son, Yuri."

"But we've come all this way to surprise him! Please, just let us see him for a few minutes."

"I'm sorry," Myra said. "Patients who left the ICU less than forty-eight hours ago are only allowed approved visitors, and you're not on the list."

Natalie narrowed her eyes. Convalescent homes couldn't be that different from hospitals or sanitariums and she knew those institutions thrived on protocol—pointless bureaucracy that enforced a power structure. All they had to do was find out who had the power. "How do we get on the list?" she asked.

The sympathetic furrow slipped from Myra's brow. "I'm sorry, ma'am. You can't just 'get on the list.' It's a long process that involves paperwork and documentation of your relationship to our patient."

The doctors did this on purpose, Belial said. *They want to kill him without witnesses.*

Constantine bent over the reception desk. "Are you absolutely sure there's no way we can see him? Perhaps it would help to see a friendly face."

"I'm sorry, sir. I wish I could help."

"Listen," Natalie said, shoving past Constantine. "His son's been murdered. Someone needs to tell him. Do you want it to be you or do you want it to be me?"

Myra gasped and looked back to Constantine. "Is this true?"

Constantine sighed. "I'm afraid so. The police contacted us yesterday."

"Why didn't you say something?" She jiggled the mouse at her desk and refocused her eyes on the screen. "It says here that Gregory's son is his only living relative."

"Grigori," Natalie snapped. "His name is Grigori."

Myra leveled her with an arctic glare. "That's what I said."

"Can you at least give him a message? Tell him Nicholas and Alexandra sent us here. Tell him it's about the girls."

The woman hesitated, glancing down at her mouse.

"It's important," Constantine added.

She sighed and ripped the top sheet from a stack of sticky notes. "What did your wife say again?"

Natalie repeated her message and watched with satisfaction as the woman shuffled off to fulfill their request. *She'll tell the doctors about you,* Belial said.

"It doesn't matter," she said. "As long as I see Grigori."

You must be careful with him, little one. His mind is fragile.

"What do you mean?"

He is near the end of his journey. He will see through a heart that is not surrendered.

"I was afraid of that," she said. She looked up at Constantine and wondered if his willingness to pretend to be married to her counted as a surrendered heart.

"You look worried," Constantine said. "Did Belial tell you something about the letters?"

She nodded. "Apparently, getting in is the easy part."

"He's an old man. Just tell him he needs to give us the letters or Yuri will die. There's no way he knows it's already happened."

Natalie thought of the way she and Beth could spend afternoons in the campus library, wrapped up in research. All of a sudden, Beth would look up from her desk and gasp, fully aware that halfway across town, her son had just fallen off his skateboard in the driveway. "He'll know," she said.

"Natalie, that's impossible."

As she opened her mouth to retort, Myra shuffled back into the room. Natalie pushed Constantine aside. "What did he say?"

"He wants to see you," Myra said. "He said he's been waiting for you."

CHAPTER THIRTY-ONE

Grigori had a single room with a double-paned observation window facing the hallway. Everyone who walked by could look in and see him, whether he curled up and slept or sobbed alone and waited to die. The man on the bed looked older than his eighty years. His skin had withered and darkened, like fruit dried in the sun.

Natalie put her hand against the door and absorbed the feeling of cold and dread it gave her. *I can't help you in there,* Belial said. *My brother's hand is already upon him.*

"I understand," she said. Then she turned to Constantine. "You have to wait outside."

He shook his head. "I'm coming with you."

"No," she said again. "It's like a séance. You have to believe."

"Natalie, he's just an old man."

"Keep the doctors away. I'll call for you if I need help." Before he could follow, she slipped through the door and locked it from the inside. She pressed her palm to the observation window and mouthed, "I'm sorry."

Then she turned to the rheumy-eyed man on the bed. The sleeves of his gown barely covered his shoulders. The armholes were cut so wide she could see the slack flesh of his forearm, now empty of muscle, lying useless against his chest. "Mr. Voloshin," she said, pulling up a rolling stool at his bedside. "My name is Natalie."

"Natalia," he corrected. His right index finger lay encased in what looked like a plastic pencil sharpener, and at least half a dozen tubes snaked out of his gown, connecting with bags and machines that surrounded the head of his bed. "Did Yuri send you?"

"No. But he gave me your box."

"How much did he sell it for?"

"Nothing."

"You're lying, Natalia." He sighed, the exhale interrupted by liquid pooling in his lungs. "That poor family will never know peace."

"Peace is a luxury we don't all get." She thought about how hard it was to make her shrinks understand that angels and the afterlife were real things, not the made-up invention of Israel's lost tribes. "You don't have to be afraid of me."

"Of you?" he said, a tiny smile curling his lips.

"Lots of people are afraid of me."

"They can't see it, can they?"

"See what?"

"The angel. Standing behind you."

Natalie gulped. "That's Belial. No one's ever seen him before."

The old man smiled, wrinkling his parchment-thin cheeks. "He thinks you're beautiful."

"I need to know where the real letters are, Grigori."

"Did your angel tell you about my little trick?"

She smiled at him. "I figured it out myself. The paper wasn't right. It was too new."

"I knew Yuri would sell them as soon as I was gone."

"How did you get them?"

"My father carried them from Ekaterinburg to Korea. He gave them to me on his deathbed." He took a deep breath but couldn't fill his lungs without coughing. She poured a glass of water from the carafe on his nightstand and held it to his lips. "Thank you," he said, eyes glistening with cough-induced tears. "They tell me it will only get worse until the end."

"They're doctors. It's their job to lie to you."

"It is what I deserve. God gave me one chance, and I ruined it."

"I can make it right if you tell me where the letters are."

"Letters," he mumbled, turning his head into the pillow. He closed his eyes and stopped breathing for a single count. Then he choked, coughed, and blinked his red-veined eyes. He looked at the plastic curtain hanging around the bed and then at her, as if he were confused at where he found himself. "What has happened to us all?"

"We're fighting a war," she said, reaching for his hand. "I swear to you, Grigori, I won't let anything happen to your letters. I'll help the girls find the peace we can't."

The old man's eyes glowed with tears and fervor. He leaned over and opened the drawer of his nightstand. From the Bible resting inside, he pulled an onionskin envelope that contained several folded pieces of paper. Natalie gasped. "You had them with you all along?"

"I knew God would send the right person to me when it was time."

"You're a good man," she said, touching his cheek. "Thank you."

The old man turned his head, letting the pillow absorb the tears streaming down his face.

"Thank you," she whispered again, as she placed his clammy hand beneath the blanket. What gave men like Grigori the strength to defy dictators and entire countries to do what they believed was right? It wasn't fair that these men died alone and forgotten when they were the best of humankind. "I wish I could be more like you."

She stood up, kissed him on the forehead, and pulled the blanket over his shoulders. Then she saw it — an old rotary phone on Grigori's bedside table, next to a Russian-language magazine and the weekend edition of the *Chronicle*. She glanced out the observation window. Constantine stood with his back to it, arms crossed over his chest.

She picked up the receiver and twirled the phone's plastic ring. After a brief click on the line, it began to ring.

Then she heard the telltale click of the answering machine. "Hi, you've reached Beth and Seth, but we can't come to the phone right now." There was a brief shuffle as Seth stepped up to the recorder. "Don't be lame and hang up. Leave us a message so my mom feels cool."

The beep echoed in her ear.

"If you're there, pick up," she said. "Come on, Beth, this is serious." Natalie glanced out the observation window. "I'm all right, but I need your help. I need you to come and check on a man named Grigori Voloshin in the Seaside Oaks nursing home in Daly City. Tell Seth I'm sorry I missed the sharks. Lock your doors and don't let Seth or Roo out of your sight. I'll be home as soon as I can. I love you, Beth."

CHAPTER THIRTY-TWO

JULY 2013

SAN FRANCISCO, CALIFORNIA

Beth picked up the phone for the tenth time that morning. She held her right thumb over the "9" and her left over the "1," promising that this time she'd tell the police about Natalie's condition. But then she pictured Sergeant Lopez tossing Natalie in the back of a patrol car, hauling her to a county hospital, and dosing her with a month's worth of mind-destroying drugs. She put the phone down.

All her life, she'd protected Natalie from the clutches of the system — lying to social workers, lying to doctors, and lying to anyone who asked why her sister was "weird" or "mental." After their parents died, Natalie was all she had. Never, she vowed, would those vultures sink their claws into her own flesh and blood. Even now, she couldn't betray a lifetime's worth of trust.

In the den, there was a sideboard that doubled as a bar. She opened it up and stared at the dust-covered bottles. Her fingers closed around a bottle of single-malt scotch and she took a shot straight out of the bottle. The burn rose from her belly with the speed of mercury on a hot summer day. She closed her eyes and concentrated on relaxing.

That's when she heard it. A soft click, like a doorknob latching, coming from upstairs.

There had been strange noises all over the house since early that morning, like the walkie-talkie noise in Seth's room. Every time she investigated, it turned out to be nothing. Still, she couldn't shake the feeling that something wasn't right. Lopez had promised a squad car would patrol the area until they found her sister, just in case.

Images of Natalie's bed, spattered with bullet holes, sprang to her mind. *Don't be a victim,* she told herself.

Beth tiptoed to the kitchen and slid a chef's knife out of the wooden block. Long and triangular, the blade was sharp enough to slice through a shoe. She held it at eye level and moved toward the stairs. One at a time, she crept up to the second floor.

The first room off the hallway was her office. She glanced at the phone, resting on a storage cube beside the desk. The handset hadn't been removed from the console or switched off. *That's a good sign,* she thought. *Don't the bad guys usually cut your power or phone before hacking you to bits?*

She glanced around the room. The papers on her desk were lined up properly and the shelf of books was still in order. Then she saw the closet doorknob. What if there was someone behind it?

She tried to make her feet move forward, but they held firm. *You can do this,* she thought. *You gave birth without drugs. You ran a marathon. You gave the commencement speech at graduation.*

Beth shuffled forward, gaze fixed on the closet door. If the noise had come from this room, the closet was the only place to hide.

She transferred the knife to her left hand and wiped her sweaty right palm against her jeans. Then, with the knife hefted in her right hand again, she reached for the doorknob.

One twist. One pull.

One glimpse of a face behind the door — smiling at her.

Beth screamed and slashed. A hand grabbed her wrist, immobilizing the knife. She wasted three seconds trying to press the knife closer to the intruder's face before she changed tactics and kneed him in the groin as hard as she could.

The man howled and his grip slackened. She pressed her advantage, double-fisting the knife and plunging it into his shoulder. Then she ran.

Beth took the stairs two at a time, wishing she'd kept her cell phone on her instead of in her purse. Downstairs, in the garage, there was a spare car key. She'd back straight through the garage door before she'd let this creep catch her.

Heavy footsteps thundered behind her. She felt the air move as his hands reached out for her, clasping nothing as she ducked to avoid his grasp. The lunge left him off kilter as he reached the next stair.

He fell, crushing her against the staircase.

Beth's head slammed against the next-to-last stair and the world went black for just a moment. Her body contorted painfully against the stairs, but every burning nerve ending urged her to fight, get up, run. She flung out an arm and grabbed one of the stair rails, using it to pull herself out from under her attacker.

Kicking like a swimmer, she caused enough damage to force him to roll over. Her body slithered out from under him and she darted for the kitchen. *The phone,* she thought. *Call 911 and grab another knife.*

Her fingers reached for the handset as it began to ring. Caught off guard, she paused a second too long. The attacker came up behind her, circling her neck with his arm. Beth clawed and scratched, kicking out behind her.

The phone continued to ring. Two times. Three times.

Black spots floated across the room. She shot her hand back, hoping to poke him in the eye.

The answering machine picked up. When the voice on the other end began to speak, white-hot lightning coursed through her veins. "If you're there, pick up," her sister's voice said, low and anxious. "Come on, Beth, this is serious."

She fought the press of darkness, summoning her strength for one last attack. She slipped her elbow forward, then slammed it into the man's stomach. He grunted and wheezed but didn't lose his grip. Her hands flew up to his arm, pulling with everything she had. Her lips shaped her sister's name as the last gasp of air flew from her lungs.

CHAPTER THIRTY-THREE

Natalie slipped through Grigori's door, onionskin envelope in hand. "I have the letters. Let's get the hell out of here."

Constantine glanced back at the old man. "Are you crying? What did he say to you?"

"The world is a fucked up place and I don't want to talk about it." There was no hope in a world that punished a man like Grigori with a painful, lonely death. If the angels couldn't stop bad things from happening to good people, there was even less hope for someone like her.

As she passed through the sliding glass doors of the lobby, a voice called out. "Wait! Ma'am, I have something for you!"

Told you, said Belial. *I told you they wouldn't let you leave.*

Natalie's blood turned to ice. She gulped and turned around.

"Mr. Voloshin said to give you this." Myra held out a ring with a mauve pearl surrounded by small diamonds. "He said it belongs to you."

For a moment, the world swam before her eyes. She reached out for it, afraid it was being used as bait to lure her back inside. But Myra just dropped it into her palm and turned away.

Belial fluttered his wings and peered forward through her eyes. *Oh, dear. This is getting serious.*

"What's that?" Constantine asked. "Don't tell me the letters need a decoder ring."

"I've seen this before," she said. "It was Alexandra's. Nicholas gave it to her for Christmas in 1903." She put the ring on her finger and watched the diamonds sparkle in the dreary light. "It feels heavy. Like a part of her has followed it."

"Okay, take it easy," Constantine said, pulling her back to the Monte Carlo and opening the passenger door for her. He closed it behind her, got in the driver's seat, and started it up. "What's our next move?"

"You're asking me? I'm the crazy one, remember?"

"You're the one who figured out the letters were fake," he said, putting the car in reverse. "At Voloshin's, all you had to do was put your hands on that man's face and you knew where the letters were. I'd have had to beat him to a pulp to get that out of him. I couldn't have gotten this far without you."

"That's the nicest thing anyone's ever said to me."

"You can thank me when we find the password and get rid of Vympel. Where can we find a quiet place to translate these letters?"

Natalie directed him to I-280 North. They drove into the city and parked around the corner from the San Francisco Public Library's Civic Center branch. "We can work on the translations here," Natalie said. "Then we'll figure out what happens next."

They rounded the corner of Larkin Street and slipped through the library's columned entrance. Natalie looked up at the domed skylight, illuminating the central atrium. Each successive floor spiraled around the atrium, with silver pendant lights illuminating the dim passageways. She'd come here many times to pick up books or journal articles for Beth's research. It was a peaceful place, one she felt at home in. She took Constantine's hand and led him to the elevator bay.

They rode to the third floor and wound through the stacks until they found an alcove with a beat-up table and chairs. Natalie sank into one, pulling the onionskin envelope from her bag. Constantine pulled a pen from his pocket, stolen from the desk of the nursing home. "I'll translate them on paper and pass each one to you as I finish," he said. "Does Belial have any last words of advice?"

"He's quiet. It scares me."

"Why?"

She tapped her finger over the onionskin envelope. "These are people I've read about my whole life. I've obsessed over them, dreamed about them, helped Beth write a book about them. Now I'm part of the story, and Belial has *nothing* to say?"

Constantine slipped the envelope out from under her grasp and pulled out the letters. "Maybe once you read the letters, he'll have something to tell us."

"Wait," she said, reaching for his hand. "Before we do this, I just want to say thank you. For believing in me."

He wrapped her hand in his and pressed his lips to the tender webbing between her fingers. The pressure of his lips on her skin made her blood tingle in her veins. She closed her eyes and her breath came out in a sigh as she imagined his lips tracing their way from her hand to the soft flesh of her inner elbow. "Don't let go," she whispered.

"Natalie, open your eyes." She obeyed and found his crystalline gaze locked on her face, so bright a blue she blinked under his scrutiny. His mouth crinkled at the corners in a bemused smile. "We're in a library, with some of the world's best killers after us. If you keep distracting me, they're going to sneak up and kill us because I'm too busy staring at you."

She nodded, unsure whether to feel disappointed or flattered. Then she put her arms up on the table and buried her head in them, waiting for the flames in her cheeks to subside.

He laughed and caressed her bent head, then started the translation. It took only a few moments to finish. "All right," he said. "I've got it. But I don't think it will help."

He slid it over to her. She snatched it and read as quickly as she could.

DEAR IVAN,

THANK YOU FOR THE BIRTHDAY CAKE. I'VE NEVER TASTED ANYTHING SWEETER, NOR WILL I IF MY SISTERS ARE RIGHT. OLGA BELIEVES WE WILL NEVER LEAVE THIS HOUSE, AND OLGA IS ALWAYS RIGHT. TATIANA BELIEVES GOD WILL SAVE HER, AND ANASTASIA DOES NOT WANT TO BE SAVED. I AM THE ONLY ONE WHO WANTS TO LIVE! I AM THE ONLY ONE WHO WANTS TO EXPERIENCE SOMETHING OF THIS LIFE BEFORE IT IS BLOTTED OUT LIKE A DROP OF INK. AND I WILL TRY… I PROMISED YOU I WOULD TRY. IF I SUCCEED, WE WILL RUN AWAY TOGETHER AND PRETEND WE ARE AMERICAN. PAPA SO ADMIRES THE AMERICAN PRESIDENT AND ALL HE DID FOR US IN 1905. HE TOLD US THAT SHOULD ANYTHING BAD HAPPEN HERE, AMERICA WOULD SHELTER US. SOME SAY THE AMERICANS ARE UNCOUTH, BUT MAMA ALSO SAYS YOU ARE UNCOUTH. IF AMERICA IS A NATION OF PEOPLE JUST LIKE YOU, I KNOW I CAN BE HAPPY THERE. THERE IS NOTHING TO BE HAPPY FOR HERE. EVEN MY BONES ACHE FOR MISSING YOU. IF THERE WERE ONE MAGIC WORD I COULD UTTER THAT WOULD BRING YOU TO MY SIDE, I WOULD SPEAK IT, EVERY DAY OF MY LIFE. SOMETIMES GREATER RICHES ARE TO BE FOUND IN A SINGLE WORD THAN IN A GOLDEN PALACE.

MARIA NIKOLAEVNA

Constantine frowned. "Does any of this make sense to you?"

With a shaking hand, she pointed to the first line. "None of the sources say exactly what happened, but on her nineteenth birthday, Marie was discovered with one of her guards in a position compromising enough to get the guard dismissed. After that incident, Marie lost her family's trust. Alexandra wouldn't let her carry any of their hidden jewels."

"Doesn't that give her even more of a reason to get the password to Ivan?"

"It wasn't about the money. She wanted to be in love and do everything normal girls do, but her family thought she betrayed them. They punished her for it."

The same way mine punished me, she thought.

After the hospital and her vision of Treblinka, she'd come home to find her room decorated with rainbow wallpaper and a yellow bedspread. The terrarium was gone, Medusa vanished. She knew what they were trying to do, but it was useless. After the ovens and the snowfall made of human ash, no one could convince her that the world was a safe and happy place. It only made her parents seem stupid, like the people who'd lived next door to the death camp and said they didn't know why it snowed all the time.

Suddenly, a hot knife-edge of pain sliced through her occipital lobe. *This has gone far enough*, Belial said. *You're getting close to things that will hurt you.*

She grasped her head with both hands. "Belial, stop!"

I care about you too much to see you hurt. Let me handle this.

Through the pain, she remembered the horror of the motel room, when Belial had killed the Vympel man using her as the weapon. "I won't let you do that again. I'll fight you."

I don't think you'll win. Here, let me prove it to you.

Suddenly, the white-hot wall of pain turned into a brittle sheet of glass. Belial flicked one wing and shattered it into a thousand pieces. She felt each shard slice through her as it fell. There were pieces of her everywhere, bleeding and broken, reflected thousands of times in each tiny falling shard. She felt herself falling, too, just as broken and sharp as the glass.

CHAPTER THIRTY-FOUR

Ivan Tarasenko rapped on the back door of the ambulance parked in Elizabeth Brandon's driveway. The red numbers and letters on its side had already begun to drip. In Moscow, they had fixers for rush jobs like this. In a foreign city, they'd done it themselves with supplies stolen from a hardware store and an abortion clinic.

Sergei flung open the ambulance doors and slid a gurney toward him. "Tie her to this," Sergei said. "The police just went around the block."

Ivan wheeled the gurney from the driveway into the foyer. The professor lay unconscious on the floor. Her throat had begun to bruise, a band of blue-and-black wrapped around it like a necktie.

He put her on the gurney and strapped her down. "You fought well, *lastochka*." His hands stroked her legs, feeling the soft flesh of her thigh. "I'll give you your reward later."

Before he left the house, he used his cell phone to record the phone message that had stopped her dead in her tracks. Then he wheeled the gurney out to the ambulance, shoved it inside, and jumped up into the vehicle. Sergei signaled to Yakov, who punched the gas so hard the gurney slammed against the back of the driver's seat.

"Easy!" Sergei barked.

Ivan rotated his shoulder and grimaced. The woman had stabbed him just outside his body armor. An inch to his left and he would have been unharmed. "Sergei, listen to this," he said. He played his superior the recording of the answering machine message.

Sergei's scarred face twitched with concentration as he deciphered the English words. "Voloshin," he muttered.

Ivan nodded. "A relative of the man named Yuri that we killed this morning? We should kill this one, too."

Sergei shook his head. "We have no orders to do so."

"What if he also knows about the letters?"

"The message says he is in a nursing home. Old men talk and no one believes them."

"The younger sister has already visited him. We should silence him before he helps anyone else."

"We cannot risk being caught," Sergei protested.

Ivan let his eyes flicker toward the front seat. "Send Yakov."

"And if he is caught? The American police will interrogate him."

"Not if the cleaner gets to him first."

"I don't like it."

"Do you want Starinov to hear this message? What will you tell him when he asks if we have taken care of it?"

"*Bliad*," Sergei swore. He pulled out his phone and began re-charting their course. "Yakov, we have another target."

Ivan shuffled through the bags they'd stolen from the abortion clinic until he found something useful. He pulled out a crumpled white coat and a stethoscope and tossed them up onto the van's empty passenger seat, next to Yakov.

"Here," he said. "You're going to need these."

CHAPTER
THIRTY-FIVE

Constantine watched Natalie's eyes roll back in their sockets. He caught her before she slid to the floor. "Not now," he said, feeling her twitch in his arms. Balancing her weight on one hip, he shoved the letters and his translation into his pocket. Then he swung her up into his arms and crept through the stacks.

On his left, he saw an unmarked gray door. He swung it open and hurried inside, fumbling for the light switch. It was a janitor's closet. The walls were lined with metal racks, all stacked with cleaning supplies. He set Natalie on the floor and put his hand to her forehead. There was no fever this time.

He reached into his pocket for one of the tiny bottles Viktor had brought back from the drugstore. He waved the whiskey beneath Natalie's nose, with no response. He tilted the bottle to her mouth, but she twisted in his arms and the liquid dribbled down her chin.

His parents, he realized, had gone through this kind of agony every day with Lana while he'd remained oblivious, off playing spy games for Vadim in Georgia and Chechnya. For the first time, he understood how much harder it was to be the one who stayed behind. Guilt ripped into him like an animal's claws. *Mamulya, I'm sorry*, he thought.

The doctors told him that Lana had survived the kidnapping and rape by becoming someone else inside her head. But afterward, instead of putting them back together, she tried to kill the girl to whom it had all happened in order to remove any permanent reminders. Was that what was happening to Natalie? Was Belial the part of her that felt weak and unloved, and she'd created a supernatural identity for him?

He propped her up in his arms, squeezed her cheeks, and poured a quarter of the bottle into her mouth. Then he pinched her nostrils shut and waited for her to swallow. A moment later, her throat convulsed and she sputtered and choked. Her eyes flew open, racing from corner to corner.

"You're safe," he said. "Natalie, you're safe. Can you hear me?"

She nodded, panting as if she'd run a race. Her hand latched onto his arm and held it tightly. "He wanted to fight me."

"Belial?"

Her eyes filled with tears, the clear liquid diluting their color until she looked like a transparent ghost. "I've never fought him like that before."

He bent over her until their noses touched. "Natalie, you won. You're here, with me. Belial's not in control. You won."

"I won," she repeated softly. "It doesn't feel that way." One hand reached up to wipe the tear tracks from her cheeks. "We need that password, Constantine."

"I know. But there's time. I'm just glad you're all right."

"I'm not all right," she said.

"What do you mean?"

"He's going to try again."

CHAPTER THIRTY-SIX

"It is done," Yakov said, sliding into the ambulance's passenger seat, the stethoscope still around his neck.

Sergei nodded. He shifted into gear and maneuvered down the steep driveway. "Did anyone see you?"

"*Nyet.* The old man was asleep."

Sergei glanced over his shoulder, to the blonde woman on the stretcher. Ivan sat beside her, flicking his cigarette lighter. All that remained was to communicate the password directly to Starinov.

Sergei followed the signs for the southbound interstate. Once they were headed for the airport, he reached under the seat and pulled out the rusted box they'd retrieved from Dashkov's motel room. He pulled out the Romanov letters and handed one to Yakov and one to Ivan. "Read these. We will tell Starinov the password before we get on the plane."

Sergei concentrated on the late afternoon traffic. Anyone looking closely would see the dripping paint and the impossibility of their being actual rescue personnel. He made sure to signal before each lane change and stayed two miles per hour below the speed limit.

He'd driven no more than three miles when Ivan cleared his throat. "Sergei? We have a problem."

"He's right," Yakov said. "This doesn't make sense. It's a bunch of garbage."

"It doesn't say anything about a password. Or money."

Sergei swore. A thin, nervous sweat broke out beneath his arms.

"What do we do?" Yakov asked.

Ivan flicked his lighter and held it close to the woman's hair. "Let the woman help us. If she doesn't, we'll kill her."

"No," Sergei said. "Starinov wants her alive."

"She doesn't know that." Ivan pinched the woman's nose shut. Within three seconds, her eyes flashed wildly and she struggled against the restraints of the stretcher. "Good afternoon," Ivan said.

"Who the fuck are you? What do you want?" Her blonde hair had fallen into her eyes and she tossed her head to shake it away. "Are you the one who shot up my sister's apartment?"

"You put up quite a fight. I'm proud of you."

"Where's Natalie?"

"Right now, you will help us get the tsar's password."

"You've got to be kidding me." The woman blinked twice, then rested her head on the stretcher. "This isn't happening. I'm dreaming. This must be how Nat feels all the time."

Ivan held up his letter. "This looks familiar, doesn't it? Voloshin showed them to you and now he's dead. Give us the password or you'll die, too."

The blonde woman snarled at him. "What are you talking about? I told Nat and I'll tell you — the password doesn't exist."

"You should hope it exists. Your life depends on it." Ivan dangled the letter in front of her face.

Her eyes followed it like a child tracking a hypnotist's swinging coin. "Untie me," she said, rattling the restraints on her arms.

"Do it," Sergei said. "And shoot her if she moves."

Some of the color drained from the woman's cheeks. Ivan unbuckled her wrist restraints, but left her legs shackled. "Read," he said, pointing the gun at her. "Tell us the password."

Yakov tossed the other letter into the back of the van. Ivan scooped it up and she snatched it out of his hand. When she reached the end, she flipped back to the first letter. "Where's the rest?"

"What do you mean, the rest?"

"I mean the rest of the goddamn letter," she said. "There's no password here. There's nothing about a bank, a branch, a type of account, the name the account is under … nothing."

Sergei felt the sweat pool above his belt. He signaled right and moved out of the passing lane. The airport signs were all pointing to the right, to an overpass that veered up and over the freeway. "We must have that password," he said. "You are not looking."

"There's nothing else to look at," the woman said.

Ivan growled. "Voloshin said you verified the authenticity of these letters."

"I have no idea what you're talking about. I've never seen these pieces of paper before."

"You're lying!"

"Even if I were, those letters are still missing vital information. Unless you have something else you're not showing me, I can't help you. Please, just let me go."

"I can't do that," Sergei said. He followed the signs for cargo, directing him away from the main passenger terminals. When they'd left behind most of the traffic, he pulled over in a loading zone and put on the vehicle's emergency flashers. "Go," he said to Yakov, pointing at his stethoscope. "Stand over her with that."

Yakov clambered into the back of the van and bent over the woman. Sergei pulled his phone from his pocket and pressed the primary speed dial.

"Do you have it?" Starinov asked.

"We have the letters and the woman. But there's a problem."

"Solve it."

"The letters appear to be missing vital information. They don't specify a bank or an account number."

The line fell silent. Sergei heard his own breathing amplified by the fiberoptics. Even his lungs sounded scared. "What about Voloshin?" the prime minister asked. "Make him tell you."

"I'm afraid that's not possible, Your Excellency. We killed him."

"*Zavali yebalo*," the prime minister swore. "Should I send the Red Cross or the Youth League to replace you? Either one could do a better job." Then he paused. "Vadim," he said in a smooth, silky voice. "Oh, Vadim, you cold-hearted son of a bitch."

"Your Excellency?"

"It's Dashkov. You said he took the wrong sister, but Vadim allowed it. It must be because she knows something we don't."

"Do we go back into the city to find them?"

"No," Starinov answered. "Hold your position and wait for my signal. I know how to locate them. Give me an hour to make the arrangements."

CHAPTER THIRTY-SEVEN

Two letters, one woman, one password. He ruled nearly one-sixth of the world's land mass, but these three things continued to elude him. Starinov looked at the first portrait hung on his wall. What would Ivan the Terrible have done to a subordinate who professed to be stymied by these things? He would have tied the disobedient one to a pole and slow-roasted him over hot coals.

Things had been simpler before the advent of mass media, microjournalism, and satellite imagery. Modern rulers were forced to hide behind religious terrorists and organized crime. These shadow organizations got the glory for doing Russia's dirty work, and he took the blame for not curtailing their nefarious activities. But it was impossible to reveal how connected they all were — the members of the Duma and the press wouldn't stand for it.

He pulled the blue curtains open an inch, watching the rays of the morning sun warm the slanted rooftops of the buildings inside the Kremlin. The world was waking up and he had more business to attend to. The first part, the hardest part, had already been done.

He picked up the phone, pressed the button that scrambled the caller ID, and dialed. His prey answered on the second ring. "*Da?*"

"Good morning, Vadim Petrovich. I wasn't sure you'd be in the office yet."

"It is a busy day, Your Excellency."

"It is indeed," Starinov said. "I know what you've done, Vadim."

"Oh?" The strain in the other man's voice wore it filament-thin. "What is that?"

"Don't be coy," he said, gazing into Great Peter's hypnotic brown eyes. "I know everything."

"Then why bother asking?"

"Because I wanted to test you, Vadim, and you failed. Your little game is over. I have the letters. I even have one of your agents."

The older man's voice revealed his pique. "Then just have me killed and be done with it."

"Oh, I will. But before you die, I will ask you for a favor."

"Go to hell, Maxim."

"You first," he snapped. "After you deliver Dashkov and the woman to me."

"I will do no such thing."

"I suspected you would feel that way, but Valery thought you would be much more agreeable."

"What does Valery have to do with it? This isn't a matter for the Criminal Intelligence Department."

"But it is, you see. How else could I learn that your granddaughter's favorite color is purple? That she loves it so much she would follow a man waving a purple scarf right into a waiting van instead of continuing on to school?"

He heard Vadim suck in his breath. "You bastard! What have you done?"

"I have done what I do best and you know it."

"Maxim, she's just a child. She has nothing to do with this."

"I never thought she did." Starinov paused. "Tell me where Dashkov and the woman are. When I have word they are in my custody, I will release your granddaughter."

"Maxim, I need time."

"How long does it take to make a call? Two minutes? Maybe three?"

"I've been calling Dashkov for hours. He won't answer."

"That's not my problem."

"An hour. Give me an hour."

"You have ten minutes."

"I need more than that to run a trace! Give me an hour, Maxim."

"You have ten minutes. Then I will tell the officer holding a gun to your granddaughter's head to pull the trigger. Unless, of course, he has other things he'd like to do first."

"If you do that, I will hunt you for the rest of my days, Maxim."

"Chivalrous indeed, but don't you think this time could better be spent in search of—"

The line went dead.

Starinov smiled. In the twenty-four years he'd worked in government circles, he'd never known Vadim Primakov to lose his composure. "It's your move, old friend," he said.

CHAPTER THIRTY-EIGHT

Constantine tapped his pocket, where he'd shoved the letters and his translation. "Are you sure you're ready for this? I don't want to see you go under again. You scared the hell out of me, Natalie." His hand smoothed a flyaway hair beside her face and she leaned into his caress. Tucked within the protective circle of his arms, she felt warmer and safer than anywhere else she could possibly be.

"I didn't mean to scare you," she said. Their faces were so close that his lips hovered over hers. She imagined losing herself inside him, becoming a part of his body so that Belial and Vympel wouldn't know where to find her. "But I came back. I always come back."

"Yes, you did." His eyes glowed with hunger. Then his lips descended on hers. Heat surged from her belly and she pressed her body against his. His hands pulled through her hair, sweeping across her skull. Everywhere he touched her, she felt a tingling that pulsed with the same rhythm as the heat in her core. Deep inside her, something began to twist and ache with pleasure. She arched against him and moaned just as he broke away from her.

"We can't," he said.

"But I want to."

"So do I," he said, tucking her hair behind her ear. "But you deserve better than this."

Despite everything, she felt her lips curl into a smile. *Even if I die tonight, it will be with him.* The thought gave her a sudden burst of energy. If they managed to survive, she would get to go on a real date, like a normal person. "Let me see the translation," she said.

He pulled it from his pocket. She read it again, but it didn't make any sense the second time, either. Something was missing. Then she stopped. "Are you sure this is all?"

"What do you mean?"

"Go back to the originals."

Constantine unfolded the two yellowed rectangles and spread them out on the floor. "What are we looking for?"

"That," she said, pouncing on Marie's letter. "What's that?"

At the top of the letter, someone with different handwriting had written two brief lines in pencil above the date. Her eyes jumped back to Olga's letter, the one he hadn't translated yet. "Look! It's here, too." She pointed at two faint lines added to the letter just below the signature. "The added lines are in different places. What do they say?"

Constantine picked up Marie's letter and held it closer to his eyes. "It's so faded, it's hard to tell. It looks like… oh, Jesus."

Natalie reached for his arm. "What is it?"

"It says 'Bank of England.'"

"I knew it!" She giggled and clapped her hands. "I knew they were lying!"

He squinted, turning the paper slightly. "And there's a name."

"What name?"

"It's hard to read. Let me spell it out." He pressed out a fold in the paper. "In English, it would be S, L, V, E, V. I can't read all of the letters."

"Oh my God," she breathed.

"What—" Suddenly, Constantine's phone vibrated in his pocket. He reached for it and glanced at the incoming number. "It's Vadim."

Natalie looked up at him. "Do you still trust him?"

"Right now, you're the only one I trust." He put his finger to his lips then put the call on speakerphone. "What the hell is going on, Vadim? Vympel took Viktor and the letters."

"I know!" Anger crackled like electricity in Vadim's voice. "I had to hear about it from Starinov himself! You made me look like a fool."

"Did he tell you where they took Viktor?"

"No. Where are you?"

Constantine clenched his jaw, but didn't answer.

"Listen, my boy," Vadim said, "we're all upset. But Starinov said he won't recall Vympel until I bring you and the girl in."

"If he has the letters, why does he care about us?"

"Just tell me where you are. The ambassador will send an escort and it will all be over."

Something in the older man's voice set her on edge—a desperation that sent his natural baritone pitch into a tenor. Natalie felt her gut clench. *No,* she mouthed. *Don't do it.*

"Please," the older man begged. "We'll get Viktor back and I'll make sure they don't hurt the girl. I swear to you."

Constantine held the phone in both hands, squeezing until his knuckles went white.

"You won't make it out of there without help," Vadim said. "You know that."

Constantine bent his head. "I know," he said softly. "We're in the library. Ninth Street."

"Just stay where you are."

"I'm trusting you, Vadim. With my life and hers."

"I know, my boy."

The line went dead and Constantine shoved the phone back in his pocket. Natalie touched his arm. "Why didn't you tell him we have the real letters?"

"Something's wrong," he said, shaking his head. "It's in his voice."

"What happens when the ambassador comes to get us?"

"He'll put us on a plane to Russia."

She scooted backward, bumping up against a metal rack. "But I've never been anywhere! I don't know what Belial will do."

He grasped her forearms and looked into her eyes. "I won't let anything happen to you, I promise. We're going to turn these letters over to Vadim and let him fight Starinov. End of story."

"What about Viktor?"

"I won't hand over the letters until Starinov lets him go."

Natalie's gaze fell to the pieces of paper on the floor. "But what if I can figure it out?"

"No. All they want is the letters."

"What happens when they can't decipher them? Will I get kidnapped again?" The thought of waiting for another Vympel squad to break down her door made her feel sick to her stomach. "I have to go to the bathroom. I'm going to throw up."

"I'll come with you." He put the letters back in his pocket.

"I don't need a babysitter. I can hurl on my own."

"Fine." He kissed her on the forehead. "If you're not back in five minutes, I'm coming in there for you."

She nodded and clutched her purse to her chest as she walked out of the closet to the restroom. She wished Beth were here. Beth would calm her down and shoot holes in her theory wide enough for elephants to stomp through. Soloviev — the letters written in pencil must refer to him. He was Maria Rasputin's husband, a man usually vilified for stealing money and jewels collected to help fund the Romanovs' escape from captivity. But what if he hadn't stolen them? What if the jewels and money had ended up somewhere else?

No one would suspect it, she thought. *No one ever has.*

She pushed open the door to the restroom and something hard struck her on the temple. The world went as black as Lucifer's wings.

CHAPTER THIRTY-NINE

Constantine finished his translation of the second letter and re-read it quickly. It made no sense. There was no password, and the girls didn't even talk about the same things. One referenced America, the other a ship. Nothing was constant except the two extra lines: Bank of England and SLVEV. If Natalie couldn't make sense of the girls' non sequiturs, this whole mission would end with nothing.

He glanced at his watch. He'd given Natalie five minutes and she'd already been gone fifteen. Something was wrong. He ran down the hall to the women's bathroom and knocked. "Natalie! It's time to go."

There was no answer.

"Natalie!" He flung open the door and saw five empty stalls. A silver faucet dripped like a metronome, but there was no splash of water in the bowl to indicate it had been used recently. He dashed from one end of the floor to the other, looking for her purse or signs of a struggle. He found nothing.

Liquid panic burst in his veins. There was only one person who could have informed on them. He wiped sweaty palms on his pants and reached for his phone. As soon as the older man answered, he bellowed into the speaker. "Did you take her?"

"Constantine, what the devil are you talking about?"

"You're the only one who knew where we were. Tell me where they're taking her."

"I don't know what you're talking about."

"I'll burn them, Vadim. I'll burn those goddamn letters before anyone else sees them if you don't tell me where she is."

Vadim sighed. "They're bringing her to Starinov."

"It won't do him any good. Natalie's only seen one of the letters. I have the other one."

The older man grunted. "Maxim underestimated you, my boy."

"You tell that bastard that if they hurt her, those letters are as good as gone."

"You aren't the only one with something at stake, boy."

"But I'm the only one trying to do anything about it. Are you going to help me or not?"

The air between them crackled with static.

Constantine slammed a fist into the wall. "Goddamn it, Vadim, I've killed for you! Now I ask for one thing and you can't find anything to say." He rested his forehead against his reddened fist. "I need your help. Please."

He heard the movement of Vadim's left hand, crossing himself. "There's a pilot," the older man said. "He's on standby just north of you, waiting for another agent. If you can get to the San Rafael airstrip, he and the plane are yours."

Constantine exhaled. There was still hope.

CHAPTER FORTY

This time, her head ached from the outside. The pain radiated from a central point on the left side of her skull. She reached up to touch it and her fingers slid over a bump as raised and round as the Palatine.

I'm sorry, little one. Belial tucked his head to his chest. *I should have been there to warn you.*

"Go away," she said. She blinked and waited for her eyes to focus. She was on a leather-covered bench, beside a tiny oval window that displayed blue sky, clouds, and a wing. A memory of the library flashed before her and her cheeks burned with anger at how easy a target she'd been. *Constantine,* she thought. *Does he even know what happened?*

She rolled over and saw two men, big and dark-haired with small features squished into pockmarked faces. Two more stood at the rear of the plane. One of them had a lanky form with a familiar shoulder line. "Viktor," she mumbled.

He turned around. "You're awake!" he said, hurrying to her side.

She searched his face for any signs of harm from the motel attack. "What's happening? Have they hurt you?"

"Don't worry about me, lamb." He reached out to touch her cheek and Belial flapped his left wing — the one closest to Viktor. She flinched at the sudden pain.

"What's wrong?" Viktor asked. "Are you hurt?"

"It's Belial. I need a drink."

"Leave it to me." Viktor went up to a blond man standing at the rear of the plane. The man opened a panel in the wall, pulled out a bottle, and poured generously into an old-fashioned glass.

When Viktor's fingertips brushed hers to hand off the glass, Belial twitched. Then Belial's entire left side began to vibrate, knocking painfully against her skull. She downed the scotch as fast as she could and pressed her hands to her head, waiting for the alcohol to send Belial to sleep.

"I thought alcohol helped," Viktor said. "You look terrible."

"More," she whispered. "Hurry."

Viktor took the glass from her hand. As soon as he stepped away, the pain stopped — instantly, as if Belial had flicked a switch.

Belial never did anything by accident.

She eyed Viktor, standing at the makeshift bar, covering two ice cubes with a generous pour of scotch. He'd shaved and changed his clothes since the abduction. There were no bruises or black eyes, no scratches or grazes on his hands or head. She thought about every time she and Constantine had escaped Vympel—one or both of them bleeding, limping, bruised, broken.

Do you understand now, little one? Belial said. *He told you the truth, but you did not see it. He said it out loud, for all the world to hear.*

"Philby," she whispered.

Viktor looked up, one dark eyebrow raised. "What was that?"

"Nothing."

"Don't be shy. I'd really like to know what you said." He knelt to meet her gaze, his eyes dark and satisfied.

You asked for it, she thought. "You're a traitor, aren't you? Just like Philby."

"A traitor to whom? Not myself, and I'm the only one I care about."

"But you saw them kill Yuri! Vympel shot at you as we tried to escape. Why would you turn to them after that?"

"Who said anything about after?"

"You were helping them the whole time?"

"I was helping myself." He stood up and shook his head. "I can understand why Constantine never figured it out. He's so goddamn dull. But you… aren't you supposed to be psychic?"

"Psychotic. There's a difference."

"To-ma-to, to-mah-to." He handed her the glass of scotch. "You put your faith in the wrong things, love. Constantine, your ridiculous delusion, and a dead man murdered for crimes against the Russian people. Do you know they called the tsar 'Nicholas the Bloody'?"

"It's better than 'Viktor the Asshat.'"

"When I find the tsar's money, I'll write my own nickname."

"You won't find it. I won't help you."

"Yes, you will, lamb chop. I'll kill your sister if you don't."

She tossed the glass of scotch at him. He ducked and it shattered against the hard plastic of the plane's cabin. "Don't you ever mention my sister again."

"Yakov, show her."

One of the bulky men on the bench reached into his pocket and pulled out a phone. There it was, on a high-definition screen: an image of her sister, bound and gagged, lying in the shadows. Beth's face was turned away from the camera, but Natalie recognized the blonde hair and the gray Yale sweatshirt.

Belial jumped to his feet, slamming into the back of her skull. *O God, to whom vengeance belongs, show thyself!*

Natalie barely felt the pain in her head. All the pain she felt was in her heart, as if God himself had put on a pair of steel-toed boots and kicked her in the chest. "Belial will kill you for this," she said. "And I won't stop him."

"Can Belial give you the code you need to land in Russian airspace?"

"He doesn't care if we land. He just wants you to die."

"He should care. Your sister's in the cargo hold."

Natalie dropped to her knees, pounding the floor with her fists. "Beth!" she screamed. "Can you hear me? Beth!" She dug at the carpet like a dog searching for a buried bone. Her fingernails bent backward and broke as she raked them across the surface.

Viktor snapped his fingers and one of the men on the bench plucked her from the floor by the waist. "Stop it," Viktor hissed, reaching back to slap her across the face.

"Let her go!" Natalie cried. "I'm the one who should die."

"No one has to die." Viktor grabbed her chin and wrenched her head upright. "What the hell is the matter with you?"

Natalie sagged against the muscular arm holding her. Her eyes drifted to the floor, littered with broken glass. She imagined using it to slice through Viktor's femoral arteries… laying bare his bones and carving into them a summary of his perfidy. A strangled laugh croaked its way out of her throat.

"You're laughing." Viktor took a step back. "Tell me why."

"I'm going to carve my name into your bones."

"Not quite the souvenir I had in mind. Let's have another drink, shall we? We'll sing 'God Save the Tsar' and you'll tell me what the password is."

"You don't know the words to 'God Save the Tsar.'"

"Christ, you're impossible. I don't know how Constantine did it. Just tell me what the password is and this will all be over."

"I don't know it yet."

"What do you mean?"

"I've only read one of the letters. Constantine didn't finish translating them for me."

"I have the letters, you silly girl."

"That's why they're going to call you 'Viktor the Asshat.'"

"What are you talking about?"

"There are two sets of letters. One is real. One is fake. You can guess which set you got away with."

Viktor's upper lip began to twitch. Natalie watched with satisfaction as the twitching moved across his face, spreading to his cheek and his brow.

"You have nothing," she said.

Belial smiled. *Good girl. Now let's tattoo his bones.*

CHAPTER FORTY-ONE

The Beechcraft turboprop hugged the California coastline, chugging toward the Mexican border. The pilot had said there would be one stop before crossing the Pacific. Constantine wanted to stay awake until they were in international airspace. He didn't trust Vadim, not yet.

He leaned his head against the window and tried to let the drone of the propellers silence the doubts in his mind. The lights below grew sparse as they flew south over Mexico. Just outside Culiacán, the plane banked westward for its descent. The pilot landed on a deserted airstrip carved into the fertile hills east of the city. "We switch planes here," the pilot said. "It's too dangerous to go into Culiacán."

The pilot led him toward a weathered shack, with windows covered by tattered scraps of fabric. With a flick of the wrist, the pilot tossed a duffel bag through the window. "Bribe?" Constantine asked.

"More like a rental fee. We have to hand-deliver the bribes."

"Where's the other plane?"

The pilot grinned. "You don't work the Mexico desk, do you?"

He led them behind the shack, where they found a rusted U.S. Army jeep from the Stalin era, complete with the key in the ignition. The pilot started it up and drove slowly over the ridge. Inside a lonely beige hangar, they found a second plane with an angry co-pilot. "You're late," the co-pilot said.

"Can't be helped," the pilot grumbled. "Primakov re-routed everyone for this."

Constantine felt more secure once he saw the new plane —a Challenger 605. Vadim wouldn't destroy a Challenger and two pilots without a good reason. In all likelihood, he was safe until Moscow. "We'll need one fuel stop," the pilot said, closing the hatch. "Try and sleep through it if you can."

Constantine sank into a seat and calculated their arrival time. They would land in Moscow early the next day, a half-day behind Vympel. Starinov would question Natalie as soon as Vympel brought her to him, but since she hadn't seen the translation of the second letter, there was nothing she could tell him.

She'll be all right, he told himself. *She has to be.*

His mind circled back to Vadim. Without his support, taking on Starinov and his thugs was a suicide mission.

He needed access to the bureau's armory and computers. If Vadim turned on him and revoked his access, he'd have to bribe one of the analysts to let him back in. It was too much to think about without a few hours of sleep.

He stretched out across a row of seats and closed his eyes.

⚜

They approached Moscow in daylight, morning sun glinting on the winding Moskva River. From several thousand feet, Constantine saw the thick Kremlin walls and wondered if Natalie was already inside them. He set his watch to local time and touched his injured shoulder. It was crusted with blood.

When the plane's wheels touched down on Vnukovo Airport's private runway, the pilot's voice came over the loudspeaker. "Mr. Primakov's escort has arrived for you."

Constantine looked out the window and saw a black BMW 5-series parked near the nose of the plane. What if Vadim had betrayed him again? Was there a Vympel death squad waiting in the car? He pulled his gun from his waistband.

When the co-pilot exited the cockpit and moved to open the hatch, Constantine raised his gun. "If anyone other than Vadim gets out of that car, I'll kill you. Do you understand?"

"Y–yes, sir." The man opened the hatch and descended quickly, followed by the pilot. Constantine stopped on the bottom stair, gun in hand. When the BMW's rear passenger door opened, a figure stepped out and waved the two pilots away.

Constantine held his ground.

The figure walked toward the plane. Constantine recognized the older man's stooped walk and lowered his gun. "Why?" he asked. "Why did you do it, Vadim?"

Pouches of dark skin puddled beneath the older man's red, watery eyes. "Maxim took my granddaughter. Liliya won't see me until I get her back."

"I'm sorry," Constantine said. "But now Starinov has your granddaughter, Viktor, and Natalie. Why did you let it happen?"

Vadim blinked and two tears ran down his cheeks. "Everything I've done to create a better Russia was for her. I can't jeopardize her life."

"You can't trust Starinov."

"I have no choice. He has a gun pointed at her head."

"So let's take away his gun."

The older man looked around the airstrip, as if confused by his own surroundings. "Everything I dreamed this country could be has vanished."

"We can get it back," Constantine said, "but we have to show Starinov he's not the only one who knows how to lie."

"And put Marya in more danger? I can't do that."

"You will if you want her back."

"What are you going to do?"

"They've got Natalie. I'm going after them."

"The girl," Vadim said. "Is she truly mad?"

"She hears something that she thinks is an angel. But it's just her heart, and she listens to it." He looked pointedly at the older man. "I don't know anyone else with the courage to do that."

Vadim hung his head. "What can I do?"

Constantine held out his hand. "Tell Starinov what he wants to hear, but promise me you're still one of us."

Vadim clasped Constantine's outstretched hand, his grip cold but firm. "He will tell you I have turned on you. Do not believe him."

Constantine nodded and slid into the backseat of the BMW. "Tell the driver to stop at the bureau. I need weapons and supplies."

Vadim sat beside him as the driver sped toward the Kievskoie Highway. "Starinov has Marya at the Ussov building. I tracked the convoy with satellite imagery."

"How many cars?"

"Two, both G55s."

"Plus the men who kidnapped Natalie. That's eight to twelve men, total."

"This is madness. They'll kill you on sight."

"Not once they know I have these." Constantine patted his chest pocket. "When Starinov asks Natalie for the password, the first thing she'll tell him is that his letters are fake. Once he knows she needs these to figure out the password, he'll be the one looking for me."

"And you plan on walking right into his trap?"

Constantine shrugged, wincing when the dried blood pulled at his skin. "It's the easiest way in. Besides, Viktor will be there to help."

"What about the password?"

"Once I get Natalie and Marya out, Starinov will chase us all the way to the Bank of England if we let him. We're dead unless we get that money first. I need a plane and flight clearance. Can you do it?"

"General Alexeev can," Vadim said. "He is Marya's godfather."

"Then call the bank. Tell them we'll be coming."

"They'll never believe me."

"Make them."

The BMW turned onto Bolshaya Nikitskaya. Constantine looked up at the bureau building and prepared a shopping list in his head. Then he turned to Vadim. The old man's eyes were still red and puffy, but a little color had returned to his cheeks. *He has hope now,* Constantine realized. *And so do I.* "Thank you," he said.

Vadim held up his right hand with the first two fingers raised in blessing. "God be with you, my boy."

CHAPTER FORTY-TWO

"D efine 'nothing,'" Viktor said. Fear dappled his black eyes with shades of gray, and the muscles at the bottom of his cheek clenched as he swallowed.

"I want another drink," Natalie said. "And I want this jerk to let go of me."

Viktor snapped his fingers. The goon holding her dropped her onto the floor. She held her palms against the carpet. *Beth, I'm here*, she thought. *I'll get you out.*

Viktor brought her another finger of scotch in a fresh glass. "Now," he said, "what's this nonsense about fake letters?"

She snatched the glass and drank quickly. "Yuri's letters were fakes. They were copies of the real thing."

"If they're copies, love, the words will be the same."

Natalie shook her head. "The real ones have two extra lines written in pencil. I'm assuming you read both letters?"

"A bunch of rubbish about soldiers, sailors, and dancing girls."

"It's a code. I have to see complete translations of both letters, the real ones, before I can even start to figure it out."

"And your dearly beloved has both letters in his possession?"

She watched the way he held himself, the way he braced his shoulders and tilted his nose into the air, and wondered why she hadn't seen it before. "You hate him, don't you?"

"It's not that I hate him, pet. It's that I love me. As long as he's in the spotlight, I get nothing."

"Why do you want to be in the spotlight?"

"Because that's where you get everything you want in life."

"That's not what it's for."

"Then what, pray tell, *is* it for?"

In the hospital, after Treblinka, the doctors had hooked her up to electrodes. They shone a spotlight on her, trying to induce another seizure and record her brain waves. They left it on her for hours, until she could see nothing but painful bursts of red when she closed her eyes. Finally, she passed out. When they revived her, they kept her awake for three days straight, still trying to induce a seizure. Then they tried strobe lights and forced hyperventilation. After five days, they simply shocked her with a current of 500 mC. In the end, she had learned a valuable lesson. "The spotlight," she said, "is where you learn to give them what they want."

Viktor pointed at the largest guard, with thick brows and a scarred face. "Sergei, did you see Dashkov in the library?"

The man frowned. "You told us to bring you the girl, not to look for Dashkov."

"I sense a rebuke coming on. Go on, speak, you great brute."

"Starinov needs to know Dashkov has the real letters. He's expecting us to give him the password as soon as we land."

"I'll handle it," Viktor said.

"The way you handled the order to bring the letters to Moscow?"

Viktor pointed at the big man sitting next to Sergei. "What do you think, Yakov? Shall we vote and pretend this is a democracy?"

"I agree with Sergei," Yakov said. "Tell Starinov."

"And you?" Viktor asked, turning to point at the blond thug. "I suppose you also think he's right?" When the blond man nodded, Viktor raised his hands to the ceiling like a convert at a prayer meeting. "Consensus! The majority has spoken!"

"What about me?" Natalie said. "Do I get a vote? Or are you just another antediluvian misogynist who disenfranchises the weak and downtrodden?"

"By all means, love, cast your vote."

"I agree with you. Don't call Starinov."

Viktor straightened. "I appreciate the vote of confidence, my dear, but I'm afraid we're still outvoted three to two. You know what that means." He reached into his pants pocket.

"No," Natalie said. "Don't call him, Viktor, please…the less he knows, the better."

"I'm sorry, lamb, but the majority rules." He pulled his hand out of his pocket. In it, he held a gun that looked just like Constantine's. He squeezed the trigger and a spray of liquid exploded against the cabin wall. The man called Sergei slumped against the far side of the bench, his head trailing a stream of red as it fell.

Natalie screamed and covered her face with her hands.

The man sitting next to Sergei jumped up and cast a wide-eyed look of fear at Viktor. "What the hell are you doing?"

"Evening the odds," Viktor replied. "Now it's two against two. Anyone want to change their vote?"

CHAPTER
FORTY-THREE

Vadim slid his access card through the reader and waited for the keypad to unlock. He typed his ten-digit code and unlocked the electric door of his office.

The message light on his office phone was blinking, but he ignored it. He picked up the phone and removed the back panel, inspecting it for listening devices. When he found none, he replaced the panel and switched on his computer. Anyone monitoring office activity would now be able to see he was on the network, but it couldn't be helped.

He accessed the bureau's database and pulled up everything coded with threat level white — world bankers, businessmen, and prominent individuals who posed no direct threat to Russian security but who warranted monitoring simply because of the wealth or resources at their disposal. The system asked for a username and password before displaying the files.

Liliya had written him a program he used when working from home—a software map that scrambled keystrokes, creating unique associations for each login attempt. He activated the program from a flash drive.

A mock keyboard appeared on screen with random letter placement. He proceeded to log in and pulled up a list of dossiers on the Bank of England's governor, executive directors, and monetary policy committee. He clicked on the governor's name and read the file. When he was finished, he looked at the clock. It was 8:15 a.m. and London was three hours behind that. Vadim dialed anyway.

The phone rang four times before a man's scratchy voice answered. "What the devil do you want at this hour, Berkeley?"

"Mr. Perry, I apologize for the ill-timed nature of this call. My name is Vadim Primakov and I am the Director of the Public Security Intelligence Bureau of the Russian Federation. I need to speak with you about an urgent matter regarding the account of Tsar Nicholas II."

The Englishman did not respond. The line crackled with an awkward, frozen silence.

Vadim took a deep breath. "Sir, I beg you, don't hang up. This is not a training exercise. You may be contacted shortly by Prime Minister Maxim Starinov. I wish to explain what is happening here, and how it affects your bank."

The man didn't reply, but Vadim heard the rustling of bedclothes, as if Perry were sitting up and paying attention.

He continued, relaying what Constantine had told him in the car. "We have recently come into possession of information written by the tsar's daughters — Olga and Marie, to be exact. The daughters each wrote down your bank as the source of the tsar's funds. These letters also include the name on the account and the password," he lied. "We will need to access this account very soon."

"I'm terribly sorry, sir, but I don't know anything about — "

"Yes, you do," Vadim interrupted, pulling the Rumkowski file up on his screen. "We are well aware of the defensive maneuvers your bank has used over the years to deflect scrutiny from this account. Bark and Peacock hid it well, but the money does not belong to you. It belongs to the Russian government, according to Soviet decree. In the interests of European solidarity, I advise you to forgo any further defensive action."

"Sir, I will need proof of your allegations. And our prime minister will need to be notified, as will the bank's executive directors."

"I will get you anything you need as long as the necessary people are informed and in place for the account's opening later today."

Perry sputtered, as if he'd choked on his morning tea. "Today? But surely you know that's impossible."

"People are going to die unless this can be solved."

"But I don't even know where the paperwork for such an account would be, if it exists at all."

"Then find it. Prime Minister Starinov will not want to be kept waiting."

"He's coming?"

"He is in the air as we speak," Vadim lied.

"But…but we might have to get clearance from Buckingham Palace."

"Then I suggest you do so immediately." Vadim replaced the phone in its cradle and put his head in his hands. His mind tormented him with images of Marya, bound and gagged, tossed into the back of a van. He pictured her choking on her own sobs, gasping for air and believing everyone had abandoned her.

How could Starinov do it? he wondered. *How could a little girl's life be worth a few bundles of tsarist rubbish? Who, other than God, claims the power to decide such things?*

A memory surfaced deep in the recesses of his brain: a day at Sokolniky's School Number One, when he'd been paired with Maxim Starinov for a geography drill. The two of them, no older than six or seven, had been given a map of the Soviet Union and told to label as many cities, rivers, and mountains as possible in two minutes. The entire class had been paired up to compete, with the winner to be awarded a pair of gold-trimmed fountain pens. He remembered Starinov's eyes, cold and ruthless as they watched the pens, held up for display in the teacher's hands.

"I want that pen," Maxim said. "We have to win."

Vadim turned up his nose. "It's ugly. What do you want it for?"

"Look at all that gold. I can sell it to someone and get what I really want. Hurry." The boys had set to scribbling, their pencils flying over the map: the Urals, Sverdlovsk, Lake Baikal, Irkutsk, Kamchatka, Arkangelsk. In the end, they won. The teacher beamed when Maxim clasped the pen to his chest and sighed, a perfect facsimile of a proud winner. Anyone would have believed he'd wanted the pen all along.

Is that what's happening here? Vadim wondered. *Is there more than the tsar's account at stake?* Kadyrov had hinted at it and he'd forgotten.

He looked back to his computer screen, still filled with the contents of the Rumkowski file. There were at least two levels of clearance he didn't have, each of which presumably contained more information about the tsar's account. There was only one person who could get that information for him. Unfortunately, she had locked him out of the house and was no longer speaking to him. Still, he had to try. He reached for the phone and dialed his home.

"Liliya, please," he said. "It's for Marya."

CHAPTER FORTY-FOUR

When the plane's hatch opened, Viktor ordered Ivan and Yakov off first. "Take the cargo. I'll follow with this one," he said, squeezing Natalie's arm.

The Vympel men hurried to obey, studiously avoiding Sergei's body. Natalie heard a squeak as the cargo hold opened, followed by the sound of a body being dragged across the floor. A car's engine started, doors slammed, and the car sped away. Beth didn't make a sound.

Viktor pushed her into the back of a black sedan with tinted windows. The car pulled onto a crowded highway, two lanes in each direction separated by a thin guardrail. Soft green embankments rounded away from the highway on either side. The cars looked strange to her — metal squares in bright colors, like animal cracker boxes on wheels. She realized how far from home she was, and how unprepared she was to pull off any sort of rescue for Beth.

Natalie glared at Viktor, settled in the seat next to her. She imagined a boy who idolized a traitor, someone who became famous for how well he lied. "Why do you do it?" she asked.

"Do what?" Viktor said.

"Philby. The British shit. Why can't you just be yourself?"

"Darling, I'm a spook. There's no such thing as being oneself."

"You're running from something."

"The law, the truth, a particularly unsatisfying childhood … take your pick, love."

"I know the difference between the truth, a lie, and what people want to hear. You lie, Viktor, all the time. Why?"

Belial snickered and shuffled his feet. *You know all about that, little one. Or have you already forgotten how it works?*

No, she thought. *I haven't forgotten.* She remembered the day her parents had told her they were taking her out of public school, in sixth grade. They said the principal didn't want her around other students until the cause of her "episodes" could be determined and addressed with medication. But later that week, she heard Beth telling their mother that Natalie's teachers wondered what had happened to her, that homework was piling up. The school knew nothing about her absence.

Up to that point, she'd done her best to hide the fact that Belial was with her all the time, but it hadn't been enough. Her own parents were made afraid and embarrassed by her.

There was no point in fighting it after that. *And you still hate them for it*, Belial said.

Suddenly all of Viktor's lies made sense.

"They didn't believe you," she said. "That's how it started, isn't it?"

"What the bloody hell are you talking about?"

"Your parents, family, friends…someone accused you of lying, or doing something you didn't do. No matter what you said, you couldn't make them believe you."

"You're insane, love. Surely even you know that?"

"It's easy to become what people already believe you to be. No one's disappointed that way."

"I'm asking nicely—please stop talking."

"Did it work? Did it make them accept you?"

He slapped her across the cheek. "One more word and I'll lock you in the trunk."

Natalie absorbed the sting of his palm and compared it to others she'd felt. Anger hurt less than fear, she realized. Viktor was angry, but her mother had been afraid.

They drove in silence for another twenty minutes before the driver turned off the Leninsky Prospect and veered east. Natalie saw a green park on her right, followed by spaced-out office buildings. Except for the Cyrillic signs, it looked to her like pictures of the South: trees and lots of grass. The driver sped toward a tall building shaped like a capital "I." He pulled up to a guard station and flashed a badge. The guards opened the single-armed gate and they sped beneath the building, stopping beside an elevator bay.

"Let's go," Viktor said, pulling her from the car. She stumbled behind him into the elevator. When it docked on the twelfth floor, he marched her into a mahogany-paneled office and closed the door behind them. Natalie scanned the conference table, leather settee, and assortment of salon chairs. "Where's Beth? Where did they take her?"

Viktor flipped a switch, igniting gas logs in the marble fireplace with a comforting orange flame. "Posh, isn't it? This place belongs to the Ussov family, but *they* belong to Starinov."

"I don't care. I want my sister."

Viktor stepped closer to her and touched the neckline of her blouse, spattered with drops of Sergei's blood. "You need to clean up a little, pet." He pointed to a set of double doors on the far side of the room. "The powder room is through there and to the right. But don't take too long. If you're not back in ten minutes, I'll tell Ivan to slice off one of your sister's fingers."

CHAPTER
FORTY-FIVE

Algernon Perry, governor of the Bank of England, hung up the phone and sighed. He was sick of the way Russian oligarchs behaved as though London were merely a satellite of Moscow. "Buying up our property, jetting around as if they owned the place," he grumbled. "Barbarians, the lot of them."

In bed beside him, his wife lay silent as a stone. She never had trouble sleeping. Instead, she snored like a jackhammer as he sorted out the bank's Asian affairs with the Hong Kong office in the early morning hours. If anyone inquired about the noise, he told them he was on a turbo prop plane.

"Just one more call, sweetheart," he said. He dialed the number he'd been given, still unsure why he was complying with the head barbarian's request.

"*Da?*" the barbarian answered.

"It happened just as you said it would, Your Excellency. A man claiming to be Vadim Primakov requested access to the tsarist account. I told him what we'd agreed upon."

The Russian prime minister sounded pleased. "Exactly right. As I told you earlier, this man is a fanatic who must be stopped. It's unfortunate—his granddaughter has been kidnapped by a prominent crime syndicate. I'm afraid he has become mad with grief and will do anything they tell him."

"Dreadful," Perry said dryly. As far as he was concerned, all Russians were gangsters. Things like this were bound to happen when one handed policing tasks over to men who were criminals themselves.

"I will make sure the man doesn't cross your borders, Mr. Perry. In the meantime, there is one more thing you can help us with."

"Delighted," Perry said, stifling a yawn.

"I would like to access the tsar's account."

"Have you the password, Your Excellency? You hadn't yet located it the last time we spoke."

"The password is no longer a problem, but based on the number of interested parties, we cannot take any chances. I wish to restrict the account's access. No generals, no ministers, no ambassadors. Only me."

Perry shivered. The room was cold and he longed to slip beneath the duvet. "I must warn you, Your Excellency. There is one provision that has never been made public." Algernon Perry told the Russian about the only stipulation on the account, enshrined shortly after the bank's officers learned of the tsar's murder. "It's highly unusual," he finished. "But it was authorized by Sir Peter Bark, with the full knowledge and approval of His Majesty George V."

Perry heard nothing but long-distance crackles on the other end of the line.

"Your Excellency?" he said. "Are you still there?"

Perry heard a torrent of Russian swear words, followed by the crash of the phone being tossed at the wall. *Bloody barbarian,* he thought.

CHAPTER
FORTY-SIX

Cold water removed the last trace of Sergei's blood from her skin, but it did nothing to erase the stains on her blouse. The red circles faded and spread, looking like impressionist cherry blossoms against the lavender fabric. She stared at them in the mirror, transfixed.

Belial had told her that blood held no secrets from those who could read it. *Why do you think we have no books in heaven?* he'd said. *We read your blood instead. It tells us everything about you. Sometimes we can't wait to read the next chapter, so we open you up.*

Sergei had no more story to tell. Neither did Yuri. *What about you?* she wondered, staring at the pale, half-dead thing in the mirror. With her smeared eye makeup, she looked like a creature from a black-and-white movie, the bride of

Frankenstein. *All the better*, she thought, *for fighting the devil and his emissaries.*

She returned to the office the way she had come. Sunlight streamed through the floor-to-ceiling windows, burnishing the mahogany desk until it was the color of blood.

Viktor clapped his hands. "Much better, my dear. Now come here and sit down. I'm making you a drink."

Natalie obeyed, perching on a leather settee beside the desk. He handed her a cut-crystal glass filled with vodka and pulled a matching footstool out from beside the settee. Gently, he put his hand beneath her ankles and lifted them onto the stool.

"You've had a stressful day," he continued, moving to stand behind her. "I think you've earned the right to relax." He groped her neck, sending a slither of unease across her shoulders.

"What do you care if I'm happy?"

He found the elastic holding her hair in a ponytail and pulled it out. His hands dug into her shoulders, strong thumbs grinding into her back.

"You're hurting me," she said.

"Just relax."

"I am."

"Don't lie to me, pet."

"Why not? You do it all the time."

"I'm trying to be kind to you. This is my apology in advance."

"Most people apologize for things they've already done."

"I'm not sorry about any of that. But I do feel badly for what's about to happen."

She felt her heart beat too quickly. "What's that?"

He bent close to her and whispered, his warm breath tickling her skin like a feather. "Constantine will die once he's given us the letters. You know that, don't you?"

"Belial won't let you do that."

His fingers paused in their kneading, moving to encircle her neck. "Starinov wants everyone who has seen the letters to die."

"Including you?"

"Starinov can't kill me."

"A gun and a bullet beg to differ."

Viktor chuckled and came around the settee to face her. "For a nutter, you've got quite a good sense of humor. If only you'd met me first, lamb…think how different your life would be right now." His index finger traced the diagonal path of her cheekbone and she shivered.

"Your finger's cold," she said.

"I'm sorry." He put it in his mouth, licked it, and stroked her cheek again. "Is that better?"

She willed herself not to pull away. "You can still do the right thing. Let my sister go."

"This is Russia, darling. No one gives a damn about the right thing."

"Starinov isn't going to give you any of Nicholas's money."

"He will. Or I'll leak the story to the press."

"What story?"

"The story of how he killed a pair of American sisters to get his greedy hands on the tsar's money." Viktor smiled ruefully. "You'll be another Daniel Pearl, my dear — cut down by a rabid nationalist desperate to take out his hostility on the United States. I promise not to behead you, though. I'll leave your pretty face intact." He tapped his wet finger against her nose. "Merry Christmas."

"It's July, asshole."

Viktor smiled. "I've got something that will cheer you up." He moved to the desk chair and picked up his suit jacket, flung over the back. From the pocket, he pulled out a handful of things that sparkled. "I took the liberty of searching your purse when Sergei and his men brought you onto the plane. I was quite surprised to find your little cache." He dropped the handful into her lap. "Put them on. I know you want to."

She combed through the pieces, making sure they were all there: the buckle, hairpin, earrings, and brooch. *I almost lost this*, she thought. *All Grigori's sacrifice would have been for nothing.* As much as she hated to indulge Viktor, wearing the jewelry was the only way to make sure he didn't take it away from her. She put everything on except the shoe buckle, which she tucked into the edge of her bra for safe keeping.

"I can't see that last one," Viktor said. He gripped the fabric of her blouse and ripped it until the buckle's diamond gleam peeked out. "That's better. Carbon suits you, my dear."

CHAPTER FORTY-SEVEN

JULY 2013
MOSCOW, RUSSIA

From the outside, the Ussov building looked no different than any other on Profsoyuznaya Street. This area of southwest Moscow had become a business park, home to some of Russia's richest oil companies, banks, and engineering firms.

Like many powerful Moscow families, the Ussovs had learned that power came not from money, but from connections. They forsook their dreams of a luxury railway empire and threw in their lot with Cobalt, a private security company allied with the FSB. Their private empire of railways became invaluable to the government during the first and second Chechen wars. Constantine remembered seeing boxcars painted with their emblem on tracks outside Grozny.

After wartime profits had made him unspeakably rich, Ussov leased his building to the FSB. It became an unofficial fortress used as a halfway house for valuable foreign prisoners. Ordinary citizens drove past it on their way to eat at the Goodman Steak House or work at the Paleontology Institute, never dreaming it held secrets the government would kill to keep.

Constantine parked his bureau-issued Volga on the access road paralleling Profsoyuznaya Street and studied the building. Vympel would never drag captives, conscious or unconscious, through the front door. The underground garage would be their best point of entry.

Natalie, he thought. *Please let her be all right.* He still blamed himself for her involvement, but it was more than that now. She wasn't a stand-in for Lana. She was simply herself: frightening, infuriating, and impossible to forget. The letters in his pocket were her life and he would do anything to give it back to her.

He headed straight for the garage. Two guards sat in a booth next to the gate, dressed in security uniforms with FSB M2s at the hip. "Where do you think you're going?" one asked him.

"Upstairs," Constantine said. "Your boss is waiting for me."

The guard came out of the booth pointing his M2. "Against the wall," he said, shoving Constantine against the glass and kicking his feet apart. As the man patted him down, Constantine observed the guards' monitor bay. One square on their screen was black — all others displayed empty rooms inside the building.

The guard turned Constantine around by the shoulder and asked his name. Constantine gave it to him. One call upstairs and the guard marched Constantine to an elevator. When the doors opened, he saw a large, brown-haired Vympel man holding a TT pistol. "Get in," the man said.

Constantine obeyed. When the elevator doors opened, the man jammed the muzzle into his back and pushed him forward. He proceeded down the marble hallway, aware of a strange electricity in the air. *It's Natalie*, he thought. *She's still alive, I can feel it.*

At the Vympel man's prodding, he pushed open a set of double doors and walked into an executive suite. A black-suited figure stood with its back to him, staring out the sun-drenched window. He ignored everything except Natalie, huddled on a backless couch, spangled with diamonds in her hair and on her ears. "Natalie!" he called. "Are you all right?"

The figure at the window snapped his fingers. The Vympel man behind him pistol-whipped the base of his neck. "I didn't give you permission to speak," the figure said.

A wave of leaden fear engulfed him, as cold and deep as Lake Baikal. "No," Constantine said. "Tell me you didn't."

"Didn't what?" Viktor said, turning around. "Didn't find a way to make something of myself in this godforsaken country?"

"We were friends, Viktor."

"Were we?"

"You're making a mistake."

"The one making a mistake is the one with a gun pointed at his head. Now give me the letters and let's get this over with."

"Don't!" Natalie warned, standing up. "He'll kill you."

Viktor backhanded her and Constantine leapt at him. The Vympel guard behind him sprang to action, clubbing him with the pistol. He stumbled and spun to face his attacker. He kicked at the guard's hand to knock away the gun and charged. They tumbled to the floor, scrambling for position.

The guard wrapped one thick hand around Constantine's neck. With his other, he reached into his pocket and flicked a carbon-fiber knife into action. Constantine pushed on the man's knife hand as hard as he could. The man switched tactics, jerking their linked hands to the right. The tip of the blade made a long, shallow groove across Constantine's chest.

Constantine growled and slammed a fist into the man's nose. The man lost his concentration long enough for Constantine to roll away and stand up. He felt blood leaking from the slash in his chest, but his anger masked the pain. He pointed at Viktor. "Hit her again and I swear you will not live."

"Neither will you," Viktor said. "Yakov, kill him."

"No!" Natalie cried. "If you hurt him, I'll give you the wrong password."

"The hell you will." Viktor pointed at Yakov, holding a hand to his bleeding nose. "Call Ivan and tell him his presence is requested."

Yakov wiped his reddened blade against his pants and reached for his phone. Constantine kept his eyes on Natalie, searching for signs of strain. An empty glass of vodka sat on the table beside her. There were no marks on her that he could see.

Behind him, the office doors were pushed open by a blonde woman with her hands tied behind her back and a scarf looped around her mouth. A little girl followed her, similarly bound. *Marya*, he thought. A tall blond man with dark red lips and crooked teeth brought up the rear, a TT pistol pointed at the girl's head.

"Beth!" Natalie cried, launching herself toward her sister.

Viktor grabbed her wrist and jerked her back. "Not until I have what I want."

Ivan marched the captives to the conference table and pulled out a single chair. Beth sat down and Marya scrambled into her lap as best she could with bound hands, leaning into Beth's chest and keening softly. As soon as Ivan pulled down her gag, Beth spat at him. "Get the fuck away from me," she growled, "or I swear I'll cut your throat with my toenails."

Constantine's gut clenched with a renewed wave of fear. When had they kidnapped Natalie's sister? Now there were *three* captives he had to get out safely. With Viktor's help, it would have been difficult; now it felt impossible. He scanned Beth and Marya's bodies, looking for any incapacitating wounds, but he found none. Beth's face was scratched, but she appeared otherwise unhurt.

Viktor made a courtly bow in Beth's direction. "I apologize for detaining you against your will, but I assure you it is necessary. Your sister holds the key to our nation's biggest treasure, unclaimed for nearly a hundred years. She's going to help me get it in order to save your life."

Marya began to whimper and rub her head against Beth's chest, loosening her gag until it slid down around her neck. "Where's my grandpa?" she cried. "I want to go home!"

"Be a good girl," Viktor said, "and let the grown-ups talk now."

"But I want to go home!"

"She's just a child," Beth said. "If my sister and I are the ones you want, fine. Leave her out of it."

"Please let me go! I want my mama!"

"Oh, for the love of God," Viktor said, "make her shut up."

Ivan, the blond Vympel man, stepped forward and smacked Marya across the face. Marya wailed once and fell silent, curling into Beth's chest. "It's all right, sweetheart," Beth said. Then she looked up at Ivan. "After I cut your throat, I'll cut off your balls and feed them my dog one at a time. Assuming you have any, that is."

"Beth," Natalie said. "You're not helping."

"Somebody has to," her sister snapped. "Nat, what the hell is this about? Did you really find the tsar's account?"

"We found letters from Olga and Marie to men on the outside. They coded the password, and a boy carried them out of the Ipatiev house. His family's had the letters ever since."

"Then how the hell did *you* get them?" Beth asked.

"It's a long story. Check your messages."

"Messages," Ivan said, turning to smile at Natalie. "*Da*, I forgot to thank you for helping us find the old man so easily."

Natalie's face drained of all its color. "What did you do to Grigori?"

"What do you think? We killed him, of course."

She turned to Viktor. "Did you order this?"

Viktor held up his hands. "Don't look at me."

Natalie moaned. Constantine kept his eyes on her face — something strange was happening. It looked like she was shaking, sobbing without a sound. Her forehead creased, as if she were in great pain. "Which one of you did it?" she asked.

"Yakov did the honors," Ivan said. "But I would have been happy to oblige."

Natalie turned to Yakov, his bristly brown beard stained with blood from the nose Constantine had just broken. "You did this thing?" she asked.

"Yes," he answered.

"How?"

The big man shuffled his feet. "He didn't feel it. He wasn't awake."

"I don't believe you."

Natalie closed her eyes and tilted her head to the ceiling. The window's bright light washed over her like a sunrise and Constantine felt his muscles tense. What if Natalie lost control, the way she had in the motel room? Would Viktor shoot her? He caught Beth's eye and noticed the same look of dread on her face.

Finally, Natalie tilted her head down and opened her eyes. They were filled with tears. "Belial says you're lying."

"I'm not," Yakov said, glancing at Ivan for support. "Tell her."

Beth tucked her chin over Marya's head. "Don't look, sweetheart."

Natalie stepped toward Yakov. "It's not me you have to convince. It's Belial. Do you know who he is?"

Yakov shook his head. Constantine looked to Viktor to gauge his reaction, but his former friend was watching the proceedings with a bemused smile.

"He's an angel," Natalie continued. "He lives in my head, but sometimes he gets out." She blinked and two tears fell down her cheeks. "Grigori was a good man. You didn't even know him."

"I was doing my job," the big man said. He looked to Viktor for help, but Viktor's gaze had locked on Natalie. Constantine glanced around the room. They were all watching her, succumbing to her strange energy.

"Have you ever seen an angel when he's angry?" A smile played on Natalie's lips. "His face looks like lightning."

"Stop it!" Yakov snapped.

"The angels read our blood. It tells them everything, like whether we're sorry for the crimes we commit." Yakov stepped backward. Natalie followed, holding one hand to her heart. "Are you sorry for what you've done? For murdering a man who never hurt you?"

"Yes," Yakov whispered, crossing himself.

"You're not telling the truth," Natalie said, leaning closer to him.

Yakov couldn't back up any further without inserting himself into the fireplace. "I swear I am."

"Let's see." Her fingers moved from her heart to her shoulder. Something glimmered in her hand. Then she slammed it into the side of Yakov's neck. Over and over, she slammed her hand into his neck until thin streams of red began to flow between her fingers. "Read it, Belial! Read it and tell me how sorry he is!"

The brooch, Constantine thought. *She's using it as a weapon.*

Yakov's eyes widened with horror as he saw the red on her fingers. He shoved her to the floor and reached for his gun.

Beth and Marya screamed in unison.

"Don't move!" Viktor cried, raising his gun.

Constantine saw Viktor's finger waver on the trigger and leapt at him, fingertips outstretched.

He wasn't fast enough.

The gun went off, its muzzle flash shooting like a star.

CHAPTER FORTY-EIGHT

"There," Liliya said. "You're in."

Vadim held the phone between his shoulder and his ear and watched Liliya's password-breaking program disappear from the screen. In its place, he saw a version of the FSB data warehouse he'd never seen before. It was organized in color-coded layers, with two layers visible above his own security clearance. "Where did you learn to do that?"

"Where do you think?" she snapped. "In prison."

"Thank you, Liliya."

"I didn't do it for you."

"I'll get her back. I promise you."

He heard Liliya sniff and try to cover it up with a cough. "I'm standing at the door with a pistol. I will shoot anyone who comes through it without my daughter. Do you understand me, old man?"

"Liliya, I'm sorry."

"You have five minutes before they find you and cut off all access. Don't speak to me again unless you have my child."

The line went dead. He tried to take a breath, but his lungs felt full of water. *I am drowning*, he thought.

If he lost Marya, he lost Liliya, too. They'd never been demonstrative with their feelings, but their bond remained solid, like the foundation of a house. You couldn't see it for all the rugs and furniture and carpeting, but without it, everything fell apart and sank into the earth. He could feel her anguish. It was closing in on him, too.

He turned his attention to the screen and clicked on the security level above his. A directory opened, filled with folders he had no time to search. He swore out loud. He could never look at all of these files in five minutes. It was hopeless.

He closed that directory and moved on to the highest level of clearance — the level only Starinov and his chosen directors had access to. He'd memorized the file number assigned to Rumkowski's collection of documents. He typed it in and clicked on the result.

The folder contained dozens more documents than he'd ever seen, all labeled with numeric codes. He clicked wildly, opening as many as possible. Once the reports began to open, however, he saw one name that told him exactly what Starinov was after.

"Holy Mary, mother of God," he breathed. Like the pen they'd won in grade school, the tsar's account was just the decoy. *It was never about the money,* he realized. Starinov was after something much more valuable.

CHAPTER FORTY-NINE

The bullet sliced through the air inches above Constantine's fingers. Helplessness seared his heart like acid as he fell at Viktor's feet. He flopped onto his injured shoulder in time to see the bullet hit its mark. But it wasn't Natalie whose eyes flew open with shock and pain. It was Yakov. The Vympel man's shocked gaze floated over Viktor's smoking pistol, then he collapsed to the floor.

Ivan drew his gun. "What the hell did you do that for?"

"Don't point that thing at me," Viktor said. "He was about to shoot the only person who can give us the password."

"How do I know you won't kill me next?"

"Do you think I *want* to even the odds here? I need you alive."

Constantine scrambled over to Natalie and helped her to the settee. "It's okay," he said. "Everything's going to be okay."

"Grigori," Natalie sobbed, tucking her head into his shoulder. "I led them right to him."

"It's not your fault. Grigori knew that." He looked down at Natalie's right hand, spattered with red. He pried it open and found her weapon—a diamond brooch with a long, sharp pin coated in blood.

In Beth's lap, Marya fidgeted and turned her head. She caught sight of the bloody body on the floor and began to wail. "I want to go home! I want to go home!"

"Hush, sweetie." Beth pressed her cheek to the girl's head, offering what comfort she could with her hands tied behind her back. It didn't help. Marya's piercing cries echoed in their ears.

"God, that noise," Viktor said. "Either you shut her up or I will."

"Untie me and I might have more luck," Beth said.

"I'd say you're having *no* luck. Ivan, why don't you give it a try?"

The blond man knelt over Beth and jerked Marya's chin toward him. "If you don't stop crying, I will find your family and skin them alive. I'll tell them they're dying because you couldn't keep your mouth shut. Do you want them to die because you couldn't keep your mouth shut?"

Marya's face turned white. She gasped, but held back her cries.

Ivan caressed her cheek with the muzzle of his gun. "Good girl. You'll be quiet now, won't you?" Marya nodded and Constantine ground his teeth. That poor child would remember this day for the rest of her life, and there was nothing he could do to help her.

"Let's get back to business," Viktor said. "Have a look at our golden goose, will you, Con? Make sure she isn't hurt."

"I'm fine," Natalie said. "I can speak, you know."

"I know, darling, but it's so much easier when you don't."

"Are you sure you're all right?" Constantine asked, pointing at her blood-spattered blouse. One shoulder was torn, where she'd ripped the brooch free to stab Yakov. But the other…the other had split the blouse straight down the front. "Did he do this to you?" Constantine asked.

"Viktor didn't hurt me."

"That's not what I asked." But it didn't matter, because he already knew the answer. Enemies were supposed to look different, speak a different language, and wear different clothes. They weren't supposed to be behind you in the trenches, aiming a gun at your head the entire time. "I trusted you with my life, Viktor. Vadim did, too."

Viktor curled his lip. "Vadim is a relic. Refrigerated and dry like week-old borscht."

"Then why bother betraying him?"

"Because he never saw what I was worth. No one did."

"Take a hint," Beth said.

"Enough! Con, I want those letters and I want them now."

"You don't need Marya or Natalie's sister for that. Let them go."

"Jesus, Mary, and Joseph, I'm tired of you telling me what to do."

Constantine held up his hands. "Fine. You win, Viktor. You're in charge."

"Is this the conciliatory phase of the negotiation? You forget, Con, I went through those training classes, too. You're a bad liar, and negotiating involves lying to people."

"Negotiating is about compromise."

"Not if you want to win!" Viktor yelled, slamming his fist against the desk. "And I always want to win."

Marya, startled by the noise, let loose a whimper.

"Ivan, for the love of Christ, I don't care how you do it, just make sure I don't hear one more word out of her!"

Ivan nodded. He pulled his gun, pointed it at the girl's forehead, and pulled the trigger. The bullet shot through Marya's head and knocked her body to the floor. Beth screamed as blood and brain matter splattered on her neck and face. She jumped to her feet, knocking the chair backward. Ivan pressed the barrel of his TT to her forehead. "You're next, *lastochka*."

"How could you?" Beth screamed. "All you had to do was untie me, and I could have held her!" Tears streaked through the dirt and blood on her face, creating shapes that forked like lightning strikes.

"It is done," Viktor said. "Starinov wouldn't have released her anyway."

Constantine growled. "She was a child, Viktor, not a disposable *mafiya* thug."

"Spare me the lecture, you bloody hypocrite! We killed hundreds of people in Chechnya and you didn't bat an eye. Do you think our reports on Chechen positions didn't lead to bombing raids? Do you think women and children didn't die when our rockets obliterated the villages their generals tried to hide in? A soldier either feels guilty all of the time or none of the time. I happen to be the latter. Which are you?"

"He's a better man," Natalie said. "And you know it."

"None of you understand how the real world works! I can't wait to be rid of you all."

Suddenly, his thick brows drew together. He reached into his pocket and pulled out a vibrating phone. He gulped when he saw the number on his screen. "Shut up, all of you. It's Starinov."

CHAPTER FIFTY

"Well, ladies and gentlemen," Viktor said, putting away his phone. "It appears we've been given a change of venue. The cleaning crew will arrive soon and we want to be well out of their way."

Constantine felt Natalie's warm hand slip into his and he squeezed it, tracing out two words in English on her palm. *Be ready.*

"Here's how this works. We'll all march to the elevator like one big happy family," Viktor said, pistol in hand. "Con, you'll go first, hands on your head. Ivan will follow and shoot you if you do anything he finds disagreeable. Ladies, you'll follow Ivan. If you try to run, I'll shoot you in the leg. It won't be fatal, but it will hurt like hell."

"Wait," Beth said. "Bring some of that vodka for Natalie."

"I have some in my purse," Natalie said. "May I have it back?"

Viktor grabbed the bag from the mahogany desk and tossed it to her. "By all means, take it and drink absolutely everything in it once we're in the car. I don't want to hear any more of this avenging angel rubbish."

"Is it because you're scared of the angel or of me?"

"Both," Viktor said. He nudged Constantine's arm with his gun. "Go."

They proceeded out of the blood-spattered office. Constantine heard Natalie whisper something — the same line over and over. Something with the words "courage" and "change." He marched down the marble hallway and stopped at the elevator. Ivan reached around him and pressed the "down" button with the muzzle of his gun.

When it opened, Constantine moved all the way to the back, knowing Viktor would never allow him to remain there. It was standard Stealth procedure: get into the elevator first, wait for your enemy to follow, grasp the handrail in back and use it to balance yourself for a kick, striking your opponent above his ear, preferably with steel-toed boots.

"Goddamn it, Con," Viktor said. "How stupid do you think I am?"

Constantine tried to look chagrined. He moved forward and stood next to the control panel as the rest of the group filed in. Viktor placed himself at the rear, with the women in front, facing the doors. Ivan stood with his gun jammed into Constantine's back. When the polished metal doors closed, Constantine could see each of their reflections. He watched

Natalie take her sister's arm and squeeze it. *She knows*, he thought.

Ivan punched the button for the garage and the elevator descended. There was a pause as it landed and settled. Then, in the space of a single breath, the doors slid open and Constantine ducked.

From the ground, he snatched Ivan's ankle and jerked him to the floor. The Vympel man hit the ground hard, head slamming onto the grooved strip separating the elevator shaft from the concrete floor.

"Run!" Natalie cried, shoving Beth forward.

Viktor aimed his gun at them. Constantine reached for Viktor's legs, forcing his shots off course. Then he catapulted to his feet, grabbed Viktor's head, and slammed it into his upraised knee. Beneath him, Ivan groaned and tried to stand, but one kick to the head left him motionless. "That's for Marya," he said.

A scream echoed against the low concrete ceiling. *Natalie*, he thought. *The guards.*

He pulled Viktor's gun out of his unconscious grip and sprinted around the corner. Natalie wrapped her arms around her sister, shielding her from the two men firing on them from the guard station. Constantine fired back, catching one guard in the chest. The other ducked into the booth.

"The street!" he called. "Go — there's a car on the frontage road."

Her frightened eyes met his. "What about you?"

"I'll be right behind you." He pulled her to him for a quick, fierce kiss, reaching into his pocket for the car keys.

He dropped them into her hand and turned toward the guards' booth. "Go!"

He swiped the M2 from the dead guard's hand and rolled past the entry, aiming his shots inside. There was a grunt and then silence.

Constantine popped out of his crouch. The guard's feet were outstretched in his field of vision, but what if the man was luring him into a trap? His finger twitched on the trigger and a bullet shot straight through the guard's foot.

No movement.

He sighed, touched his shoulder, and groaned. In the booth, he found what he'd expected—an SR-2 on the gun rack beneath the monitor bay and an M2 pistol in the dead man's hand.

He paused just long enough to look back over his shoulder. Before that morning, he never would have left Viktor behind. But everything was different now, and he had only himself to blame. He vaulted over the garage gate and ran toward Natalie and the Volga.

⁂

"Where was Viktor going to take us?" Natalie asked. She sat beside him in the front seat, with Beth in the back. They made an eerie sight, both sisters spattered with blood and streaked with tears.

"I don't know," Constantine said, speeding toward the Transportnoye Koltso. He glanced from mirror to mirror, waiting for the armor-plated Mercedes G55 to come flying up behind him. "But as long as we're in Moscow, Starinov will keep sending Vympel after us."

"What do we do?" Beth asked softly. "Should Nat and I go to the embassy?"

"They'd just send you to the airport with an armed escort. All Starinov would have to do is wait until they put you on the plane and then pull it off the runway."

"So we're sitting ducks."

"Wait." Natalie reached out and put her hand on his arm. "Can you get us to London? If we unlock the account first, it's all over. Starinov won't have a reason to hurt anyone else."

He smiled at her. "I asked Vadim to arrange the flight before I came after you."

"So this is really happening," she said, squeezing his arm.

"Wait a sec," Beth said. "The account really exists?"

Natalie nodded. "There are pencil markings on both letters that say 'Bank of England' and 'Soloviev.'"

Beth wrinkled her nose. "Soloviev? What does that douchebag have to do with it?"

"I don't understand," Constantine said, swerving past a smoke-spewing Lada. "Who is Soloviev? That name wasn't in the file Vadim gave me."

"Boris Soloviev is Rasputin's son-in-law," Natalie explained. "I never would have picked him, Beth, but it makes sense, doesn't it?"

"No, it doesn't. Soloviev's the one who fucked it all up. He took money, promised to set up an escape for that poor family, and absolutely nothing happened. Hell, some of the sources even claim he's a double agent."

"I'm confused," Constantine said. "He was a double agent for the Bolsheviks?"

"No one knows for sure," Beth said. "The guy was a liar, and official records from that time are so spotty that it's impossible to prove one way or the other."

"Look," Natalie said, "we know Boris Soloviev married Rasputin's daughter, Maria — that's his Romanov connection. We also know he was a dick. Maria said she didn't trust him, even though she was married to him. But that doesn't mean he didn't do one good deed."

Constantine frowned. "But how did he get the Romanov money in the first place?"

"He followed them to Tobolsk and then Ekaterinburg, the two places they were imprisoned. That's when their friends and employees tried to slip them money."

"What did they need money for? I thought the tsar was richer than God."

"Before World War I, he might have been. But the war drained most of the treasury and his personal fortune. When Nicholas abdicated in 1917, most of the things he considered his personal property became the property of the state."

Beth leaned forward. "It's like a divorce. Imagine being married to the richest man in the world for, oh, 300 years, and then having to go through and separate your stuff, his stuff, and the community property. It's a pain in the ass."

"So his assets were frozen and he was short on cash," Constantine said.

"Exactly," Natalie agreed. "And once the Soviets took over the government, they decided Nicholas and his family should pay for their own upkeep during exile. So they barely had enough money to eat, let alone plan an escape or a more comfortable exile in another country."

"And this Soloviev guy, possibly a double agent, followed them into exile. Then what?"

"He was a go-between for the Romanovs and the people who wanted to give them money. But he was also a world-class dickweed who ended up pocketing most of that money… or so we thought." She stopped to take a breath. "Beth, what if Soloviev didn't steal anything? What if he put that money in the bank, anticipating the day the imperial family was rescued and needed money to support themselves?"

Beth bit her lip. "It's possible. Soloviev's father was the treasurer of the Holy Synod. He might have been able to make contact with bankers and financiers by dropping his father's name."

"Plus, if the account isn't under a Romanov name, the bank holding the money can deny it has any Romanov property without telling a lie."

"But when did Soloviev do it? And how?"

"I don't know," Natalie said, shaking her head. "It must have been after Tobolsk. Remember Yaroshinksy?"

"You're losing me again," Constantine said.

"Yaroshinsky was a businessman who gave the Romanovs 175,000 rubles in 1917, but they never got all the money. That must be what Soloviev started the account with."

Beth grabbed the back of his seat. "But Soloviev didn't go to England, you guys. He never left Russia. He even got arrested at one point, didn't he?"

Natalie nodded. "In early 1918. It doesn't mean he didn't sneak out of the country before that or send someone else, pretending to be him."

"It's a shitty theory," Beth said. "Even if we tally up all the money Soloviev collected from royalists, we're not talking that much. Maybe half a million rubles total? Why are we being hunted by lunatics and murderers over half a million defunct tsarist rubles?"

"There must be more," Constantine said. "Starinov wouldn't care otherwise. What happened to the rest of Nicholas's money?"

"It evaporated," Beth said. "Whatever survived the war effort got destroyed by post-war inflation or confiscated by the Soviets."

Natalie pressed her fingers to her temples. "There's more. There has to be."

"But even if there are hundreds of millions of rubles we're missing, how does a Russian walk into the Bank of England in 1918 with boatloads of cash and not end up in front of Lloyd George? The Russian government owed England big time — they were behind on war supply payments. Wouldn't someone have raised a red flag?"

"They got around it somehow."

"How?" Beth said. "With a hall pass?"

Natalie sat up straight. "The Romanov girls passed notes to their friends on the outside whenever they could. Why couldn't Nicholas or Alexandra slip something to Soloviev? Something he or his representative took to England to set up the account?"

"That's weak, Nat."

"Not if there's an inside man who can connect the bank, the king, and the tsar. Think, Beth."

Constantine felt their eyes on him and sighed. "Don't look at me. I have no idea what you're talking about."

Natalie turned to face her sister. "You know who I'm talking about, right?"

"Nat, are you saying what I think you're saying?"

The sisters looked at each other, the same tentative smile playing on their lips. "Bark," they said in unison.

CHAPTER FIFTY-ONE

Starinov slammed the phone and swore. What was wrong with the world? Why was there no one in it who could follow simple orders? Viktor had failed him; the American women and Dashkov were gone. Primakov's granddaughter was dead, as were three Vympel men. Viktor hadn't been able to give chase and now the letters and the captives were loose in Moscow. Even if he marshaled every man and woman in the FSB office, it could be days before they were found.

Still, there was only one way they could get out of the country. Whether the women fled to the U.S. or went after the tsar's money in London, Primakov was the only agency head not loyal to him who had the authority and reach to get them out of Russia. Stopping their escape was as simple as stopping Vadim from helping them.

It will be my word against theirs, he thought. *Who will he believe?*

Starinov looked up at his portrait of Ivan the Terrible and smiled. Ivan was the one who had commissioned St. Basil's Cathedral. When the glorious cathedral was finished, Ivan summoned the architect and asked him to describe his achievement. The proud architect called it the most beautiful cathedral ever built. Ivan agreed, showered the man with praise, and ordered the man's eyes put out. If the architect capable of such greatness were blinded, he would never build another, more glorious cathedral for a local *boyar*. Ivan knew how to possess and keep beauty. *I, too, know how to keep what's mine*, Starinov thought.

He picked up the phone and dialed Primakov's number. "Vadim Petrovich, I have a problem you are going to help me solve."

"What is it?" the older man said. "Is it Marya?"

"It is your agent, Constantine Dashkov. He broke into the Ussov building, where I was entertaining your granddaughter, the American women, and your agent, Viktor Igorovich."

"Are they alive?"

He could hear the hope in Primakov's voice. The man wanted only one response and he would question nothing if he received it. Starinov smiled to think how easily even men bred in the old Soviet system still believed the lies their betters told them. "Yes," he lied. "But instead of surrendering, Dashkov escaped with the Romanov letters and the women."

"Then where's Marya?"

Starinov didn't respond. Instead, he listened to the heavy breath on the other end of the line. He pictured Vadim, red-eyed and shaggy-haired, wearing a wrinkled tweed jacket. He would be crying or cursing or praying, none of which were of any use to a man of action. *That was always your problem, Vadim. Too much thought. Too little action.*

"Tell me," Primakov said. "Where is she?"

Starinov got up from his desk and went to stand beside the portrait of Ivan. With the tip of his pen, he counted the jewels visible in Ivan's collar. Twenty-six in total. He stood back to admire the painting's gold leaf border, glinting even in the curtain-shrouded lamplight.

"Maxim! Tell me!"

"All right," he said softly. "If you truly want to know."

"So help me God, if you don't tell me where she is —"

"She is in my care, but only because Dashkov left her behind. Viktor was wounded in the fight and Dashkov left him, too."

He could hear the confusion in Vadim's voice. "Constantine wouldn't do that. Why are you telling me this?"

"I want the letters. You want your granddaughter. I propose an exchange."

"I don't have the letters, Maxim."

"But you will. Dashkov will bring them to you. He will ask you to arrange his transportation — it's the only way he can flee the country without alerting me. I want you to agree to whatever he asks, but deliver him to me. When I have the women and the letters, you will get your granddaughter back."

"What will you do with Constantine?"

"That is not your concern."

"I don't believe you, Maxim. Constantine would never leave Marya and I know you would lie to God in order to get what you wanted."

"Your belief in your agent is touching, Vadim. But consider the facts: he left his own partner and a six-year-old girl behind. His judgment is obviously impaired."

"He's the best man I have, Maxim."

"It's a question of honor, then." Starinov leaned in closer to study the thin, cruel eyebrows the artist had painted over Ivan's Mongol eyes. *Fascinating,* he thought, *how a simple line can turn a man's visage from a source of comfort to a source of terror.* "I will pose the question to you like this — do you trust Constantine more than you love your granddaughter? If the answer is yes, I will tie your granddaughter into a pillowcase full of bricks and drop her into the Moskva. If the answer is no, you will deliver Dashkov to me and I will return her to you unharmed. The choice is yours."

Starinov looked up at Ivan. He imagined the ancient tsar's rosy lips curling into a smile of approval.

CHAPTER FIFTY-TWO

"Who the hell is Bark?" Constantine asked, heading southbound on Tulskaya. He made an illegal u-turn, watching for any trailing cars parting the traffic behind him. Viktor was out there somewhere, and so were more of Starinov's goons.

"Sir Peter Bark," Natalie explained. "Last finance minister for Tsar Nicholas II. During World War I, he made several trips to London to carry messages between Nicholas and his cousin, King George V of England. He fled to London in 1919 to escape the Soviets and landed a job managing a subsidiary of the Bank of England."

Constantine tried to process the information and monitor the surrounding traffic at the same time. "So Bark is the one who set up the account?"

"I don't think so," Natalie said. "The timing is off. But I'd bet money that Bark knew about the account. He must have been nervous when news of the tsar's death broke, especially when Nicholas's relatives started yammering about foreign deposits that should now belong to them. But he was in the ideal position to lock that account down. He was already in England, employed in finance, and handling money for Nicholas's sisters, who had both escaped the revolution."

"We're never going to be able to prove this," Beth said.

"The proof doesn't matter if we decipher the password." Natalie turned to him. "Vadim will help us get to England, won't he?"

"He gave me his word."

Beth shook her head. "I wouldn't count on it. How would *you* feel if three out of four captives show up on your doorstep, and none of them are the one actually related to you?"

Constantine's fingers clenched over the steering wheel. "I have to look him in the eye and tell him I failed him."

"But Viktor's the one who betrayed *us*," Natalie said. "He's the one to blame."

"Blaming Viktor won't bring Marya back and it won't make Vadim more likely to help us."

"I felt that bullet go through her." Beth clasped her arms around her body and rocked back and forth. "How could they do it?"

"They're killers. They weren't thinking of her as a person."

Beth sniffed and looked out the window. "How are we going to tell him?"

Beside him, Natalie took a deep breath, reached into her purse, and handed one of the small vodka bottles to her sister. "First, you rinse her blood off your face. Then you drink whatever's left."

Constantine took one hand off the steering wheel and rested it on Natalie's thigh. It was the only way he could tell her he was proud of her for giving her sister the luxury of breaking down. Without looking at him, she clasped his hand in hers.

They drove the rest of the way without speaking, Beth crying quietly and Natalie squeezing his hand every time her sister sobbed. Eventually, the drone of the car lulled them both into a doze. He was grateful. They needed the rest, but their sleep also left him free to scan the roads for an ambush.

He turned onto the MKAD ring road and headed for Vnukovo Airport, dreading the moment when he had to shape the words that would destroy Vadim's faith in the future. He knew Vadim believed in God and wondered whether that belief would help soften the blow. To him, it seemed more comforting to believe in randomness than in a deity who targeted the innocent.

Finally, he reached the winding access road that led past Vnukovo's commercial runways. He stopped at a checkpoint to flash his bureau identification. The guard waved him through to the ring of private airstrips leased to government entities, each of which came with a hangar and administrative trailer.

A Challenger sat in the bureau's open hangar with its hatch closed and lights off. Constantine pulled up beside the aluminum-shingled office trailer. He couldn't see anything through the window, and there was no car parked beside the trailer.

This doesn't feel right, he thought. *No car for Vadim? Or the pilot or maintenance crew?*

He parked the Volga and touched Natalie's shoulder gently. "We're here," he said. She blinked sleepily, nodded, and reached into the back to wake her sister.

Beth woke quickly, sitting up to look around. "It looks deserted. Are you sure this is the right place?"

"It feels wrong to me, too. Keep your eyes open." He divided the cache from the Ussov guard booth between them, giving the women pistols and taking the assault rifle for himself.

"Is this a trap?" Natalie asked.

"It might be, but we have no choice. We leave here with Vadim's help, or we don't leave at all."

He got out, rifle in hand, and walked up to the trailer. He flung the door open and jumped sideways, but no spray of gunfire rocketed out from the doorway.

Inside, an old man slumped in a folding chair beside the single window. A lit cigarette dangled from his lips, ash collecting in a pyramid on the floor. His lank hair hung like gray straw around his head.

"Vadim?" Constantine asked. "Is that you?"

"Come inside, boy." The other man's voice was buried under an avalanche of grief and nicotine. "I have done as you asked. The pilot is waiting for my signal."

He met Vadim's eyes and recoiled from the black grief in their smoke-reddened depths. "About Marya —"

"None of that," Vadim said, waving the words away like a fly.

He knows, Constantine thought. *Starinov must have called to gloat.*

Beth stepped out from behind him. "We couldn't help her," she said softly. "I tried to keep them away from her, but they..." She broke into a sob and couldn't finish. Natalie put her arms around her shaking sister and stared over Beth's shoulder at Vadim.

The older man pointed at Natalie. "This is the one?" he asked in Russian.

"*Da,*" Constantine answered.

"She is a *rusalka.* An evil creature. She must take life in order to live." Vadim crossed himself. "There is no soul behind her eyes. Something has taken it."

Natalie narrowed her eyes. "Belial has something he wants to say to you."

Constantine's throat tightened as he listened to her enunciate the guttural sounds of Russian, a language she didn't speak: *At least my soul is spoken for. Yours is still available to the highest bidder.*

Beth raised her head from her sister's embrace. "Nat, what did you just say?"

"I don't know," Natalie said. "Belial told me to say it."

Constantine tightened his grip on the rifle. "Tell Belial to be quiet until we're on that plane. He's going to get us killed."

Vadim looked at Constantine. "You understand this madness?"

"Whatever it is," he said, "it isn't madness." *Madness,* he thought, *was shooting a helpless child at point-blank range.* "Go back to Liliya and let me take care of Starinov." The foggy look in Vadim's eyes made his bones shake the way they did before a bombing raid or rescue mission. Something wasn't right, but he had to keep going until he knew what it was.

"Let's go," he said, ushering the women to the door. Vadim followed them onto the tarmac, raising one hand as a signal. The pilot unlocked the hatch and pushed it open, dropping the stairs. "Go on," Constantine said, touching Natalie's elbow. "I'll be right behind you."

"Promise?" Natalie said, a ghost of a smile on her lips.

"Promise," he said.

She held his gaze, as if she weren't sure whether to believe him. Finally, she nodded and climbed the stairs.

Constantine turned to Vadim. He wondered what he could say that would carry any weight when placed next to a human soul. He opened his mouth to speak and heard a scream. He spun and saw Natalie at the plane's hatch, in Viktor's arms, a knife at her throat. An enormous strip of white tape held Viktor's broken nose in place.

"Let her go!" Beth cried. She fumbled for the gun tucked into her waistband.

"Don't," Vadim said, raising a pistol in his black-gloved hand.

Constantine roared in frustration. They were all working against each other, and they'd all end up dead because of it. "Why, Vadim? Just tell me why."

The old man pressed his thin lips together. "She's my granddaughter. What choice did I have?"

"But she's already dead!" Beth cried. "She died in my arms. I tried to tell you…"

Vadim shook his head. "She's alive. I know the truth."

The truth, he thought. *Whose truth?* A cold lump of fear formed in the pit of his stomach. "I told you not to believe anything they said."

"They'll trade her for you," Vadim said. "You and the *rusalka.*"

"Starinov's men killed her and he lied to you about it. I would never have left her behind." He focused a long, hard look on his boss. "Not after Lana. You know that, Vadim."

"Get on the plane, boy." Vadim waved the gun at him with shaking hands.

"You!" Beth pointed at Viktor. "You were there! Tell him what really happened."

"He'll find out soon enough." Viktor shoved Natalie behind him and motioned for Beth to follow. With a bent head, she obeyed.

Constantine knew he could kick the gun out of Vadim's hand and overpower the older man. But if he did, Viktor might close the hatch and leave him behind. He couldn't abandon Natalie and her sister. His best chance of saving them was staying with them, watching, and waiting. He'd failed his own sister, he'd failed Marya, and he'd be damned if he did it again.

"I tried to save her," he said, meeting Vadim's pain-sore eyes. "When you come to your senses, you'll see that." Then he tossed the rifle onto the tarmac at Vadim's feet and walked up onto the plane.

CHAPTER FIFTY-THREE

Natalie heard the plane's hatch click shut. Viktor marched her toward a blue-eyed man with sharp features. The top of his head reflected light, and the hair on the sides was cut so short as to be almost invisible. He looked too young to be bald. His red lips were thin and well-defined. "Welcome," he said.

Belial twitched. *Beware, little one.*

Viktor pushed her into a seat across from the red-lipped man, with Beth next to her. In the front of the plane, two armed guards kept watch over Constantine.

"I am Maxim Apraximovich Starinov," the man said. "And I believe you know why you are here. I find it amusing that two Americans will be the ones to help me unlock our tsar's last secret."

"Why is that?" she asked.

"Because after supposedly winning the last cold war, you are going to give me what I need to defeat your country in the next one."

Natalie watched his eyes, but they registered no humor, no anger, not a single flicker of human emotion. *He'll kill us and feel nothing,* she thought.

Belial seconded her opinion. *Do not let him see your fear, little one. He feeds on it.*

"Please," Starinov said. "Relax. We will not arrive in London for several hours. Let us get to know each other."

"We know you already," Beth said. "We don't like you."

Starinov grimaced. "I fail to understand why the world's worst citizens are considered its best moral police. Your Uncle Sam is a bad parent who gives you vodka before school, ice cream before bed, and a whore for your fourteenth birthday. He steals the wallet from your pocket and when you ask him for money, he gives back what he has already taken from you. Still, the world idolizes him and turns its back on its true savior."

"Let me guess," Beth said. "That's you?"

"When children cry, for whom do they wail? Not an uncle, surely."

Natalie thought about the ancient nicknames for Russia's tsar and tsarina — "little father" and "little mother." The parent/child relationship was sown deeply in the soil of Russian culture. "A mother," she said. "He's talking about Mother Russia."

Starinov smiled. "What could be more natural than a mother taking care of her children? Deciding which children should be punished and which should be rewarded?"

"Mothers don't punish their children by killing them."

"Perhaps that is why there are so many bad children."

"That's what Hitler said."

Starinov shook his head. "Americans always invoke Hitler when a strong ruler does something of which they disapprove."

"How long did it take you to realize Chechnya wasn't Poland?"

"As long as it took your country to realize Iraq wasn't France."

"Just because Vichy and al-Maliki rhyme doesn't mean they're the same thing."

"By all means," Beth interrupted, "feel free to continue this exercise in narcissistic megalomaniacal tendencies *after* you tell me what the hell this has to do with the Romanovs."

"Nothing," Natalie said, holding Starinov's gaze. "It's just foreplay."

"Call it what you will." The prime minister took a sip of vodka from a crystal glass. "But the world has never seen a man as wealthy as the tsar. You cannot tell me you've never imagined being that rich or powerful."

"Try me," she said.

"Why not?"

"Because angels don't take bribes."

Viktor leaned over Natalie's shoulder. "Don't let her start

with the angel rubbish. It's a voice in her head and she does whatever it tells her to. It told her to stab Yakov in the neck."

"I had a good reason," she said.

"Oh?" Starinov asked. "What was that?"

He won't like this part, Belial said.

Natalie leaned forward, looking Starinov in the eye. "Have you ever felt your heart stop in your chest, just long enough to miss a beat? Afterward, once you've caught your breath, your heart pumps a little faster to catch up. Do you know what that is?" Starinov shook his head. "That's an angel. They read our blood like a book. Sometimes they want the pages to turn a little faster."

"I see." Starinov blinked twice. "You've quite the imagination."

"You can call it that if it makes you feel safer."

Viktor snorted and pointed at his broken nose. "You see what I've been up against?"

Starinov wore the same dismissive look as her shrinks — a false smile that failed to hide his disdain. He pointed at the bloody brooch pinning her blouse closed. "Where did you get that?"

"A man gave it to me."

"And where did he get it?"

"The Ipatiev house."

"All property of the former tsar belongs to me."

"It belongs to the people of Russia and the Russian state."

"I am the Russian state!"

"Your legislative branch would disagree."

"Enough," he said. "Bring me the letters!"

Viktor walked up the plane's center aisle to where two Vympel men held Constantine. She heard the rustle of fabric and paper, then a muffled groan. Over the seat backs, she saw Viktor's face go pale.

"What is it?" she asked, more afraid for Constantine than herself.

Viktor held the letters up. They were soaked through with blood. "Yakov," Natalie whispered, remembering the slash he'd given Constantine. "Viktor, do something before he bleeds to death!"

"Like what, love? Call an ambulance?" He carried the sodden letters to her and dropped them on the table. "All yours."

At her side, Beth gasped. "That's Marie's writing!"

"I told you," Natalie said. "I've read that one, but I haven't read Olga's."

She separated the top letter from the bottom letter, but the blood had already dissolved the ink. All that was left were a few charcoal smudges across the page, impossible to decipher beneath the stain. At the top of the page, the date remained untouched: JULY 13, 1918.

She couldn't even make out a signature at the bottom.

It was gone, all of it, along with any chance of finding the password.

CHAPTER FIFTY-FOUR

Vadim heard the Challenger take off, a breathless god's hurried exhale of heat and air. He leaned his head against the trailer's window and reached into his jacket pocket for a small picture frame.

In the photo, Marya wore her favorite purple dress and a purple ribbon in her hair. In her arms, she clutched an irate cat that belonged to their neighbors. She'd tied a matching ribbon around the cat's neck. The animal hung stiffly from her grasp, as if willing the girl to put it down. No matter how many times Marya teased and tormented the cat, it tolerated her caresses with remarkable good grace for a full five minutes. Marya loved it as if it were her own, smuggling smoked salmon in her pockets in case she saw it on the way to school.

He stroked the glass over her cheek, unable to believe he would never touch her or hold her again. Constantine was right. Starinov had lied to him and he'd swallowed it up. *But who could blame me?* he thought. *Who would believe someone could murder this tiny person, a girl who'd barely begun to live?*

His lips quivered and a pile of ash fell from his cigarette to the floor. Now he faced the prospect of telling Liliya. He knew his daughter's temperament. She would want to hate him, but because of what he and Valery had done for her, she would feel unable to express that anger. The resentment would build inside her every day until it grew and spread, killing her like a cancer.

For himself, he was finished. He'd heard stories of snipers with hundreds of kills whose steady hands never faltered until a single shot went astray and killed the wrong person. Then the sniper lost his confidence and abilities, thanks to shaking hands or cloudy eyes. Despite hundreds of repetitions and the body's own muscle memory, the mind lost what had made it special in the first place — control. How long had Viktor been working for Maxim? How long had he been feeding the FSB information from the bureau's private databases?

He could never trust his own judgment again.

Maxim had done more than kill Marya. He and Liliya had been destroyed, too. Maybe that had been the plan all along. Had Constantine's *rusalka* been right? *At least my soul is spoken for,* she'd said. *Yours is still available to the highest bidder.*

But he hadn't sold his soul. He simply hadn't used it. *You must leave Liliya with more than this,* he thought. *You must make her believe you tried to set it right.*

He ground out his cigarette on the floor and texted his driver. There was still one person who might be able to help.

CHAPTER FIFTY-FIVE

Natalie glanced out the window as the Mercedes S-class flew down the M3 from Farnborough to London. It was late afternoon and most of the cars were moving in the opposite direction, away from the city. The Mercedes, closely followed by a second identical sedan, had little difficulty weaving past Peugeots and Vauxhalls.

Separated from Constantine and her sister, Natalie rode in the lead car with Starinov, Viktor, and a bodyguard. At first, she noted landmarks as they passed: the ring road, a reservoir, a big stadium, and two separate river crossings. But the Romanov letters, clutched in her hand, thrummed with a life and energy all their own. Part of her hoped that if she stared at them hard enough, the dissolved ink would reappear. *Belial, I need a miracle*, she begged.

I'm sorry, little one, he answered. *You know it doesn't work like that.* The angel shrugged his shoulders in defeat. Every wingtip brushed her brain case, delivering the sting of a needle piercing flesh. She closed her eyes before Starinov or Viktor could see her cry.

From the safety of the darkness behind her eyelids, she tried to piece together what she remembered from Marie's letter. Somewhere there had to be an unusual word or phrase, a bit of diction that seemed wrong. If she could just find one loose thread and pull it until it unraveled, maybe she could guess the password.

Suddenly, it occurred to her that she was looking for help in the wrong place. What could Belial possibly know? If the Romanovs had selected the password, they were the ones she needed to ask. She tried to clear her mind and let images of the Romanov children float over her, the way she'd seen them in hundreds of photographs and film reels. She saw Tatiana standing in the snow, Anastasia with her skirt bunched around her ankles in the waters of the Black Sea, Olga turning her head sideways from a book to bare the beginnings of a smile, Alexei holding a ball above his dog's head. They were one of the richest families in the history of the world, yet one of the most tragic. What could it all mean in the end? How would they have chosen a single word to encapsulate their lives?

"Help me," she whispered to them. "Help me understand."

"Understand what?" Viktor said. "How insane you are?"

His words broke the spell. Natalie took a deep breath as the car pulled through a wrought-iron gate and slowed to a stop. In front of them stood a pale but imposing Gothic mansion with a three-story tower at its center. The Russian flag flew to the right of the entrance and two armed sentries stood between the car and the porch.

Natalie wiped the sweat from her brow. She could feel Belial, nervous and restless, as he prowled the space beneath her skull. She ground her teeth and concentrated on containing him. *You have to help Beth*, she told herself. *Nothing's more important than getting her out of this.*

Starinov led them into the house and through a red-carpeted ballroom with staircases ascending on either side. Natalie looked up in awe at the light streaming from the third-story window, falling brightly over golden urns, paintings, and detailed fretwork. But Starinov kept marching toward the back of the house, to a golden ballroom with a parquet floor, crystal chandeliers, and marble bar. At the far end of the room, Natalie thought she saw a bank of windows and realized they were mirrors framed in curtains. There were no real windows, no view of the outside.

Starinov closed the ballroom's double doors behind them. "A good place, yes? I announced my candidacy for prime minister here. I have many happy memories of this room. Today, you are going to give me another."

"Where are Beth and Constantine?"

"Gregor and Arkady are bringing them now."

"Please let them go. They can't help you."

"Don't ask for the impossible."

"*You* are," she snapped. "Why do you think I can do what decades of Soviet flunkies couldn't?"

Belial shifted his weight, raising his head to stare at the door. *They are closing in on us. I don't like this.*

A scuffling sound from beyond the threshold grew louder as two guards marched Constantine and Beth in at gunpoint. They locked the doors from the inside and flanked Starinov and his other bodyguard, staring straight ahead with no expression on their faces.

That one is ill, Belial said. *Shall we tell him how he will die? He won't like it.*

"It's death," Natalie said through clenched teeth. "No one likes it." She felt a drop of sweat slide between her shoulder blades.

Beth rushed over and reached for her hands. "Nat, you don't look so good. It's Belial, isn't it?"

Natalie nodded. "He's trying to get out again. He's scared and angry."

Beth turned on Starinov. "She needs alcohol. She's no good to you without it."

The prime minister raised one pale eyebrow. "Aren't you the noble nurse. I've never heard of anyone prescribing alcohol for insanity."

"I've been taking care of her my whole life. I know what she needs."

Constantine came up to her and touched her face softly. The lines around his eyes had grown deeper, like canyons cut into a relief map. "Will it happen like before, in the motel?"

"I don't know," she whispered.

"You need to help us," Beth said to Starinov. "Now."

"I don't have to do a thing. If she can't give me the password, you will."

"The hell I will. Both those letters are ruined. If Nat were able to tell me what the first one said, I might have a shot. But if she goes under, you'll never get that goddamn password."

Starinov's face, devoid of all expression, studied each of them in turn. "Five minutes. If you don't have the password when I return in five minutes, I will shoot you, one by one, until you tell me what it is. Is that clear?"

Natalie felt her heart quiver. *Belial,* she thought. *Stop reading.*

"You have," Starinov said, glancing at his watch, "four minutes and fifty-nine seconds."

CHAPTER FIFTY-SIX

Constantine ran to the wall of mirrors. He peeled back the curtains, looking for a hidden exit. "Nothing," he said. He patrolled the rest of the room, looking for anything they could use as a weapon.

Beth's lower lip trembled. Stray hairs, visible wrinkles, smeared makeup — everything she usually had under control had gone awry. "Nat, he's going to kill us. What the hell are we going to do?"

It's all because of me, Natalie thought. *And there's only one thing I can do to fix it.* "We're going to give him the password."

Beth's blue eyes widened. "You know what it is?"

"No. But I know who does."

It took Beth a moment to follow. "Nat, you can't be serious."

"What are you two talking about?" Constantine asked. He'd finished his circuit of the room and brought a half-empty bottle of vodka from behind the marble bar.

"No," Natalie said. "I don't want any more."

Just like Beth, it took him a moment to understand. "You can't be serious."

"Do either of you have a better idea?"

"We convince Starinov to get those letters to a spectroscopy expert," Constantine said. "Maybe there are traces of ink deep down in the paper that we can't see."

"He won't give us that much time."

Beth reached for her hands. "Nat, we've spent twenty years fighting this. How can you just give in?"

"Because I want you to see your son again." She turned to Constantine. "And I want you to see your sister. Belial will tell me what I need to know."

"Wait," Constantine said. "Is this..." He paused. "Is this real?"

"Six years ago..." Beth shivered and began again. "If you'd seen that wall, six years ago, and what Dante told her to write...you'd believe, now, too." She touched Natalie's forehead gently. "But Dante almost killed you, Nat. Who's to say Belial won't kill you now? What if you get lost in there? What if you don't come back?"

"I'll come back. I always have."

"I don't want you to go somewhere I can't come with you." Beth sobbed and squeezed her hands. "It's my *job* to fight for you."

Natalie looked into her sister's eyes. Grigori said he'd seen an angel behind her, standing ready to defend them.

Maybe, she thought, *that angel was me.* "I'm not a baby, Beth. This time, I'm the one who has to protect you."

Belial's lips curled — Natalie felt the movement as surely as if she saw it. *This is a very interesting conversation, little one.*

"Of course it is," she said, closing her eyes and surrendering. "It's all about you." She let the pain in her head wash over her in waves. Instead of fighting it, she sank into it. "Belial," she whispered. "I need your help.

I thought you'd never ask, my dear. Belial's voice echoed within her bones. She rescinded all control and let herself fall to the floor.

"No!" Constantine yelled. "Natalie, open your eyes."

Natalie kept them shut. She felt his fingers sweep her face, caressing her cheeks. Still, she kept her heart closed. She focused on Belial's movements — his lips, his wings, his fingertips. She shut out everything else, locking the pain and hope away in her heart. When she spoke, it was only to him. "Belial, I need you to ask them what the password is."

They aren't going to tell us. It's their secret.

"It will save my family. They'll understand. I know they will."

I need to give them something, a token that proves my intentions.

"Why would they doubt you? You're an angel."

My brother put his hand upon them and someone must atone.

"Tell them I have this," she said, pulling at their diamonds in her ears, kept safe by Grigori's family for more than ninety years.

I'm going to release you while I look for them.

"I don't care what you do, just get me that password."

You should care. I've always wanted you to care. Belial lifted his wings. They carried him past the corporeal limits of her skull. She felt a rush, as if a gust of wind passed through her. The pain in her head vanished so suddenly that its absence hurt as much as the pain itself.

"He's gone," she muttered. When she opened her eyes, she was propped in Constantine's lap. Beth knelt beside her, holding her hands. There were red marks on each of her wrists. "What happened?" she asked.

Over her head, Beth met Constantine's glance. "Should I tell her?" When Constantine nodded, Beth opened her hand to reveal one of the earrings Natalie had been wearing. The wire loop that went through the ear was coated in blood.

Natalie raised her hand to her left ear and felt the earring's mate. Then she tried her right ear and her hand came away red.

"You tore it out," Constantine said. "You didn't know what you were doing."

"I told Constantine to hold you down," Beth added. "I knew he wouldn't hurt you."

"I'm sorry, *lastochka.* We were afraid of what you'd do to yourself if we let you up."

Natalie flicked her eyes to each corner of the room. Something was missing. *The noise,* she thought. *The rustle of Belial's wings. The pressure of his presence in my skull.* Without him, the world felt flat, like a two-dimensional map. Her brain felt thick and useless, like a limb that had fallen asleep. "How much time do we have left?" she asked.

"Two minutes."

"That's not enough. Belial needs more time."

"Is that really our best option?" Beth said gently. "If you tell me what the first letter said, we can try to do this together."

"We wait," she insisted.

"They're going to start shooting people, Nat."

"Then we stall them! I can't do it without Belial." She looked up at Constantine, needing the warmth and solidity of his body. He'd protected her from everything, never asking anything in return. "Please," she said. "Make them wait."

"Natalia."

Her heart clenched at the sweetness in his voice as he pronounced the Russian version of her name. He brushed the sweat-dampened hair from her face and kissed her softly. *Remember this forever*, she told herself as she closed her eyes. *If you die, at least it will be with his breath on your lips.* When he pulled away, she felt cold and wanted to curl back into his embrace.

"Natalia, open your eyes," he said. "It's not Belial. It never was. It's *you*."

"You're wrong. I black out and Belial does the rest."

"It's always been you."

I wish that were true, she thought. *But I'm just the puppet.* It was Belial who told her the answers, Belial who warned her when danger was near. Without his voice, she was lost. She was simply herself, and the world had already told her that she wasn't good enough.

The ballroom doors burst open as Starinov, Viktor, and three guards returned. The guards formed a line behind the captives, pointing assault rifles at their spines. Natalie felt her throat run dry with fear. *Belial, where the hell are you?*

Constantine lifted her to her feet, keeping an arm around her waist. Starinov's cold eyes swept her from head to toe, blinking as they passed over her torn earlobe. "You will give me the password now."

"I–I need more time."

The prime minister curled his upper lip, giving her a glimpse of small, childlike teeth. "When I give an order, you will follow it. Perhaps this will convince you of the gravity of your situation." He drew a pistol and pointed it at Constantine's forehead.

"No!" she screamed.

Starinov aimed, smiled, and pulled the trigger.

CHAPTER FIFTY-SEVEN

The guard standing behind Constantine fell backward, legs crumpling beneath him. Beth screamed and Natalie felt her heart vault into her throat.

"Are you convinced now?" Starinov said. "Because there is one minor detail I have not yet shared with you. The Bank of England will seal the account forever if you give me the wrong password."

"What?" Viktor said. "But then who would get the money?"

"No one. The bank will destroy everything associated with the account." Starinov stepped over to Natalie and tapped her forehead with the muzzle of the gun. "So you see, my dear, you have quite an important task. I'm prepared to give you more time to think, so long as you know that I will kill one person in this room every three minutes until you're done thinking."

The floor seemed to sway beneath her feet. "What if I'm wrong?"

"Then you will all die." Starinov pushed back the sleeve of his jacket to look at his watch. "Three minutes." He folded his hands behind his back and paced. The two bodyguards behind Beth and Natalie crossed the room to join him, exchanging nervous glances.

Beth pointed at Viktor. "I say we tell Starinov to kill him first and buy ourselves another three minutes."

"You ungrateful bitch! I'm management."

"Then why are you standing with the help?"

Viktor glanced at Starinov, glanced at Natalie, and stalked back to Starinov's side of the room.

"Jackass," Beth said.

Natalie sank to her knees, painfully aware of the emptiness in her brain. "Belial," she moaned. "Belial, where are you?"

Images of herself and Beth as children flowed through her mind, two pretty girls in white dresses. Then she began to confuse those girls with the Romanov girls, and Seth's features grew to look like the tsarevich, Alexei. "I don't know who I am," she whispered. "Belial, please tell me who I am."

All her life, she'd never known why Belial chose her. She'd never asked him to intervene in the spiritual realm — if that's where he was — on her behalf. Now, the one time she did, he was going to let her down. "Belial, just tell me what to do!"

Suddenly, she felt a searing heat beat down on her. She closed her eyes and saw a white light, stronger than any bulb or candle. There was a roar, as if the air itself were being torn to pieces, and then her skull rattled with an enormous vibration. Feathered wings wrapped themselves around her brain as Belial gripped her and landed. She screamed as an electric jolt of pain rocketed through her entire skeleton.

Did I hurt you, little one? I didn't mean to. I'll be still now.

"The password," she whispered.

Ask your sister. It's written on her face.

And then all was still. Belial tucked his wings over his shoulders and crouched in silence.

It's hopeless, she thought. *We're going to die.*

Natalie opened her eyes so the tears would have somewhere to go. Constantine and Beth hovered over her like worried parents. She looked into her sister's eyes, blue and bright and filled with hope. *Everything I know about love I learned from you*, she thought. Beth had defended her, sheltered her, fought for her, and taught her how to fight — not that she was doing a very good job. Her cheeks burned as she realized how badly she'd let her sister down.

Natalie reached for Beth's hand. "I'm so sorry," she said.

Beth shook her head. "Why?"

"Without me, your life would have been perfect. It's the only thing I ever wanted to give you, and..." Her eyes floated down to the scars on her arms. "I screwed it up."

"Stop it." Beth blinked back tears. "You and Seth are my family. That's what's perfect."

"I'm always going to be someone's problem."

"Not t–true." Beth bit her lip to control the sob. "Nat, I wouldn't know what faith is if it weren't for you. No one else could have taught me that."

Natalie threw her arms around her sister. Beth felt thin and frail in her embrace, and she wondered how long it had been since someone had taken care of her. "I'll do better," she whispered. *In the last minute of this life left to me, I'll swear I'll do better.*

"I love you, babe," Beth whispered back. "Nothing will ever change that."

Nothing. The word made her smile. Beth was smarter, stronger, faster, braver, and better in every way. If Beth believed it, it must be true.

Across the room, Starinov's voice echoed like a drill sergeant's. "Three minutes," he said, pointing his gun and pulling the trigger. Another of his bodyguards tumbled to the ground, folding in on himself like a marionette being put away. "Next time, I'll choose someone from your side."

Viktor edged closer to them.

Natalie watched a thick red pool spread from the lifeless body's skull. "It's not supposed to happen like this."

"How *was* it supposed to happen?" Viktor snapped. "Was God's gift to women here supposed to save you so you could live happily ever after?"

As Viktor spoke, Natalie felt something shift inside her brain, as if Belial had twitched his wings. It was swift and purposeful, like the stroke of a finger on a piano key, or the tap a blackjack player made to request another card. She'd never felt him move that way before.

"That's it," she said softly. "That's the answer."

It made so much sense. Of *course* that was how they would have encapsulated their lives. All their love, all their pain, all their suffering revolved around one thing and one thing only — and now she knew what it was.

CHAPTER FIFTY-EIGHT

The tale had taken almost twenty minutes to tell, with interruptions on both sides to correct and clarify. "I don't know how much time they have left," Vadim said. "And I don't know where else to turn."

It was the literal truth. His driver was circling aimlessly, waiting to be given a destination. In the back of the sedan, Vadim clutched the phone in one hand and a cigarette in the other.

Rockwell Marshall, the American ambassador in Moscow, sighed. "I could have done something if you'd told me while they were still on U.S. soil, but as of now, we're out of luck. You have no idea what kind of incident report this is going to generate."

"Are you listening to me?" Vadim snapped. "Maxim Starinov sent Vympel into the U.S. and killed two men, both U.S. citizens. Two more of your citizens will be dead if you don't help me stop him!"

"Mr. Primakov, if they aren't on Russian soil, there's not a hell of a lot I can do. I'm sorry."

"If you hang up on me, Mr. Rockwell, my next call will be to Atlanta and then to London. I'll tell CNN and the BBC what's happening. I doubt they'll share your cavalier attitude."

"Listen," the ambassador said, "the best I can do is call Gordo and tell him what's going on. Britain is our friend and friends don't poke around in other friends' garbage cans. I can relay the message, but I can't ask for any sort of rescue team to be sent in. They have to offer it."

"And if they don't?"

"Union Jack's going to have a real bad press day when the bodies are found."

"I'm trying to avoid having any bodies in the first place!"

Marshall sighed. "Let me conference in Gordon Wilson, our ambassador in London. Maybe he can get us some traction."

The line went silent and Vadim put his finger over the "disconnect" button, ready to hang up and dial Atlanta. Surely the free press would care more about innocent people about to be murdered than cold-hearted bureaucratic cogs whose only business was to sweep up murder, not prevent it. But even the American press couldn't bring down a foreign prime minister, not single-handedly—his plan still needed the official channels to work.

In his pocket, he caressed the glass that shielded Marya's image from his fingerprints and tears. Three minutes later, the line clicked back to life. The undersecretary to the American ambassador to Britain had managed to drag his boss out of a dinner meeting and slip a phone into his hand.

"Rocko," a deep voice boomed. "How's the caviar?"

Rockwell Marshall laughed. "Not bad, Gordo — a hell of a lot better than fish and chips. Listen, buddy, we have a problem. I'm on the line with Vadim Primakov, director of the Public Security Intelligence Bureau of the Russian Federation."

Gordon Wilson paused, leaving a palpable chill on the line. "Yes?"

"Gordo, there's a hostage situation in London. Maxim Starinov has two American women and one Russian man held prisoner. They're under duress, traveling without passports."

Wilson gulped. "Starinov's here?"

"He's headed for the Bank of England. He's after some old account, something hidden during World War I."

Vadim cleared his throat. "If I may add to that, sir, one of your citizens is being forced to divulge the account's password. Maxim will kill her, and her sister, once he's got it."

"Jesus," Wilson said. "Who else knows about this?"

"Mr. Primakov spoke to the governor of the Bank of England."

"Did the bank's governor speak to the British PM?"

"How the hell do I know? I'm sitting here rotting in Moscow. That's why we need you, Gordo."

Wilson exhaled. "Let me see if I can get the prime minister on the line. If the governor of the bank did his job, Davies already knows everything."

Vadim sat through one more connection, waiting for the chance to plead his case. This time the wait was much shorter. The prime minister of Britain, Steven Davies, acknowledged him last, after cordially greeting the two American ambassadors. Londoners, Vadim knew, feared and resented the wealthy Russians who owned much of their city.

"Good evening, Mr. Primakov," Davies said in a cultured Eton accent. "I am aware that you spoke with Algernon Perry, the governor of the Bank of England. You told him Prime Minister Starinov was coming to claim the tsar's account. This is an irregular form of diplomatic contact, to be sure, but not illegal."

Vadim took a deep breath and crossed himself. "I told you Starinov was coming, but I didn't tell you he brought two kidnapped American citizens and one of my Russian agents. He'll kill them when he has what he wants."

The line fell quiet for the space of a breath. "Are you sure he'll do it on British soil?"

"Is that all you care about? Who's responsible for cleaning up the mess? How about preventing the mess in the first place?"

Davies sniffed. "You elected the man. What he does is not my business until he does it in my backyard."

"He's already in your backyard. He's going to murder three innocent people in it."

The British prime minister sighed. "Even if Starinov is traveling incognito, he is still a head of state. I cannot pull him over like a common criminal and risk an incident. Until he commits a crime on British soil that I can prove without a doubt, I'm afraid I can't help you, gentlemen."

CHAPTER FIFTY-NINE

"I think I know what it is," Natalie said.

It was all coming together. Thoughts and images shot through her mind like fireworks, and it was all she could do to grasp their burning, sparkling essence before they vanished into the black.

Alexei, Nicholas II's son and heir, was born in 1904. No little boy could have been more loved. To Alexandra, his birth was proof that God had heard her prayers. The only thing most Russians expected of her as tsarina was to produce an heir, and after ten years and four daughters, she had finally fulfilled their expectations. The boy was cherished by his doting father, fierce mother, and four adoring older sisters. They called him "God's gift."

What the world didn't know was that Alexei was ill. Every day the boy lived and breathed was a gift, one that might not be repeated. He suffered from hemophilia — at that time, an incurable disease that doomed him to an early death. Nicholas, Alexandra, and the girls kept Alexei's hemophilia a secret, so most of the Imperial court never knew how fragile the boy's hold on life really was.

Natalie's brain began to thrum with the soft whir of a mental photo album — snapshots she remembered of Alexandra and Alexei. In most of them, Alexandra's eyes were lifeless and helpless, staring back at the camera only because she didn't have the energy to turn away and hide her pain. Hemophilia was a mother's nightmare. How do you raise a healthy boy when everything that could make him happy might kill him? Still, God had answered Alexandra's prayers by bringing her a son. If there was anything the family would have wished to commemorate, Natalie knew it was their own private miracle.

But nothing in Marie's letter mentioned Alexei. Natalie remembered her references to each of the other sisters, but she said nothing about her only brother. Was that a sign in and of itself? The password is the only family member not mentioned? *Too easy*, she thought. Marie's letter also mentioned running away to America with her soldier, which seemed unusual. None of the girls had ever visited America. Was there a common factor linking Alexei and America?

"Nat," Beth said. "What's going on? Talk to us."

"God's gift," she replied.

"Bleeding Christ," Viktor groaned. "I didn't mean for the name to stick!"

Natalie looked up at her sister. "Belial told me where to find the answer, Beth." *It's written on her face,* he'd said. But what had Belial intended her to see? She saw specks of Marya's blood on the ridge of Beth's ear. On her cheek, there were four parallel scratches in the process of healing. The unevenly spaced scabs looked eerily like Morse code. "What happened here?"

Beth reached up and felt the scabs. "That was Roo. It's nothing."

Natalie held four of her fingers over the scratches, mimicking the dog's paw.

The dog.

Then her heart began to pound. Roosevelt had a Romanov connection. He'd brokered the peace deal between the Russians and the Japanese following the Russo-Japanese War. Embarrassed by a quick and unequivocal defeat, the Russians should have had their asses handed to them by the Japanese, but Roosevelt brokered a sweetheart deal that helped them save face. Marie's letter even mentioned him, although not by name: *Papa does so admire the American president and what he did for us.*

"Oh my God," she said. "That's it."

Roosevelt's first name was Theodore.

In Greek, "theo" meant "god." And "dore" meant "gift."

Of course, the girls couldn't tell their lovers the password was Alexei's nickname. If the letters were intercepted, former servants or courtiers could be consulted to get that information. But how many of those people shared Alexandra's religious fervor? How many would know the Greek origin of the American president's name?

"I know what it is," she said.

And in that instant, she knew what she had to do.

CHAPTER SIXTY

Vadim gripped the phone so tightly he worried it would break and disconnect the call. Simple humanitarianism wasn't working. It was time to try something more effective: greed. Without his daughter's password-cracking abilities, he would never have found the necessary information. *I thank God for you, Liliya,* he thought, *more than you know.*

"Your Excellency," he said, addressing the British prime minister directly. "I don't think you see how serious this is. Have you stopped to consider there might be more than money in the account?"

Davies paused. "What else could there be?"

Vadim pulled his purloined copy of the Rumkowski file from his briefcase. Rumkowski's infiltration of the Bank of

England remained a secret in the intelligence community, but the lies would end here, with him. "Gentlemen, let me tell you a story."

One of the Americans on the line coughed to cover up a click. *All the better,* he thought. *Let everyone hear the truth.*

"In 1921, a Cheka agent named Rumkowski recruited a small team to help him infiltrate a number of prominent European banks, including the Bank of England. Lenin authorized the mission, hoping they would be able to find what he had not — any remaining money belonging to the tsar … and millions of dollars of missing tsarist gold."

"Gold?" snapped Rockwell Marshall. "Primakov, you didn't tell me this had anything to do with gold."

"I shouldn't have had to. Tell your president to read J. Edgar Hoover's file on Admiral Kolchak's missing gold."

"Admiral Kit-Kat? What the hell are you talking about?"

"Kolchak was a former tsarist naval officer. He led the anti-Bolshevik resistance in Siberia from 1918 to early 1920. While this area was under his control, he seized the tsarist gold reserve in Kazan, worth $332 million. He used some of the gold to finance his fight against the Bolsheviks, but he couldn't hold the region. The Red Army closed in on him and he was eventually captured and executed. The counter-resistance fell apart and $120 million of the gold went missing. It vanished from a train headed to Irkutsk in December of 1919."

"Vanished?" Davies asked. "How can that much gold simply vanish?"

"It can't," Vadim said. "And Rumkowski knew it. He tracked down two of the soldiers who'd seen it last — the ones who had loaded the gold onto the train and traveled with Kolchak. He found them in a gulag, half-starved and near death. They told him the gold had vanished on a night Kolchak heard the Red Army was near. Kolchak fled for his life and left the gold behind. These two men remained at their post with the gold, hoping to bribe their way to freedom if the Red Army found them. Before the Red Army got to them, however, a man dressed as a tsarist officer came and offered them a hundred thousand rubles to sneak him onto the train and bring him a small list of items while on board. The soldiers accepted. They hid him in one of the cars and brought him what he asked for — black paint, white paint, and brushes."

"What the hell did he want with paint?"

"I think I see where this is going," Davies said.

"The missing $120 million in gold was nailed into the only storage containers Kolchak had on hand — coffins. The soldiers painted the coffins black and the tsarist officer labeled them with words in a language the soldiers couldn't read. When they had finished, the tsarist officer shot all four of the men. Two survived, but they were unconscious while the officer made off with the gold."

"Wait just a damn minute," said Rockwell Marshall. "How did one man lug that much gold off a train? And where did he put it?"

"Obviously it wasn't one man," Vadim snapped. "Imagine a guerilla warfare scenario, under the cover of darkness, with multiple armies fleeing and fighting and no one truly in charge. It was chaos. It would have been easy for a small band of men to cart off as much gold as would fit into the available supply of coffins, load it into a few trucks, and make their getaway before the Red Army stormed the train."

"But if the soldiers who survived couldn't read what went on the coffins, what did they tell Rumkowski about its destination? Why would Rumkowski assume the gold ended up in a bank instead of in the pockets of whoever took it?"

"Where could someone have stored that many tsarist gold bars without fear of them being stolen?" Vadim said. "Certainly not in Russia. They would have to go into a safe deposit box in a bank that could be trusted."

"More like a safe deposit room," said Gordon Wilson. "How much space does it take to store $120 million worth of gold?"

Vadim continued. "Russia's allies in the war were France and England. Although Russia had signed a treaty with Germany and exited the war, anti-German senti-ment remained high. Despite technically being at peace, Rumkowski guessed that no Russian would have put money in a German or Austrian bank."

"But how did he know the money was in England and not in France?"

"He didn't. He infiltrated Rothschilds and the Bank of France to rule them out."

Davies let out a long, low whistle.

Vadim smiled, accepting the praise for his long-dead countryman. "That's not the last of it. Rumkowski's team was able to place one operative inside the Bank of England, close to the governor, but he was never able to find evidence of a tsarist account. There were no written records of it anywhere."

"That settles it, then," Davies said. "Any account opened at the Bank of England would have a proper file, all of which are scrupulously maintained. If Rumkowski's agent didn't find the file, it's because it didn't exist. The gold isn't here, gentlemen, pure and simple."

Vadim set his trap. "Then why are you prepared to let Starinov murder three more people over a treasure trove that doesn't exist?"

CHAPTER SIXTY-ONE

"Did I hear that correctly?" Starinov asked. "Are you finally prepared to cooperate?" His black shoes clicked on the polished floor as he made his way toward her, followed by his last remaining guard. He pointed at Viktor and Constantine. "Get her up."

Constantine shoved Viktor away and picked Natalie up so gently she felt like she was flying. Still, the change in position made her dizzy and she tried to remember the last time they'd eaten. Constantine's cheeks were dark and hollow, and she felt a pang of guilt for what they'd all had to endure.

Starinov flicked back his sleeve to look at his watch. "We're behind schedule." He aimed his pistol at Beth's forehead. "Give me the password now or your sister dies."

Natalie looked up at the ceiling and did something she'd never done before. *Please God*, she prayed, *let me be doing the right thing.* "Roosevelt," she said. "The password is Roosevelt."

Starinov blinked, his pale face frozen in disbelief. "Roosevelt?"

She nodded. "Grand Duchess Marie's letter mentions her father's great respect for the American president after all he did for them at the end of the Russo-Japanese War. That was Roosevelt. The final peace negotiations were held at his estate, Sagamore Hill, in 1906. He even won a Nobel Peace Prize for it. The tsar always spoke fondly of Roosevelt and America. Where else would he send his children if things got bad?" She shrugged, as if she didn't care anymore. "The password is Roosevelt."

Starinov lowered his gun. "If you are lying to me, you will be the last to die. I will burn your sister and your lover alive while you watch."

"I did everything you asked," she said. "I don't have anything else to say to you."

"Surely it's better that way." Starinov reached for his phone and barked rapid commands in Russian. When he hung up, he pointed at the far wall. "This embassy is guarded by twelve men. If you try to leave this room, they will shoot on sight." He ordered his guard to strip the two dead bodies of their weapons, then headed for the door. Viktor hurried to follow.

"Where do you think you're going?" Starinov snapped.

"With you. Part of that money's going to be mine."

"A man who turns his coat once will never know when to stop." He snapped his fingers and the last bodyguard patted

Viktor down, taking his pistol. "I have no use for traitors like you." Then he left the room, closing the door behind him. They heard the shuffle of feet as a new set of guards took their place on the other side of the door.

Viktor froze, staring at the closed doors. Natalie felt no sympathy for him.

Suddenly, Beth's angry voice exploded into the air. "What the hell are you doing, Nat? I know you prefer to live in your head rather than the real world, but I have a son and I want to see him grow up! Why did you give him the name of my dog?"

Viktor spun on his heel. "What?" He charged her, holding out his hands as if he were ready to wrap them around her throat.

Constantine jumped in front of her and pushed Viktor back. "Of course she gave him the right password. Let him have the money, right?" He turned to face Natalie. "That's what you did, isn't it?"

This was the part she was afraid of. Her body ached with the pain of disappointing the only people who believed in her. How could she give that up, now, at the most important moment of her life?

She took a step backward. "No."

"Nat," Beth said. "Tell me that's not true."

Constantine reached toward her and took her face in his hands. "Natalia," he repeated. "You did give him the right password, didn't you?"

"No," she said. "I didn't."

CHAPTER SIXTY-TWO

Maxim Starinov slid into the backseat of the waiting limousine and barked at the driver to get moving. The man slammed the passenger door and hurried to the driver's seat. He started the car, switched on the headlights, and turned onto Palace Avenue. "Where do you wish to go, Your Excellency?"

"The Bank of England," Starinov replied. "Threadneedle Street."

"Right away, Your Excellency."

Two Russian flags mounted on the front corners of the hood flapped in the wind. Starinov watched them, feeling a surge of pride in his chest. *Russia will rise again,* he thought. *I will make her great. The tsar's fortune will rebuild my army, strengthen my borders, and crush anyone who stands in my way.*

I will be another Ivan, another Peter. They will write that I am Nicholas's true heir, the only one who could give Russia back to herself.

Nothing could stop him now.

CHAPTER SIXTY-THREE

Natalie saw Constantine set his jaw, clamping his mouth shut until he could speak without anger. His eyes, normally so warm when they looked at her, had turned cold. *Belial,* she asked, *how do I explain what hardly makes sense to me?*

But there was no answer.

She looked from Beth to Constantine, hoping for a glimmer of understanding, but all she saw was hurt. A flush of fear spread from her throat to her cheeks.

Beth shook her head. "Nat, they're going to kill us. Why would you let them do that?"

"I don't know how else to fight it."

"Fight what?"

"All the evil in the world."

"I don't understand," Constantine said. "What evil?"

"It's all around us," she said, glancing sideways at Viktor. "All people want to do is hurt each other and steal from each other. All they want is money. If they keep getting it, if they keep winning, they'll forget everything else. They'll forget who we are, who the Romanovs were. Belial says things are different now, that you can't count on people being good anymore. I'm scared to live in that world. I'm scared for Seth, who has to grow up in it." She shook her head. "But if we don't do anything to change it, or at least try, then we're a part of the evil, too."

She looked up at Constantine. "Can you understand?"

He pulled her into his arms and pressed her face to his chest. She felt his lips touch her hair, then her forehead. He smelled of sweat and leather and it made her feel at home.

"I understand," he said. "All you can do is what you believe in."

Viktor sighed. "Since when does fighting the good fight involve suicide? We're as good as dead unless that wing-flapping fairy godfather of hers can zap us out of here."

"We're not going to die," Constantine said.

"Four unarmed people against twelve guards?"

"We did it in Alkhan-Kala."

"Fighting is our only option," Beth said. "Besides, what are the odds Starinov was going to kill us even if Nat had given him the right password?"

Viktor curled his lip. "He knew about the Beslan school situation before it happened and didn't do a thing to stop it. If 180 butchered children don't keep him up at night, I'm guessing the four of us wouldn't pose a big moral dilemma."

"So what now?"

They all looked at Natalie, who turned her head away. "How should I know?"

"Nat, you're running the show," Beth said. "Does Belial have anything else to say?"

"No. I think it's just me now."

Belial shifted his wings but the pain was minimal compared to what she'd already dealt with. *That's not entirely true, little one.*

"It might as well be," she snapped at him. "Would it have killed you to just say 'Roosevelt'?"

You figured it out, didn't you? Just like you'll figure out whom to call for help.

"Who?"

The only person left.

Her mind raced through the images of bodies and blood she'd seen in the past few days. She thought of Yakov and Sergei and the nameless guards spilling bone and brain matter onto the floor around her. Yuri and Grigori, both killed for the good deeds of their ancestor. But there was one more — the person who blamed her for all of it. "Vadim," she said. "We need to call Vadim."

"Are you sure?" Constantine asked. "He's the one who gave us to Starinov."

"Hell, I'll do anything that might help us survive." Viktor pulled out his phone and tossed it to Constantine. "But I don't think I'm his favorite person right now."

"He's not *my* favorite person right now," Constantine said as he caught the phone. He dialed and put the call on speaker. It rang three times before Vadim accepted the call.

"Viktor," Vadim said. In the background, Natalie heard traffic noises. "Where are you? Is Starinov with you?"

"It's Constantine. We're trapped in the consulate in London. Starinov is on his way to the bank and when he gets back, he's not going to be happy. We need your help."

"I need yours first," Vadim said. "I have the British prime minister and two American ambassadors on hold. I've convinced them the tsar's account might exist, but now they think it's just a Russian matter. They're going to let him have it unless we can prove that Starinov has committed a crime on British soil."

"Starinov won't get the account," Constantine said. "Natalie gave him the wrong password. But when he finds out, he'll be mad as hell and we won't last long."

"The promise of a crime is not enough, I'm afraid. The British don't want to provoke an incident. Unless Starinov has killed a British citizen or one of your Americans, their prime minister won't lift a finger."

"Of course not," Natalie grumbled. "They wouldn't help Nicholas and Alexandra, so why would they help us?"

And then she sucked in her breath, whistling it through her front teeth. *That's it*, she thought. The story came together like a DNA helix, twisting and twining in her head until she had no idea how much she'd made up and how much was actually true.

She leaned over the phone and spoke. "Mr. Primakov, if I convince them to stop Starinov, will you send someone to get us out of here?"

Vadim hesitated. "Constantine, what is the *rusalka* talking about? How can she get them to stop Starinov?"

"Answer the question, Vadim."

"Of course, of course. I will send an extraction team for you."

"Then do exactly what she says."

She cast a glance at each of them in turn. "No one say a word about the wrong password. This only works if the British believe Starinov has the right one."

"Nat," Beth hissed. "What are you doing?"

"I'm solving the problem, Beth. Payback's a bitch and they've been earning interest for ninety years."

The speakerphone connection clicked and Vadim cleared his throat. "Gentlemen, we are now speaking with Prime Minister Starinov's captives, including the two American women."

"I am Prime Minister Davies," said a carefully modulated British voice. "Are you all unharmed?"

"Define harm," Beth said.

Natalie put a hand on Beth's arm. "Mr. Prime Minister, my name is Natalie Brandon. I'm a research assistant for my sister Elizabeth Brandon, a professor of history at Rosemont University. Vadim says you don't want to detain Starinov when he tries to access the Romanov account, but you're making a huge mistake."

Davies replied with no little hint of derision. "Do you care to explain yourself, Miss Brandon?"

"There's more than money in that account."

"So I gather. Although quite valuable, tsarist gold is no longer a British concern."

"That's not what I'm talking about." She tried as hard as she could to sound like Beth, lecturing a freshman Western

Civ class: no doubt, no hesitation, all confidence. "That account was opened under the name of Soloviev, with the intent of providing money for the tsar and his family if they were able to escape. When it was opened in late 1917, your king, George V, had already privately rescinded his offer of asylum to the Romanovs. He was afraid of Alexandra, who had a worse public approval rating than the builder of the *Titanic*. The Romanovs, however, were counting on that offer. They had nowhere else to go."

"Get to the point," Davies snapped. "This is all a matter of public record."

"The point, Mr. Davies, is that your Queen Mary bought a shitload of Russian jewelry for bargain basement prices, knowing the Russian émigrés needed money and had no power to bargain for what the jewelry was really worth. Are you with me so far?"

"Go on."

"What if I told you Mary sent a secret letter to Alexandra in 1917, offering asylum with herself and George if she and Nicholas could bring the crown jewels with them? What if I told you that letter included a list of pieces Mary wanted, including the Romanov nuptial tiara and diamond necklace? Your queen put a price tag on the Romanovs' safety, and it boiled down to their ability to extract hundreds of pounds of diamonds from the Provisional Government."

Beth gasped. "Natalie, what the hell are you — "

Natalie made a slashing motion across her throat and kept going. "And what if I told you that Alexandra kept that letter? What if, along with property deeds and a few stock certificates, Alexandra sent that letter into safe-keeping through Soloviev, just in case? I know Buckingham Palace is quite sensitive when it comes to George V and the Romanovs. What would it pay to keep hard proof of Mary's greed out of the press?"

"You've absolutely no proof," Davies said.

Natalie smiled. "Until we got our hands on the grand duchesses' letters, there was absolutely no proof this account existed, either. But it does. Are you willing to take the chance? Are you willing to give Starinov rock-solid proof that your queen's beloved grandmother was a cold-hearted bitch who cared more about discount diamonds than her own cousins?"

Davies swore. "Christ, no."

"Then do something about it. Stop Starinov from accessing that account."

Constantine grabbed the phone from her. "He's on his way to the Bank of England right now. He probably borrowed the ambassador's state car, so look for diplomatic plates and flags."

Beth took her turn next. "There are two dead bodies in the room with us, if that gives you any more of a reason to give a shit."

"We'll pick him up," Davies said quietly. "And send a team to collect you and the bodies."

"If you lose him, we're dead," Constantine said. "He's not going to go quietly."

"We'll handle it," Davies said. "Just sit tight."

CHAPTER SIXTY-FOUR

The intercom in the limousine crackled with static when he pushed the blue button. "Can't you go any faster?" Starinov snapped. "We should have been there by now."

"There's a problem, Your Excellency," Gennady replied. "There's someone following us. I tried to lose them, but they're still there."

"Them? How many?"

"I count three. Cars with tinted windows."

"Ignore them. We have diplomatic plates. They'll have to call for approval to stop us, and they won't get it. Just go."

"Yes, Your Excellency."

Starinov fell back against the seat as Gennady stepped on the gas. He wondered who the observers might be. MI6? Local police? Were they waiting to stop him until he'd come and gone from the bank? He'd already made arrangements for his plane to be refueled and waiting for him on the Farnborough airstrip. But the airport was at least thirty miles outside the city center. If he had to retrace his steps to the embassy, kill the hostages, and then get to the airstrip, it gave the British extra time to devise a way to detain him.

It wasn't smart.

No matter how entertaining it would have been to dangle his success in front of his captives before killing them, it was time to delegate.

He reached for his phone. "Igor Yegorovich," he said, addressing the colonel guarding the embassy.

"Yes, Your Excellency? What are your orders?"

"I will not be returning this evening after all. Kill them."

CHAPTER SIXTY-FIVE

Constantine tossed the phone back to Viktor. "I need a drink," he said, heading for the marble bar. He reached for a bottle and a glass and poured three fingers of whiskey.

"You and me both," Viktor added.

He still couldn't believe Natalie had bullied the British prime minister into doing exactly what she wanted. The web of words she'd spun to catch the wily diplomat made his head spin. Where had she come up with all that? It frightened him as much as it gave him hope. If Davies really could keep Starinov away from them, there was a chance they could get out alive. It never would have happened without Natalie.

"You owe her," he said to Viktor.

Viktor tapped the strip of tape over his nose. "We're not out of this yet, lamb."

"He's right," Beth said. "Nat, there's no way Buckingham Palace is going to believe your story."

"Wait just a bloody minute," Viktor said. "Are you saying all that rot about Queen Mary wasn't true?"

Natalie bit her lip. "She did buy some Russian jewels at cut-rate prices, both from the Soviet government and the tsar's sisters. I never liked her. She looks mean."

"So you slandered her? In front of a man who speaks to the queen on a daily basis?"

"It worked, didn't it? Mary was a greedy old cow and no one would believe a story like that if there weren't a grain of truth in it."

"But what if it doesn't work? What if Davies decides to let Starinov kill us?" Viktor asked.

"Why would he do that?"

"Think about it, you stupid girl! If he's willing to risk an international incident by arresting Starinov, what's to stop him from getting rid of a whole room full of people who heard the queen's dirty laundry being aired? You've only made things worse because now we don't know whether we're waiting to be rescued or killed!"

"But there is no dirty laundry! I made it all up!"

"Davies and Starinov don't know that," Beth said, eyes clouding over. "What if Davies gets to Starinov and Starinov offers him some sort of deal? Mary's letter for our lives? We'll be dead before anyone even finds out there is no letter."

Constantine felt Natalie's gaze on him, her pale eyes wide with renewed fear. "Can we get out of here?" she asked.

Constantine ran the odds: twelve armed men and a secure perimeter against four unarmed people, two of them women. He caught Viktor's eye and saw the same calculation in his dispirited gaze. "Probably not."

"I thought I was doing the right thing!" Natalie said.

His heart clenched within his chest. At least she'd made an attempt to save them. No one else had done any better. "You did," he said. "If Davies refused to pick up Starinov, we were dead anyway. You bought us some time."

"Time to think about how we're going to die," Viktor mumbled.

Suddenly, Constantine heard rubber boot soles squeaking on marble. He pointed at the ballroom doors. They heard the harsh crackle of a comlink and a few metallic clicks as the guards disengaged their safeties.

"Time's up," Beth said.

He scanned the room, looking for something to use as a distraction. Then his eyes landed on one of the dead guards. "Komsomolskoye," he said to Viktor.

During one of their early Stealth missions, a group of Chechen rebels had barricaded themselves inside a house, using a stack of their own dead and wounded to hold the doors shut. As the Russians worked to push through the blocked door, the rebels had picked them off one by one, crouched behind the corpses of their comrades.

Viktor's head snapped up. "Do you think it can work?"

"We retreated, didn't we?" He sprinted across the room and dragged one body in front of the double doors. Viktor did the same with the second body. It wasn't much, but the bodies would keep the doors from swinging open right away.

"Viktor, you take the door on the left. I'll cover the one on the right. Natalie, Beth — get behind the bar and stay there."

He took up his position, with Viktor on the opposite side.

"Just like old times," Viktor said.

Constantine looked at his friend. He saw the same black hair, same dark eyes, same ruddy lips. Why couldn't there be a sign when the soul behind familiar features turned black? "Except this time," he said, "I know you're a traitor."

A burst of gunfire sprayed the flimsy locks and a booted foot kicked at one of the doors. The door slammed into the pile of bodies and moved a few inches. Constantine heard the commander on the other side order the first two men to go through. They turned sideways to slink through the opening.

"Now!" Constantine yelled. He and Viktor pounced, yanking the guards inside and kicking the double doors shut behind them. They wrenched the guns from the men's hands and fired. Two more bodies slumped to the floor.

He could hear the consternation in the hall outside. The other guards hadn't expected resistance, but they would only be stunned for a moment. He dropped to his knees and pushed the growing collection of bodies closer to the door.

"That won't hold for more than a few seconds," Viktor said.

"It doesn't have to. If that door starts to move, we fire. They'll back off." He retrieved the dead guard's PP90 and scuttled around the bar to the women, huddled in each other's arms. "Are you all right?"

"We're fine," Beth said. "What's the plan?"

"Hold out as long as we can. Davies said he'd send a team and so did Vadim. Even if only one of them does, someone should come for us."

"And if they don't?"

"They will," he said. "They have to."

CHAPTER SIXTY-SIX

The limo sped around the corner, fishtailing as the driver struggled to stay in his lane. The motion threw Starinov sideways, sloshing the vodka in his hand. He righted himself and pressed the intercom. "What the hell are you doing? I told you to go faster, not drive like a drunken dog!"

"It's the cars, Your Excellency. They're getting closer. I thought I could lose them, but they're still there."

Starinov spun around and counted three BMW 760Li sedans with tinted windows, all speeding toward him. "*Govno*," he swore. "If you stop this car before we get to the bank, I will put a bullet in your head. Do you understand?"

"Y–yes, Your Excellency." Gennady sped up and the car flew down the Embankment, the lights on the water rushing past them like comets.

Let them try and stop me, he thought. *I am a prime minister, a ruler in my own right.*

He sat back, satisfied. Everyone who knew about the Romanov account would soon be dead, except for Vadim and he was already broken. The moment Vadim said or did anything that irritated him, he would order him and his thieving daughter to be thrown into the Moskva River.

There were no more obstacles. He had conquered them all.

CHAPTER SIXTY-SEVEN

Staccato blasts of gunfire erupted on the street outside.

"Listen," Constantine said. Had someone finally come to their rescue? Would the guards on the other side of the door defend themselves or slaughter the captives to keep them from escaping?

Viktor dashed from the door to the bar. "What is it?"

"The cavalry's coming."

Natalie shook her head. "Don't say that."

"That's a good thing, you daft cow," said Viktor, crouching next to Beth.

"No, it's not! It's why they killed Nicholas II. The White Army was closing in and the Soviets couldn't risk him being rescued."

"You just love being the bearer of good news, don't you, darling?"

Another burst of gunfire split the night. Someone on the other side of the double doors barked an order and several pairs of boots squeaked away.

Constantine fought the urge to smile. "They're sending some of the men outside. They're just as confused as we are."

"Should we run for it?" Natalie asked.

"Not yet," said Viktor. He threw an arm around Beth's neck and pointed his pistol at Constantine. "We have some unfinished business to take care of."

"Viktor!" Natalie cried. "What are you doing?"

"I'm just being me, lamb."

Beth's wide eyes looked up at Viktor as she clawed at the arm around her neck. "You asshole!"

First Marya, now Beth. Anger shook Constantine's body until even his thoughts came out with a stutter.

"Put the gun down, Con," Viktor said.

It took all his willpower not to aim at Viktor's head and shoot until nothing was left but a bloody pulp. "Even if you kill us," he said, "Starinov's guards will mow you down the second you touch that door."

"Money has a lovely way of changing people's minds."

"There won't be any money," Natalie said. "I gave Starinov the wrong password, remember?"

Viktor cocked his head. "I don't think you did, love. I think you gave him the right password and lied to us to cover it up."

Beth gulped, still struggling in Viktor's grasp. "Nat wouldn't do that."

"Think about it," Viktor said. "Your nut-job sister didn't even know that old man in the nursing home, and she went berserk on Yakov for killing him. Do you really think she'd sign her own sister's death warrant to uphold a ridiculous set of principles?" Viktor shoved the muzzle of the gun into Beth's back. "Now for the last time, Constantine, put the gun down."

Constantine set the PP90 on the floor and kicked it behind Viktor.

"Now go unblock the door," Viktor ordered. He pushed Beth forward with the muzzle of the gun. "You help him."

"No!" Natalie cried. "They'll get shot!"

"Better them than me."

Constantine imagined snapping Viktor's spine. The pop would echo against the polished floor. It would sound so harmless, like a soda can being opened. "You will never leave this room," he said softly.

"Neither will you." Viktor shrugged. "Perhaps that's enough."

"I never hurt you, Viktor."

"I never said you did."

"Then why?"

"You exist." Viktor shook his head. "There's only one way to win and I learned it at a very early age. Let the rest of you struggle like ants carrying anteaters, sagging under the weight of things you never learned to let go."

"It's called humanity," Natalie said.

"I think you mean insanity, lamb." He aimed the gun at Beth. "Now go, both of you."

Constantine and Beth stepped toward the bodies blocking the doors. "Quietly," he whispered to her. "I'll try to pull them all away at once. Don't let any part of them touch the door. If the guards see movement, they'll shoot."

He grabbed a wrist and a leg of the body on the bottom, pulling the whole stack away from the door. One of the topmost body's legs fell sideways. Beth reached, but she was too late. One leg brushed the door, rattling it slightly.

Constantine closed his eyes and ducked, waiting for the whine of bullets.

It didn't come.

He rose out of his crouch and met Beth's frightened eyes. "Keep going," he whispered. "We'll move one at a time."

Beth nodded and leaned over the topmost body, grabbing its wrists as he grabbed the feet. The dead man's jacket rode up, exposing a swath of white stomach and a black leather belt. Constantine narrowed his eyes. He'd killed with less and there weren't many options left.

He caught Beth's eye and mouthed the word "distraction." Instantly, Beth dropped the dead man's wrists. She staggered toward Natalie and unleashed a flood of tears. "I can't do this, Nat," she sobbed. "You have to tell him the truth."

"Truth?" asked Viktor. "What truth?"

Natalie popped up from behind the bar. "Yeah, what truth?"

Beth sniffed and wiped her nose with her hands. "I can't take it anymore. All you have to do is tell him the other part of the password."

While all eyes were on Beth, Constantine stepped around the pile of bodies, moving toward the topmost body's torso.

"Don't you understand?" Beth cried. "I want to see my son! I want to go home!"

"Beth, what are you talking about?"

"This is just like you, Nat. You're always telling half the truth. If you told your shrinks everything, they might be able to help you. Don't you get tired of living in your head? Doesn't it feel like a prison? There are people who can help you. Why won't you just let them?" She threw her arms down onto the bar and buried her head in them, sobbing.

Constantine suppressed a grim smile. Beth probably had Natalie in agony. He kept his head down and moved one hand toward the dead man's belt clasp.

"Beth, don't cry, please," Natalie said. "I can fix this! Just tell me what you're talking about."

Out of the corner of his eye, he saw Viktor point the gun at Natalie. "What is she talking about? *Half* the password?"

"I don't know," she whispered. "I swear, I don't know."

Viktor let loose a frustrated roar. "Jesus, Mary, and Joseph! What the hell is *wrong* with you people?"

Constantine's fingers slid the dead man's belt from his waist. He gripped the tail end in his palm and wrapped it around his closed fist. If he kept his arm low and close to his body, there was a chance Viktor wouldn't see it until it was too late.

"Give me the whole password!" Viktor said, gripping the gun with both hands and pointing it at Natalie.

"I can't," she sobbed. "I don't know what she's talking about!"

"Tell me!"

Constantine grasped the belt in both hands and leapt at Viktor, looping the leather around his neck. He pulled it tight and jerked backwards. "Natalie, move!" he yelled.

Viktor pulled the trigger. Bullets splintered the bar and ricocheted into plaster and mirrors. Constantine crossed his hands, straining to shrink Viktor's airway.

Natalie dropped to her knees and crawled toward the PP90 Constantine had surrendered earlier. Viktor realized what she was after and shifted his aim. Beth screamed and ducked, but Natalie kept crawling for the gun.

"Got it!" she cried.

It didn't matter. Constantine felt Viktor's flailing kicks and knew they were powered by a desperate flicker of lightning in his veins, the last effort a body could make to save itself. For the space of a heartbeat, he considered letting go. He could shoot Viktor in the leg, immobilize him, and simply walk away. But that would violate the code of soldiers, written in blood on their bones, tissues, skin and sinew. They knew what it was like to stare into a man's eyes as he died, pinpointing the moment he *is* and then the moment he *is not*. They knew how to cause that moment, how to speed it up or slow it down. They were never supposed to bring it on one of their own.

But Viktor had.

Constantine thought about every shot Viktor had fired while standing behind him. How many of those shots had been meant for him?

He jerked the belt as tight as he could. "See you in hell," he said.

CHAPTER
SIXTY-EIGHT

JULY 2013
LONDON, ENGLAND

The BMW sped up along the limousine's left flank and steered into them. Gennady counter-steered to the left to avoid a deadly spiral. He eased off the gas and waited for the car to stabilize. Sweat gathered beneath his arms as he scanned his mirrors.

"What are you waiting for?" Starinov yelled from the back. The prime minister pulled a gun from his waistband and shot through the glass separating them.

Gennady ducked, avoiding the shot and the spray of glass. His hands jerked the steering wheel and the limo struck a second BMW on its right side. The BMW dropped back, then tapped the limo's bumper and floored it, nudging it into a spin. Gennady tried to correct the spin, but momentum was already working against the long, heavy vehicle.

It teetered on two wheels, then flipped onto its roof, skidding down the street and plowing through mailboxes and bike racks. Gennady let go of the wheel and covered his neck with his hands. When the car struck a building, he was thrown against the wheel. He felt it strike his head, twist his neck, and then the world went black.

CHAPTER SIXTY-NINE

Viktor made one last desperate kick, then his body went limp, held up only by the belt in Constantine's grip. Natalie stared at the red, panicked man with clawed hands tearing at his own throat. The raw flesh ballooned over the belt, like a woman's flesh spilling up out of a corset.

Belial shivered. *I tried to read him,* he said, *but everything inside was black.*

The words of Psalm 23 sprang to her mind, but she quashed the impulse. Viktor didn't deserve them.

"Is he dead?" Beth asked, calmly wiping her face with her sleeve.

Constantine let Viktor's body crumple to the floor and picked up the second gun. "Get behind the bar. This isn't over."

"Ignore everything I said, Nat." Beth gripped her sister's elbow and guided her behind their marble shelter. "Constantine needed a distraction."

"You scared the shit out of me!"

"Bet you forgot I was the president of the drama club in high school."

Natalie squeezed her sister's hand and turned to Constantine. "Are you all right?"

He looked down at his palms, scraped raw by pulling on the belt. "I should have seen what he really was."

"You saw what was good in him, just like you see what's good in me. You couldn't have helped him."

"No, but I could have killed him a hell of a lot earlier."

"Beth and I are only alive because of you." She touched his arm. "Thank you."

"So what happens next?" Beth asked. "Is this a Butch and Sundance thing now?"

Constantine shook his head. "We wait and hope that whoever's out there can overpower Starinov's men. If they can't..."

Beth nodded. "Then it's time for the Oscar-winning goodbye speech."

Natalie looked at her sister, dirt-streaked and bloodstained and blonde and petite, holding a gun as if she actually knew how to use it. *She would do anything for you,* Belial said. *You know that, don't you, little one?*

I do, Natalie thought. She rested her head on her sister's shoulder. "Beth, I love you."

Beth pressed her lips to Natalie's forehead. "I love you, too, babe."

"I missed Shark Week. Seth is going to kill me."

"He'll forgive you," Beth said. "Or he's grounded."

"Someone's coming," Constantine said. He crouched and leaned around the side of the bar, aiming at the door. "Stay back."

"The hell I will," Beth said, mirroring his position on the other side of the bar.

Natalie heard sharp commands in Russian followed by the slick sound of nylon straps sliding off ballistic vests. From the other side of the door, the crack of breaking glass erased the silence. Gunfire erupted and voices speaking English demanded surrender.

"Davies's men!" she cried.

"Wait until they've subdued the guards." Constantine held his position, gun aimed at the door. "I don't trust them yet."

Natalie nodded and listened for the sounds of the British soldiers as they shouted orders at Starinov's guards. "On your knees! Hands on your head! Drop your weapons!"

A soldier in black vest and pants kicked open one of the ballroom's doors. Splinters rained over the pile of stacked bodies and the soldier stepped backward. He held a semiautomatic rifle at eye level, making a visual sweep of the room.

"We're over here!" Beth called.

The soldier whipped his head in their direction, stepping around the pile of bodies. "Come out slowly with your hands on your head."

Natalie looked to Constantine, who nodded. He tossed the PP90 on the floor and Beth followed suit.

"Which one of you is Natalie Brandon?" the soldier asked.

"I am," she answered.

"We have orders to bring you to the Bank of England."

"Whose orders?" Beth said. "Is Starinov there?"

Two more men ran in behind him with rifles raised high. They swept the room, covering every corner before pronouncing the room clear. "Jesus," one of them said, eyes following the trail of bloodstains across the floor that marked the paths of the dead. "What the hell happened here?"

Constantine cleared his throat. "My name is Constantine Dashkov. I'm with the Public Security Intelligence Bureau of the Russian Federation. Where is Prime Minister Starinov?"

The first soldier held out his hand out for Natalie. "Come with us, miss."

She shook her head and stepped away. "I'm not going anywhere without Beth and Constantine. If you want me, they come, too."

The soldier lowered his rifle and spoke into the comlink on his collar. A second later the answer came crackling through. "Come on, then. There's a vehicle waiting outside."

"This is it," she said, looking up at Constantine. She slipped one hand into his grasp and the other into Beth's. The soldiers marched them through the embassy to the driveway, where a black SUV waited. They climbed in, followed by five armed men, and the vehicle sped off through the dark streets of London toward Threadneedle Street.

Natalie watched the narrow storefronts fly by, convenience stores and pubs and coffee shops. She closed her eyes and waited for Belial to shake his wings or shuffle his feet. But he didn't. He was at rest and she realized, with a shock, that she felt no fear: no sweaty palms, no butterflies, no dry mouth.

You have nothing more to fear, Belial answered. *You already know what you'll be asked to do. And you already know what your answer will be.*

"Smart ass," she muttered.

The man sitting next to her turned his head. "Beg your pardon?"

"I wasn't talking to you. I was talking to Belial."

"Don't ask," Beth said. "Just go with it."

The man nodded.

Twelve minutes later, the vehicle pulled up at the steps of a large columned building with a triangular cornice. Another group of soldiers surrounded the vehicle as it pulled up. Each man held a gun, and they converged on the SUV as it parked.

"This isn't a welcoming committee, is it?" Natalie asked.

"This kind of shit doesn't happen to botanists," Beth said. "Why didn't I become a botanist?"

"Botanists don't make history, Beth. Besides, Belial says we have nothing to worry about."

"That's not helping me."

"They have guns and we don't," Constantine said. "That's not helping *me*."

"Belial's right," Natalie said. "I can feel it. We've come this far—we can't stop now." She followed the soldier out of the vehicle without waiting to see whether Beth or Constantine followed her.

CHAPTER SEVENTY

JULY 2013
LONDON, ENGLAND

It was long after business hours. The bank sat empty and forlorn, its cavernous entrance veiled in darkness. For a split second, Natalie wondered what would happen if Belial was wrong. What if there were plenty of things left to fear?

No, she told herself. *It's time to stop being afraid.*

A thin man with white hair stepped out of the shadows. Deep pockets of reddened skin had settled beneath his eyes like a ship's ballast. He wore a navy suit with a yellow bow tie and pocket square. "Good evening," he said, looking them up and down. "Or perhaps good morning? I don't suppose the three of you would know."

"I don't suppose the three of us would care," Beth said.

The man pointed at Natalie's neck, still stained with blood from her torn earlobe. "Are you in need of medical care, miss?"

"It's self-inflicted. Thanks, though."

One white eyebrow rose toward the ceiling. "Of course. I am Algernon Perry, governor of this bank. I believe you know why you are here."

"I don't know anything except that people have been chasing me and shooting at me for a week straight. Belial is tired of it and so am I."

"Belial?"

"Don't ask," Constantine said. "Just go with it."

Perry blinked and nodded. "You are here because Prime Minister Davies has instructed me to give you access to a certain account, provided you have the correct password."

Shit, Natalie thought. *I still don't even know if I'm right.* "About that… I have a little confession to make."

Beth grabbed her arm. "Nat, now is not the time."

"We're in the bank, Beth. I'd say now is the perfect time."

"Perhaps," Perry interrupted, "until you're sure of the time, you'd be good enough to follow me?"

Natalie glanced back at the entrance, where the convoy remained with guns drawn and vehicle lights flashing. She gulped and followed the white-haired man across the foyer. "Mr. Perry, do you know what this is about?"

"Of course," he said. "You must understand, we have discouraged many inquiries about this account over the years. Most of them are harmless and come from reporters or authors. Some of them are less well-intentioned, like the Soviet incursion in the 1930s."

"Rumkowski," Constantine said. "We were told that one of his men got into the bank as an employee, but could never find the account itself or any written proof that it existed."

"Correct."

"But that makes no sense," Beth argued. "Doesn't every account need paperwork or at least a signature? Even this goddamn password needs to be written down somewhere, doesn't it?"

Perry turned in mid-step, eyes twinkling. "One would think that, wouldn't one?"

She glared back at him. "I'm glad you find this all so amusing. Every official statement of yours I've ever read denies the existence of any tsarist funds. How many people have you lied to about this money?"

"People have a hard time taking no for an answer."

"Why shouldn't they, especially when they're right? How have you kept this enormous lie intact for all these years?"

"How would anyone know it's a lie if there's no paperwork to be found? Any bank employee, even a vice-president, would find no evidence to prove such an account exists. When they denied the existence of the account, they weren't lying. They were simply reporting the truth as they saw it."

"So who does know the truth?"

He stopped in front of a brass-paneled elevator and made a polite half-bow. "Only the sitting governor."

"Not the prime minister?"

"Goodness, no. Why bring politics into it?" Perry pulled an electronic passkey from his vest pocket and used it to unlock the elevator. "Follow me, if you please."

The elevator opened and they filed in. Perry pulled up his identification badge and held it in front of a sealed metal panel in the elevator wall. He pressed it there for five seconds, palm against the badge. Suddenly, the panel began to glow as an intense light shone out from behind it.

"Biometrics," he said. "Combined with nanotechnology and a good old-fashioned X-ray. I don't understand a bit of it."

The panel beeped and the governor removed his palm and the badge. The metallic panel popped open, revealing another set of buttons. He pressed the bottom button and re-latched the panel.

Beth watched his movements with a pale face. "You're going to have to kill us now, aren't you?"

"If you were going to be killed, madam, I would have asked that it be done as far away from me as possible."

The elevator descended quickly, jolting Natalie's stomach. She took a deep breath, but there was still no flutter from Belial's wings. *What the hell is wrong with you?* she asked. *Are you even paying attention?*

It's all right, little one, he answered. *You'll be all right.*

Clanking and rattling, the elevator flew down an endless shaft. When it was pulled to a stop by a great squeak and clank of cables, the doors opened and revealed a dim hallway with sound-absorbent tiles on the roof and pendant light fixtures that looked like leftovers from a World War II army base. The air was chilly and damp, the cement beneath their feet littered with debris.

Perry turned left and proceeded down the hallway, stepping over the detritus in his path. She followed him until he stopped in front of a metal door with a tarnished brass knob. He reached into his pants pocket and drew out a single key. Long and old, it looked like it was made from the same brass as the doorknob itself.

"How old is that?" she asked.

"Seventy-three years," he answered. "We rebuilt this bunker in 1938, when we knew war was inevitable. It withstood the Blitz, which was all we asked of it."

"And now?"

"Now it is up to you," he said, looking at her. "I am told by the prime minister that you are the one with the password. If you are correct, this key is yours."

"And if I'm wrong?"

"I take you back upstairs and the men with guns put you on a plane." He pointed to a thin series of red wires strung over the doorway. "Then I destroy the contents of this room. There will be a press release from Downing Street that describes the unfortunate death of Prime Minister Starinov when his driver lost control of their car. I point out what a tragedy it is that the man died while harassing the bank yet again about a tsarist account that simply does not exist. In the spirit of transparency and cooperation, I may even make public our records from the Great War, to put to rest once and for all the possibility of any secret account."

"What if I tell the world you're lying?"

Perry shrugged. "You have no proof. You are here without passports, I am told, so there is no official record of your entry to Britain. I can destroy or replace any bank security footage that includes you. The only people who have seen you are now dead, in custody, or are British soldiers who will do exactly as they are told."

"Wait a minute," Constantine said. "Starinov is dead? Is that true?"

"It is," Perry said. "He was pronounced dead not half an hour ago at the Royal London Hospital, while you were en route. Davies will release a statement shortly, no matter what happens here."

Constantine grasped Natalie's shoulders. "Did you hear that? No matter what happens here, Starinov can't hurt you again."

Her whole body shook with relief. Now Beth and Seth would be safe. No more Vympel breaking into apartments and dragging people away into the night. She stared at the door and wondered why she felt nothing, no hint of angelic excitement or inspiration. Inside, she just felt numb. "What happens to the things in that room?"

"The tsar's instructions are ironclad: no one shall claim the contents except the first person to give the correct password."

"Hold the phone," she said. "The *tsar's* instructions? I thought Soloviev set up the account while the tsar was in custody in Russia."

Perry smiled. "I see you only know part of the story. The account opened by Mr. Soloviev was ancillary to the primary account, which was set up by the tsar himself, through his finance minister Sir Peter Bark. After the tsar's untimely death, Bark collapsed the accounts under Soloviev's name, in the interests of security."

Beth frowned. "But Nicholas and Bark never saw each other again after February of 1917. We know the Soloviev account couldn't have been set up before late 1917. When was the primary account set up?"

"I've seen it myself," Perry said. "The date on the charter of the first account is 1916. It was written by Nicholas II and witnessed by Empress Alexandra and her brother, Grand Duke Ernst of Hesse."

"That's impossible," Constantine said. "Russia and Germany were at war in 1916."

"Holy shit," Natalie breathed, clutching Constantine's wrist. "Anna Anderson was right! Beth, she was right!"

"Nat, what are you talking about? That crackpot wasn't right about anything, not even her own name. The DNA tests proved she wasn't Anastasia."

"But do you remember what she said? She said Anastasia's uncle, Ernst of Hesse, made a secret trip to Russia in 1916 to try and work out a peace treaty between Germany and Russia. It would have taken Russia out of the war, leaving England and France as sitting ducks. She said Nicholas refused because he was honor-bound by his agreements to the Allies. When Anderson's claim became public knowledge, everyone freaked out … especially Ernie and his relatives in Germany. Why would they have cared, unless it were the truth?"

"So where'd she get that information?"

"Someone fed it to her." Natalie started to pace, her brain whirring like a computer scanning for a virus. "So Nicholas refuses to make a separate peace with Germany, but he understands Ernie's concern about the terrible state Russia is in. He tells Ernie he's going to set aside enough money to take care of them should anything happen. Ernie witnesses the charter for this secret account, and Bark sets it up through the old-boy network. The tsar tells Bark the password, and Bark tells the governor of the bank. Each governor tells the next, like some sick Masonic ritual." She turned to Perry. "Is that how it happened?"

"I wasn't there, my dear. How could I know for sure?"

Beth narrowed her eyes at the old man. "You said you've seen the date on the charter. How?"

"The charter still exists. It is shown to each new bank governor when he assumes the post."

"By whom?"

Perry's lips twisted into a smile. "Whom do you think? The reigning sovereign, of course."

Natalie smacked her forehead. "Of course! Bark smuggled the charter to England and showed it to George V, didn't he? That's why there's no record of it in the bank. They keep it at Buckingham."

Perry nodded. "The charter and the password are separate entities. Her Majesty has custody of the charter, but no access to the password."

"Yet she's helped keep the secret," Beth said. "Why?"

"Her grandfather, George V, wanted it that way. Nicholas II wished the account to be kept secret and His Majesty honored his cousin's wishes. So has every reigning monarch since."

"That makes sense," Constantine said. "The brief I read said that Nicholas repatriated all his money in 1914 and ordered his family to do the same. He wouldn't want anyone knowing he was secretly hedging his bets."

Natalie nodded and looked Perry in the eye. Soft and rheumy, they were the color of cornflowers. They had once been the color of cold steel. "So you're the only person on earth who knows the password. What if you died without telling the next director what it is?"

"Then it all dies with me."

"What a waste," Beth said.

"I prefer to think of it as a tradition and an honor," Perry said dryly. He pulled a sealed envelope from his pocket. "While I waited for you to arrive, I wrote the password on a card and sealed it in this envelope. You tell me the password, and I'll open the envelope. If you're right, I will give you the key." He held up the slim piece of metal.

Natalie slipped her hand in Constantine's and felt his strong fingers wrap around hers. She thought of Nicholas and Alexandra, how they had stood by each other to their deaths, in love until the very end. She thought of poor Marie, how all she'd wanted was the chance to do what her parents had done — find the love of her life. *Everything about this family hurts*, she thought. *Even their love aches. I'm just a nobody with voices in my head. Why should I get to do this?*

"I can't," she said. "It's too much."

Constantine tilted her chin and kissed her gently on the forehead, cheeks, and finally, on her lips. "The stars aligned for this. Those letters made their way to you. I made my way to you. If not for this, what was it all for?"

"Nat, you can do this," Beth said. "It's time for this to end. All their bones have been found. This is the one thing they can't get away from. End it for them and let them rest."

Tears pricked her eyes and she blinked them away. "All right," she said. "Let it end. The password is Theodore."

CHAPTER
SEVENTY-ONE

"Theodore?" Beth said softly. "Are you sure?"

Natalie nodded. "That part of what I told Starinov was the truth. The clue in Marie's letter really did refer to President Roosevelt."

"I don't get it," Constantine said. "Why would the tsar use the name of the American president as his password?"

"It's more than a name. If you break it up into its original Greek components, it means 'gift of God.' It's what they called Alexei, their miracle baby. The only thing the tsar's money couldn't buy him."

Perry opened the envelope and pulled out the card inside.

Told you so, Belial said.

Constantine looked to Perry. "What happens now? Does she get the key?"

"This?" he said, holding it up. "This is worthless. This isn't even the vault. This is where we store the rubbish."

"You tricked us?" Natalie said.

Perry straightened his bow tie. "My bank has kept this secret for almost a hundred years. Did you really think I would lead you to its very door and hold out the very key you needed to unlock it, when all you had to do was knock me down and take it?"

Natalie felt her cheeks burn. "It does sound stupid when you say it like that."

"Come," Perry said. "I'll take you to the real thing."

He led them back to the elevator. This time, he took them two floors up, to another long and dim hallway. It looked just like the hall they'd come from, with one exception — Natalie noticed one door had plastic casings around it and a metal keypad.

Perry typed a long string of numbers into the keypad. It beeped and flashed a green light. "Go ahead, miss," Perry said.

Natalie grasped the doorknob. *I can't believe I'm doing this,* she thought. *This isn't real.*

She turned the knob and opened the door. Two walls of the windowless room were stacked floor to ceiling with gold bars. They reflected the dim light, producing an amber halo. The third wall held a metal shelf with several strongboxes.

"Jesus," Beth said. "What is all this?"

"Kolchak's gold," Natalie breathed. "Soloviev stole it from Kolchak, who stole it from the Soviets, who stole it from Nicholas!"

"Good God, how much did he steal?"

"They took $330 million from the reserve in Kazan. No one ever found the last hundred million or so."

"Until now," Constantine said. "Natalie, you did it."

"Unbelievable," Perry breathed.

"Rumkowski wasn't looking for the tsar's account," Constantine said, staring at the gold in wonder. "He was looking for Kolchak's gold. He knew they were connected."

"What's in those boxes?" Beth asked, pointing.

"Let's find out," Natalie said.

Constantine reached up to grab them and then set them on the floor. Natalie sank to her knees. She undid the latch of the first box and lifted the lid. Dark velvet pouches lay huddled together. She picked one up and pulled it open, revealing a small sea of uncut diamonds. The second revealed a diamond tiara, emerald brooch, ruby necklace, and diamond earrings. "This is the jewelry they smuggled out through Soloviev," she said. "They thought he would sell it and use the money to rescue them, but he deposited it."

"They'll be worth millions," Perry said.

Instantly, she put a hand over the brooch already attached to her blouse. The pieces from Grigori's cache were hers. She would never let anyone take them from her. But the treasures in this box belonged in a museum, somewhere they could be seen by everyone. They had nothing to do with her or Beth or Constantine. They hadn't been stained with her blood. They were still pure.

She set the box of jewelry aside and reached for the second. Stuffed inside were thick stacks of tsarist rubles and stacks of British World War I bond certificates, with denominations from £100 to £1,000.

The tsarist currency was worthless now, but it would have meant life and freedom to someone who'd escaped Bolshevik captivity. "This is the money Soloviev collected," she said, holding her hand over the rubles. "The money people said he stole from them."

The sight of those crumpled bills took her breath away. Real people had given money to try and save the tsar and his family. Those rubles were hope and good wishes and prayers, none of which came true. If they hadn't been locked inside a box, would they have made a difference?

She gulped and set them aside. "Perry, are these bonds worth anything?"

"Let me see them," he said.

She handed him one stack and he pulled a note loose, inspecting it on both sides. "These aren't the typical war bonds we see in the collections of investors. Those were all issued in late 1917. This looks to be a sort of pre-issue designed on the same principle as the public bonds. The king may have had these privately printed for the tsar. I've never seen anything like it."

"I have a kid to put through college," Beth said. "How much are they worth?"

"I can't give you a firm answer without calculating inflation, deflation, and the interest rate. But public war bonds are being sold and redeemed at around seventy-five percent of their face value."

"Harvard it is," Natalie said, handing Beth an inch-thick stack of £1,000 bonds. "I think Nicholas would approve of a boy getting a good education."

There was one box left and she twisted its latch slowly, almost afraid of what she would find inside. It was nearly empty, containing only a few yellowed sheets of paper tucked beneath two jewel-encrusted photo frames.

She picked up the first frame, encasing a snapshot of Nicholas and Alexandra as newlyweds. Alexandra smiled at the camera, while Nicholas stared at her in wonder. "Alix never smiled," she said, wanting to touch the image and feel the warmth it conveyed.

The next frame held a photo of the children, all five of them. From their ages, Natalie guessed it had been taken in 1912 or 1913. "They're so young," she said, looking at Anastasia's chubby cheeks. She looked at Marie, with her radiant eyes and thick, dark hair spilling over her shoulders. "You can't even dream of what will happen to you, can you?"

Natalie put the picture down, afraid to look at it with the terrible knowledge of how they died. She lifted out the remaining pieces of paper. Two of them were in Russian. "I can't read this," she said, passing them to Constantine. "What do they say?"

He scanned them quickly. "They're deeds to gold mines. One in Nertchinsk and one in Altai. What are the ones in your hand?"

"Property deeds. One in France, one in England. I don't think they're valid. Lenin nationalized all Nicholas's property, at home and abroad, a few days before he killed them."

"It breaks your heart, doesn't it?" Beth said. "This is all that's left of them. A few crumpled papers that don't mean anything anymore."

"What about the gold?" Perry asked. "That's worth something."

"I don't care about the gold," Natalie said. "It didn't help them. It can't bring them back."

"No," Beth said, "but it can help lots of other people. Nat, think what you can do with all this. Charities, scholarships, medical research…this makes the university's endowment look like chump change."

Natalie lifted the last piece of paper from the box. It was covered with spiky writing, in English, and it rested on top of a slim envelope. She glanced down at the signature. "This one's from Peter Bark."

She read the letter through. "This is all that's left of the primary account, the one opened in 1916," she said, grasping the envelope. "Bark ordered it cashed it out in 1920 because news of the tsar's death was widespread by then. He writes that the money came from a diversion of proceeds of gold bars sold to the English to aid the war effort. He says he's leaving it in this master account in case any of the survival rumors are true and a child of the tsar's can claim it."

Natalie opened the envelope. Tucked inside was a single folded piece of paper. She unfolded it and started to choke. It was a cashier's check for £15 million. Her hands began to shake and Constantine took the paper from her. He looked at the amount and whistled.

"I don't even know what these numbers mean," she said. "What do I do?"

"I can't tell you that, sweetie," Beth answered.

She felt her head begin to throb. "I'm not the right person for this. None of this belongs to me. It should have gone to them…to save them." She imagined a rescue effort, purchased with the millions lodged here in this room, and the thought alone overwhelmed her. Why should anyone's survival be so dependent on pieces of pressed metal and paper?

She turned into Constantine's arms. "It isn't fair. They could have survived if someone had used this all to rescue them! If I take it, it's like I'm helping to kill them all over again."

"No one said it would be fair, *lastochka*. You have to understand that."

Perry stared at the ground awkwardly. "If I may make a suggestion," he said.

"Go ahead," she said, turning to look at him from the protection of Constantine's arms.

"The Bank of England can buy the gold bars from you. The less attention this matter receives, the better. If you were seen carting gold bars from the bank, or repatriating them, where would you say you acquired them? Far better that they stay here and become a part of our reserve."

She nodded. "What about the rest of this?"

"It is yours," he said softly. "The deeds and tsarist bonds are worth little more than a memory. The British bonds will be honored at the current interest rate and the cashier's check at face value, of course, and I can handle that for you as well."

"I don't believe it," Natalie said. "It doesn't feel right."

"But think of what you could do," Constantine said.

"We'll start a charity or a trust," Beth said. "Think of the people you can help, Nat."

Natalie nodded, feeling like the world was spinning. It was frightening and exhilarating, like the carnival rides she'd ridden as a child. She'd close her eyes and beg for mercy, while Beth raised her arms and screamed for more. At the end of the ride, Beth would clap and smile while she'd try not to throw up on her shoes. She'd always promised herself she'd be more like Beth next time — brave, adventurous, not afraid to feel a little out of control. But she never did. *That changes now*, she thought.

"It's settled," Perry said. "I'll complete the transactions myself first thing in the morning. Shall I call the prime minister and tell him you'll be staying until morning?"

Natalie looked from Beth to Constantine. Even if it felt like sliding off a cliff, this was her chance to do something good for the people she loved. This was her chance to open her eyes, throw up her arms, and feel the wind in her hair. "Yes," she said. "I'll stay."

Perry reached out to shake her hand and clasped it warmly between his. "I can't believe I've lived to see this. But you do know the bank must continue to deny the existence of this account?"

"I understand," she said. "And I don't want to talk about it, either, believe me. Speaking of which, Perry, I need you to tell Davies something for me."

"Oh? What's that?"

"I might have … um … said some stuff about Queen Mary. You know, to convince him to rescue us. I want you to tell him it's not true. He got pretty upset over the phone."

Perry's eyes twinkled. "Then are you sure you want me to tell him? He's never been my favorite person."

"Please," Natalie said. "I just want this to be over. I want to go back to real life."

"Real life?" Constantine recaptured her in his arms, pulling her close. "And what might that include?"

"You, of course," she said, breaking into a smile. "Maybe not the broom closet this time, though."

"Definitely not." Constantine leaned over her and kissed her. She opened her mouth and his tongue swept hers gently. Then he pulled away and touched the tip of her nose with his finger. "I have an idea," he said, reaching for the first box. He pulled out the velvet bag with loose diamonds in it, and tumbled a few into his palm.

"What's that for?"

"I'm going to need something to put in your ring."

"Hey, buddy," Beth said, smacking him in the arm. "Don't you need my permission first?"

Constantine cleared his throat. "Actually, there is something I want to ask of you. Both of you. How do you feel about stopping off in Russia, one more time?"

"Are you nuts?" Beth said.

Natalie saw him clench his jaw and realized what he wanted to ask. She reached for his hand. "It's your sister, isn't it?"

He nodded. "She needs someone like you to show her a way out. And you," he said to Beth. "My sister is a lot like Natalie, and my parents are struggling with it. They don't understand. Maybe if you talked to them, about how it can be... tell them how you do it and show them there's hope."

Beth smiled. "Of course. I'll do whatever I can."

"We'll pay for anything she needs to get well," Natalie said. "But are you sure you want to use me as an example?" She pointed to her ear. "I look like Vincent Van Gogh over here."

"There is no one else," he said, holding her face in his hands. "It was always you."

Natalie smiled. "I knew you were going to say that."

So did I, Belial said. His wings shuffled, tickling her brain, and she knew it right away — he was laughing.

The End

AUTHOR'S NOTE

Thank you so much for reading! If you enjoyed the story, I'd really appreciate a brief review — even a quick star rating can help get the word out. Your support means the world to me!

What's Real...and What's Not?
The letters from Olga and Marie Romanov to their lost loves are the product of my imagination. As a teenager, Olga did fall in love with Pavel Voronov, but when her parents put a stop to the romance, Olga didn't pursue it. And Marie did have a flirtation with one of the guards in the Ipatiev house, but didn't make plans to escape with him.

As for a foreign bank account filled with the tsar's money, it doesn't exist - that we know of. Nicholas II repatriated any funds he had in foreign banks at the start of World War I. The Bolsheviks nationalized the remainder of Nicholas's fortune and possessions. The legal circus surrounding Anna Anderson (the woman who claimed to be the tsar's youngest daughter, Anastasia) prompted lawyers and writers to search for missing Romanov funds, but no significant deposits were ever found. I couldn't resist asking "what if" and created the idea of a secret account locked by a password.

But what about the gold? According to Russian author Sergey Volkov, the Russian gold reserves did change hands several times during the revolution. Admiral Kolchak sent the tsarist gold train deep into Siberia to keep it away from the Bolsheviks. In Irkutsk, however, the train was captured by Czech battalions that had been hired to fight with Russia in World War I. They'd been stranded there by the revolution, and traded the gold to the Bolsheviks for safe passage home via Vladivostok. Volkov says the Bolsheviks got all the gold in the trade, but in Irkutsk, there are rumors to this day that some of it was stolen, buried, or lost in Lake Baikal.

There's a lot more mayhem coming up for Natalie and Beth. Here's a preview of the next book in the series, *The Carmelite Prophecy*, available in paperback and eBook. If you want to be notified when the next Natalie adventure comes out, sign up for my mailing list on my website, http://JenniWiltz.com. Readers like you are an inspiration, and I love hearing from you. Email me anytime at jenni@jenniwiltz.com.

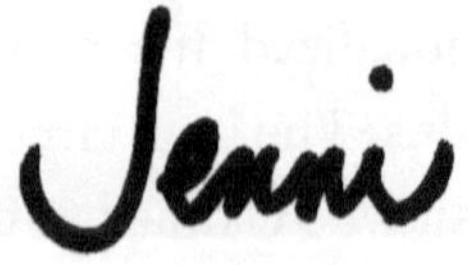

The Carmelite Prophecy: Preview

AUGUST 12, 1792
PARIS, FRANCE

other Marie-Aimée de Jésus held out the notice, delivered by special order of the Legislative Assembly. Printed on a sheet of flimsy tissue, the ink had bled in all directions. *Even the letters weep for what will come,* she thought.

Sister Léonie pulled the paper from her hand. Her gray eyes narrowed as she read it through. "They're evicting us? But why?"

They stood before the arched window in Marie-Aimée's cell. Its east-facing view had been designed to give a supplicant proof of God's glory during morning prayers. Today, though, the sun was just a clock, ticking away all the time they had left. "You know why," Marie-Aimée said.

"They're tired of waiting, aren't they?"

"You were always my best student."

The novitiate's hand fell to her side. "What will we do?"

Fight, she wanted to say. But with three hundred twelve souls in her care, she had more to think about than her principles. She sank into the chair beside her escritoire and buried her hands in the pleats of her heavy brown habit.

What the Assembly asked…it was impossible. They wanted her to abjure loyalty to the church in favor of a state that had imprisoned the anointed king, defied the pope, and failed to feed the starving populace any better than the old regime. Compliance would result in eternal damnation, she was sure of it. But rumors flew faster than crows, and every whisper spoke of terror, blood, and blades for those who refused to obey the order. Could she condemn these women to a martyr's fate? Were their lives more precious than an oath?

She looked at the girl standing beside her.

For ten years now, she'd watched and waited, wondering if Léonie's strange visions were a gift from God or the product of madness. There were times Léonie knew things it was impossible for a nineteen-year-old girl to know. When asked, the girl would only say that a voice in her head had told her.

None of the traditional means of punishment — raps on the wrist, fasting, a hair shirt — had changed her answers. By the time she'd given up on punishment, it was too late. The other women needed Léonie. They asked her where the best spot to plant a new rosebush was, or whether a beloved niece would ever find the time to write. Léonie and her voice were right too often to ignore. Outside these walls, they would brand her as a lunatic…or a witch.

But Léonie wasn't the only problem.

If the Assembly took possession of the nunnery, they would find the door hidden behind the tapestry on the far wall. If they opened the door, they would find…no.

It could not be allowed.

Marie-Aimée glanced sideways at her novitiate. The girl's face was long and narrow, with a sharp chin and long-lashed eyes. She was beautiful when she smiled, but she rarely did so. Her hands were red and rough from working in the garden and the laundry. *What if...*

No.

That could not be allowed, either, if only for the girl's safety.

There had to be another way.

A breeze from the open casement teased the Assembly's declaration from Léonie's grip. It arced toward the door, then drifted back to rest against her feet. Marie-Aimée picked it up and sighed. "I remember many mornings like this one."

"Hot before sunrise?" Léonie said, pulling at the neck of her habit.

"And the only cool place was the schoolroom. Still, the other girls couldn't wait for lessons to end."

"Not me," Léonie said.

"No, not you," Marie-Aimée agreed. "Every time I dismissed the class, you stood up like a defeated gladiator. You loved history."

Léonie offered one of her rare smiles. "I still do."

"Then you know what happened the last time a government tried to divorce itself from the one true faith."

"King Henry VIII of England. He closed the monasteries and took everything they had." Léonie narrowed her eyes. "Is that why they're doing this to us?"

"The hearts of these men are closed to me, as are their minds."

"But we have nothing worth taking! No jewels, no plate, no relics."

"That is not entirely true," Marie-Aimée said, glancing at the tapestry across the room.

Léonie gasped. Then she clamped her lips shut and closed her eyes.

"I know that look," Marie-Aimée said softly. "Is your voice telling you something?"

"Yes."

"Is it my secret?"

Léonie shook her head. "He does not know it."

"He will." Marie-Aimée opened her mouth, but found she could not speak. Forty years of silence could not be easily overcome. Deep in her belly, a feeling of sickness rumbled like hunger and her fingers sought the comfort of the rosary beads at her waist. *Is this what You want from me?* she asked. *Is this why You sent her to me all those years ago?*

But there was no answer.

God wanted her to solve this problem on her own.

"Open your eyes," she said. When the girl obeyed, she reached out and took the younger woman's hands in hers. "What do you love most in all the world?"

Léonie's forehead wrinkled. "I don't understand."

"It isn't something you understand, my dear. It's something you feel. What does your heart tell you?"

"Nothing," Léonie said, pulling back her hands and wrapping them around her midsection. "I hear my own thoughts and I hear the voice, both of them, all the time. I feel mad enough without listening to a heart, too. Even if it said anything, I wouldn't listen."

Marie-Aimée nodded.

What made Léonie blessed also made her strange, despised by the people of her village and feared by her own parents. She'd hoped to teach Léonie to hide her thoughts, to better prepare her for life outside the nunnery. The poor girl didn't belong here. She had too much anger in her heart to surrender it to God. Her plan had always been to send Léonie back out into the world, with the hope that she might expend all that anger and return of her own free will. But neither of them was ready — they needed more time.

This revolution was a disaster for them all.

Still, she had to try.

Marie-Aimée looked up at Léonie. "Have I ever told you where I was born?"

"Why should that matter?"

"I am from Reims," she said, rising to her feet. "The place where our kings are crowned and anointed by God. The place Clovis was baptized by Saint Remi, with chrism brought to him by the dove of the Holy Spirit. The place Jeanne d'Arc took from the English so that Charles VII might be crowned. There is no place more holy in all of France."

"So you love Reims above all."

"I love my city, yes, but now you know what it means when I say I love God more." She put her hand on the girl's shoulder. "What do you love most in all the world?"

Léonie closed her eyes. Marie-Aimée watched her sway, wondering what angels or demons held court inside the girl's head.

I'm the one who is mad, she thought, *trusting a girl who claims to have no heart.*

When Léonie opened her eyes, the pale gray orbs glimmered with tears. "The voice told me to say I love him. My head told me to say I love this place. But my heart told me it is you I love above all else." She sniffed and shook her head. "I have no conception of God outside this place, and no conception of a mother who isn't you. If God is love, then when I say I love you and I love this place, that must mean I love God, too."

Marie-Aimée kissed the girl's forehead. Suddenly, she felt old and tired and unequal to the task before her. *Let it be done,* she thought. "You saw the Assembly's order. You know how little time we have. There are things I must tell you before they come for us. Things you must know in case I do not survive."

Léonie gasped and stepped away. "Who would want to harm you? That's not how it happened in Henry's day."

"We are not in Henry's day, my dear."

"The voice says…" Léonie put her hands to her temples and grimaced. "The voice says we are not in Henry's day, but Mary's. Bloody Mary, who burned those who did not share her faith."

"I fear it is so." It hurt her to think of this girl, intelligent and strange, being at the mercy of the Assembly and the mob it pretended to rule. "There are things I must call upon you to do for me in the coming days. Trust me when I tell you they are more important than anything else, even our lives. Are you ready to do what is necessary?"

"I don't know," Léonie said, taking a step back. "What must I do?"

"I know you're afraid," she said. "I am, too. But we must put aside our fear, like Daniel in the lions' den. God will protect us as long as we do His work." She walked to the other side of her escritoire and opened the widest drawer. The knife, when she drew it out, trailed thin cobwebs and sprinkles of dust.

She carried it to Léonie's side and placed it in her hand, closing the girl's fingers around the handle. "Are you ready to do what is necessary?"

The Natalie Brandon Thrillers

BOOK 2: THE CARMELITE PROPHECY
A PRICELESS RELIC. A DARING THEFT.
A BLOODLINE REVEALED.

When Natalie Brandon joins her sister Beth in Paris, the past comes alive...and no one escapes unscathed.

Diagnosed with schizophrenia, Natalie is haunted by a recurring hallucination, the voice of an angel named Belial. When he guides her to the church of Saint-Joseph-des-Carmes, Natalie stumbles on two deadly secrets...a family connection to the massacre that took place there during the French Revolution, and a long-lost relic buried deep within its walls.

But Natalie isn't the only one who knows about the relic. An ultra-nationalist French professor steeped in medieval warfare and a former Legionnaire have joined forces to claim the relic and launch an uprising that will end in blood and fire on France's streets. Can Natalie and Beth stay alive long enough to save the relic and stop the next French revolution?

BOOK 3: THE SINNER'S BIBLE
A CURSE TAKES HOLD WHEN
FAITH AND LOVE FALTER.

Natalie Brandon doesn't believe in curses – except for the one that's afflicting her.

Diagnosed with schizophrenia, Natalie is haunted by a recurring hallucination, the voice of an angel named Belial. When her boss acquires a copy of the rare 1631 Sinner's Bible, Belial tells her that the book is linked to the tragic Stuart dynasty – and the curse that brought it down.

Natalie doesn't believe it until the public unveiling of the book goes horribly awry. A pair of thieves take Natalie, her sister, and her boss hostage. When Belial orders her to keep the thieves from stealing the Sinner's Bible, Natalie knows it's because he wants to unleash the curse once more. Will she stop the thieves or will she stop Belial? No matter which choice she makes, someone will die.

ALL AVAILABLE IN DIGITAL AND PAPERBACK

Readers love the Natalie Brandon thrillers:
"believable and enchanting"
"wildly entertaining, very well written,
highly inventive, and just plain fun"
"a wonderful blend of history and mystery"

Also by Jenni Wiltz

THE RED ROAD
(LITERARY FICTION)

Emma's dad has always promised to send her to college. But when an act of gang violence almost takes his life, Emma can't move on. Will she do what he wants and focus on her own future…or will she jeopardize everything to seek revenge? Available in digital and paperback.

A VAMPIRE IN VERSAILLES
(HISTORICAL HORROR)

Jean-Gabriel de Bourbon is a vampire whose survival is tied to the French royal family. As long as a king sits on the French throne, Jean-Gabriel lives. But the year is 1788, and the French Revolution draws near. Is anyone, even a vampire, strong enough to stop the force of destiny? Available in digital and paperback.

I NEVER ARKANSAS IT COMING
(MYSTERY)

Brett Sargent isn't adapting to life in Arkansas very well. A native New Yorker in the Witness Protection Program, she's trying to keep a low profile after testifying against a Mafia up-and-comer. But when a Little Falls truck driver turns up dead with a Mafia calling card stabbed to his chest, Brett knows she's next on their hit list. Available in digital and paperback.

ABOUT THE AUTHOR

Author photo by Ryan Donahue

Jenni Wiltz writes fiction and creative nonfiction. She has won national writing awards for romantic suspense and creative nonfiction. Her short stories have appeared in *Gargoyle*, the *Portland Review,* and several small-press anthologies. When she's not writing, she enjoys running and genealogical research. She lives in Pilot Hill, California. Visit her online at JenniWiltz.com.